FOOLS

The town of Fools Point, Maryland, has seen quite a few odd occurrences in the past year. Explosions, shootouts, kidnappings...and a fair share of weddings. So much has happened here, in fact, the townsfolk have taken to calling the place MYSTERY JUNCTION. This is, after all, the place where one can find danger and desire around every corner.

Folks are still wondering about our newest business owner, Jake Collins. Though gossip is flying that he has connections to the Mafia, or he was wounded in battle, Jake won't say a word about his past. But let's not forget that he has taken in that troubled teen, Matt Williams. Jake can't be all bad.

Speaking of possible relationships... Now that Amy Thomas has moved back to town, does anyone see a resemblance between her young daughter and Jake Collins? It's in the smile, I'd say. Amy has been overseas these past several years, and some insist that Jake was in the military—though no one seems to know where he was stationed. Hmm. Anyone up for a doing a little math?

Dear Harlequin Intrigue Reader,

The recipe for a perfect Valentine's Day: chocolate, champagne—and four original romantic suspense titles from Harlequin Intrigue!

Our TOP SECRET BABIES promotion kicks off with Rita Herron's *Saving His Son* (#601). Devastated single mother Lindsey Payne suspects her child is alive and well—and being kept from her deliberately. The only man who'd be as determined as she is to find her child is Detective Gavin McCord—*if* he knew he'd fathered her missing baby....

In *Best-Kept Secrets* (#602) by Dani Sinclair, the tongues in MYSTERY JUNCTION are wagging about newcomer Jake Collins. Amy Thomas's first and only love has returned at last and she's ready to tell him the secret she's long kept hidden. But would revealing it suddenly put her life in jeopardy?

Our ON THE EDGE program continues with *Private Vows* (#603) by Sally Steward. A beautiful amnesiac is desperate to remember her past. Investigator Cole Grayson is desperate to keep it hidden. For if she remembers the truth, she'd never be his....

Bachelor Will Sheridan thinks he's found the perfect *Mystery Bride* (#604) in B.J. Daniels's latest romantic thriller. But the sexy and provocative Samantha Murphy is a female P.I. in the middle of a puzzling case when Will suddenly becomes her shadow. Now with desire distracting her and a child's life in the balance, Samantha and Will are about to discover the true meaning of "partnership"!

Next month more from TOP SECRET BABIES and ON THE EDGE, plus a 3-in-1 collection from some of your favorite authors and the launch of Sheryl Lynn's new McCLINTOCK COUNTRY miniseries.

Sincerely,

Denise O'Sullivan
Associate Senior Editor
Harlequin Intrigue

BEST-KEPT
SECRETS
DANI SINCLAIR

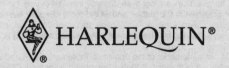
HARLEQUIN®

TORONTO • NEW YORK • LONDON
AMSTERDAM • PARIS • SYDNEY • HAMBURG
STOCKHOLM • ATHENS • TOKYO • MILAN • MADRID
PRAGUE • WARSAW • BUDAPEST • AUCKLAND

ISBN 0-373-22602-0

BEST-KEPT SECRETS

Visit us at www.eHarlequin.com

Printed in U.S.A.

ABOUT THE AUTHOR

An avid reader, Dani Sinclair didn't discover romance novels until her mother lent her one when she'd come for a visit. Dani's been hooked on the genre ever since. With the premiere of *Mystery Baby* for Harlequin Intrigue in 1996, Dani discovered she not only enjoyed reading this genre, she loved writing the intense stories, as well. Her third novel, *Better Watch Out,* was a RITA Award finalist in 1998. Dani lives outside Washington, D.C., a place she's found to be a great source for both intrigue and humor!

Books by Dani Sinclair

HARLEQUIN INTRIGUE
371—MYSTERY BABY
401—MAN WITHOUT A BADGE
448—BETTER WATCH OUT
481—MARRIED IN HASTE
507—THE MAN SHE MARRIED
539—FOR HIS DAUGHTER*
551—MY BABY, MY LOVE*
565—THE SILENT WITNESS*
589—THE SPECIALIST
602—BEST-KEPT SECRETS*

*Fools Point/Mystery Junction

HARLEQUIN TEMPTATION
790—THE NAKED TRUTH

Don't miss any of our special offers. Write to us at the following address for information on our newest releases.

Harlequin Reader Service
U.S.: 3010 Walden Ave., P.O. Box 1325, Buffalo, NY 14269
Canadian: P.O. Box 609, Fort Erie, Ont. L2A 5X3

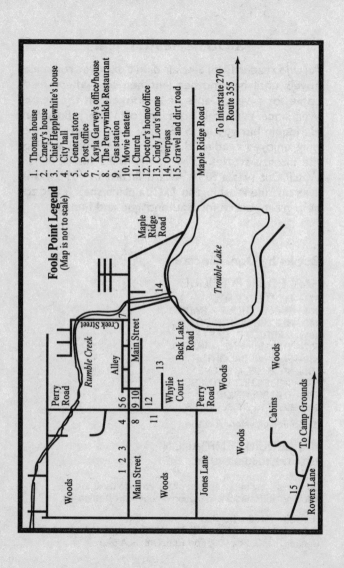

Fools Point Legend
(Map is not to scale)

1. Thomas house
2. Czmery's house
3. Chief Hepplewhite's house
4. City hall
5. General store
6. Post office
7. Kayla Garvey's office/house
8. The Perrywinkle Restaurant
9. Gas station
10. Movie theater
11. Church
12. Doctor's home/office
13. Cindy Lou's home
14. Overpass
15. Gravel and dirt road

To Interstate 270
Route 355

Maple Ridge Road

Maple
Ridge
Road

Trouble Lake

Creek Street

Rumble Creek

Perry
Road

Main Street

Alley

Back Lake Road

Woods

Main Street

Woods

Jones Lane

Perry
Road

Woods

Whylie Court

Woods

Woods

Cabins

To Camp Grounds

Rovers Lane

CAST OF CHARACTERS

Amy Thomas—Trapped in a web of lies whose origins she can't begin to comprehend, a web that threatens to destroy her family.

Jake Collins—Made a serious error nine years ago; now time is running out for him to make amends.

Kelsey Thomas—The eight-year-old has become a pawn in a thirty-year-old nightmare.

Matt Williams—Jake's teenaged nephew has a history of being in trouble and now he really wants to change his image.

Susan and Cornelius Thomas—Amy's parents share a secret that threatens to destroy their world and the family they love above all else.

General Marcus Perry—Above reproach and up for his second star, but he's been keeping a terrible secret all these years.

Millicent Perry—The general's proper Bostonian wife.

Gertrude Perry—The general's sister is slipping in and out of dementia, but just maybe, her ramblings hold the key to everything.

Cindy Lou Perry Baranski—The general's daughter who is up for reelection as the town mayor.

Eugene Perry—The general's son spends a great deal of time and money inside the local bar, with no visible means of support.

Ben Dwyer—The Perrywinkle's bartender, who may have a few secrets of his own.

John Hepplewhite—Fools Point's police chief always gets his man.

DEDICATION

For Mary McGowan, an unconditional friend.
Thank you. For Natashya Wilson and the past two years
of friendship and support. And for Roger, Chip,
Dan and Barb always.

ACKNOWLEDGMENT

Many thanks to Sgt. Rick Cage and
Officer Melissa Parlon of the Montgomery County
Police Department. They generously shared their time
answering numerous questions. Errors in police
procedure are mine alone or were purposefully done
to fit the needs of the story.

Prologue

The workman's heavy-booted foot dislodged something, causing it to roll across the ground and bounce off the side wall. The flashlight followed its course, spotlighting the dirt-encrusted skull.

"Holy sh—"

"Is that what I think it is?"

"Oh, man, oh, man, oh—"

"Come on," Will said, reaching for the ladder, not waiting to see if Buddy followed on his heels. The burly foreman stepped back as the two men scrambled over the lip of the hole and into the brilliant September sunshine.

"What the hell are you doing?" Zeke demanded.

Will pointed, angry that his hand was shaking. "We got us some bodies down there."

"In the sinkhole?"

"That ain't no sinkhole," Will told him. "There's some kinda room down there."

"What?"

"Yeah." Will hated that he was still shaking. "Buddy, you'd better go tell the boss."

Zeke stared at them. "Never mind the boss, Buddy, go get the police."

Buddy's eyes were wide, his skin strangely pale beneath his dark bronze tan. He skirted the pile of debris from the torn-up corner of the parking lot, headed around the dump truck with its heavy load of gravel and started running across the tarmac in spite of it being ninety-eight degrees in the shade. The other two men watched him head for the restaurant before turning to peer back down into the hole.

"You sure about this?" Zeke asked again.

"I know a skull when I see one," Will growled. "Even a tiny one like that."

"Tiny?"

Will sized it in the air with his hands. "There's another one. Bigger. You wanna go look?"

"Hell, no." He tipped back his hard hat and scratched at his thinning hair. "It could be an animal," he said hopefully.

Will didn't dignify that with an answer.

"You just better be sure, is all," Zeke said.

"I'm sure."

The two men resumed staring into the deep hole.

"What's going on here?"

They whirled, Zeke nearly falling into the opening at the sound of their current employer's deep voice. Jake Collins, owner of the restaurant whose parking lot they'd been hired to fix, stood staring at them, his dark eyes watching intently. He was rumored to be a gambler with Mafia connections. No one seemed to know if it was true or not, and no one had the guts to ask him. But he sure looked the part.

Everyone in Fools Point was a little afraid of Jake Collins.

"Buddy says you found two bodies," Jake said quietly.

The foreman nodded his balding head. "It's true, Mr. Collins. Down there. Reason the parking lot collapsed is someone built it over an old root cellar or something. Bodies are at the bottom.''

''Whose bodies?''

Zeke looked at Will who swallowed before shaking his head. He hoped the only thing shaking was his head beneath that penetrating gaze.

''One of 'em's a baby,'' Will told him.

''A baby?'' Jake's voice deepened a full octave.

''Yes, sir. Real tiny, the bones are.''

''Bones?''

''Yeah. They've been down there an awful long time.''

Jake Collins didn't say another word. He simply grabbed the ladder, swung his neatly pressed trouser leg over the edge of the hole, and disappeared from view.

''He's gonna get them fancy duds all dirty down there,'' the foreman muttered.

''Yeah,'' Will agreed.

Minutes later Jake reappeared. His face, as always, was an impenetrable mask. ''Don't move anything. Don't touch anything. Don't let anyone except Chief Hepplewhite or Officer Garvey down there.'' He started to walk away.

''Yes, sir. Uh, Mr. Collins, what are we going to do about the pit?''

Jake paused to pin them with a haughty stare. ''Wait for the cops to finish their investigation. Then fill the thing in permanently with that load of gravel.'' He continued across the parking lot, not even bothering to brush the dirt from his tan slacks.

''That guy gives me the creeps,'' Buddy said suddenly.

''Yeah.'' Zeke's gaze drifted back to the hole in the ground. ''Who do you suppose dumped a helpless little baby and its mother in a root cellar?''

Chapter One

A shiver stole up her spine. "Did you say Jake Collins?"

Her mother nodded, folding the last towel and placing it in the basket. "Rumor has it that he's Mafia connected, you know."

Amy Thomas shook her head even as her heart continued to pound. Jake Collins wasn't Mafia. He was the father of her daughter. But her mother didn't know that. No one knew that except her. What was he doing here, in Fools Point of all places? *And running a bar and restaurant?*

That wasn't the gung-ho navy lieutenant she'd known. Maybe this was a different Jake Collins and not *her* Jake Collins—not that he'd ever been hers except in the physical sense, and then only as a summer fling. Amy's gaze darted to where her daughter played on the floor with her mother's pair of cats and a feather toy. Kelsey giggled at the animals and their antics.

Her daughter. Jake had simply been the physical fluke that had helped in the child's biological creation.

"I don't believe that for a second, either," her mother went on, undisturbed by the cats, the child or her daughter's silence. "He's just a very private sort of man, but you know how this town is. No secrets here, they simply aren't tolerated. If he won't tell people about his past, they'll make up their own details. Look how they discuss the wife of Chief Hepplewhite. Poor woman. She just sits in that wheelchair day after day never saying a word and no one knows how she came to such a fate. The rumor is—"

Amy stopped her mother from lifting the basket of clothing or speculating any further on the lives of the residents of Fools Point. "I'll take it, Mom, you shouldn't be carrying things."

"I'm not an invalid despite what your father thinks. I have a heart condition. Millions of people do, you know."

"I'll still carry the basket."

"Have it your way. Who am I to argue with free labor? Anyhow, you should see what Mr. Collins has done with the old Perry place. Who would have thought that old eyesore could have been turned into such a fabulous restaurant? Of course, your father hates to eat out so he only took me there once, and only because I insisted. Still, it's beautiful inside. Mr. Collins did a fantastic job on the renovations. I don't think Gertrude would appreciate the changes, but then her mind is really starting to slip. I guess that's why the family sold the estate in the first place. Did you know Gertrude's niece, Cindy Lou, is the mayor now?"

Jake's name had caught Amy unprepared. While her mother had been filling her in on the latest gossip since she'd arrived in town yesterday, his name left her stunned.

"I have an idea, Mom," Amy said, barely registering her mother's words. "Why don't we get cleaned up and go over there for lunch?"

Excitement sparkled in her mother's faded blue eyes. "Oh, that would be fun, but I made egg salad for lunch."

"We'll have it for dinner instead. If we eat a big lunch

we won't want a heavy dinner anyhow. You can give Dad a steak or something. Come on, what do you say? We'll be back home before Dad finishes delivering the mail. My treat.''

It was probably a different Jake Collins, Amy mused, but she wouldn't be able to sit still until she knew one way or another. For nine years she'd dreamed of meeting Jake once again. A dozen scenarios had helped her pass many a sleepless night, especially when their daughter was a tiny infant. Being a single parent had seemed overwhelming at times.

"I'd like to go, of course," her mother said.

That was enough for Amy. "Come on, Kelsey, let's change. We're going out for lunch."

"Do I have to change?"

Oh, yes, for this lunch she definitely had to change. Amy wanted Jake to see just what he'd given up nine years ago. "How about wearing your new sundress?"

"The blue-green one that matches yours?"

"Why not? We'll dress like twins."

She saw her mother pale and reached out a hand toward the older woman. But Susan Thomas smiled quickly. "I have a blue sundress, as well," her mother announced. "We shall be the best-dressed ladies at the Perrywrinkle."

"Cool, Grandma."

More than cool, Amy decided while trying to calm the butterflies attempting to launch their way free from her stomach. If it *was* the Jake Collins she'd known nine years ago, he was in for a real surprise.

Amy dressed quickly, brushing out her long brown hair until it snapped with energy. When Jake had last seen her she'd worn it pixie-short and the color had been a much deeper brown, but a few weeks at the beach with Kelsey had lightened her hair color and darkened her skin. Otherwise, she didn't look all that different now from the woman he'd known.

As she started to put the opal studs in her ears, Amy hesitated. She turned and began hunting through the boxes she'd been storing here at the house. She found her old jewelry box after a few false starts. Almost defiantly, she picked out the crystal earrings Jake had given her so long ago and put them in her ears instead.

Staring at her image, she had second thoughts. Would Jake see the earrings as a sign that she'd been pining for him all these years? Nothing could be further from the truth, of course. Jake had taught her a valuable lesson. One she'd never forget.

Falling in love was easy. Making someone else feel the same way was impossible. Jake had wanted a summer fling and she'd obliged, foolishly picturing forever. But his only commitment had been to the navy and the secretive work he did for them. The moment they told him it was time to move on, he did. Alone.

She took heart from the way the earrings sparkled in the sunlight sweeping in through her window. Hopefully, Jake would get the message she intended. He'd meant so little she'd practically forgotten him.

The Perrywrinkle was in easy walking distance. Mindful of her mother's bad heart, however, Amy wanted to drive.

"Nonsense, darling. It's much too beautiful a day to ride in a stuffy car when the restaurant is at the top of the hill."

"Exactly. At the top of the hill."

"So we'll take our time," Susan Thomas told her.

They did, even pausing beneath the bright September sun to watch a caterpillar make its way across the sidewalk. Though they had taken a popular shortcut up the hill behind the restaurant, her mother was huffing by the time they got to the top.

"I knew we should have taken the car," Amy said worriedly.

"Don't be silly, dear. I may not be young like you, but I can still walk a block without collapsing."

Actually, it was Amy who was more likely to collapse. Her palms were sweating and her heart was beating much too fast. Surely in nine years she'd gotten over any infatuation she might have had for the man. He'd dumped her! He hadn't even responded when she'd written and told him about their baby.

No, she wasn't infatuated with Jake any longer. She just wanted him to see the beautiful, brilliant child he hadn't wanted to claim all those years ago. And anyhow, it probably wasn't the same man, she told herself for the umpteenth time.

"What's going on, Mommy?"

Amy stared at the beautifully landscaped grounds for the first time. She realized a work crew was gathered around a deep pit only a few feet away. Even as she watched, more people left the restaurant and hurried over.

"I have no idea."

"Can I go see?"

"Definitely not."

"Well, I want to see what's going on," Susan announced, and headed in that direction.

Amy should have known. In Fools Point everyone minded everyone else's business. She trailed behind her mother and her daughter. A police car appeared on the scene and a white-haired man stepped from the vehicle. Her mother came to a halt.

"That's Chief Hepplewhite," she said sotto voce. "This must be something big."

"It's true," someone in the growing crowd was saying

to his companion. ''They found a bunch of bodies down there.''

Bodies?

''I want to see! Come on, Mommy!''

''No! Kelsey…''

They'd reached the edge of the crowd. Chief Hepple-white and another police officer were descending a wooden ladder into the yawning pit. Amy's mother and daughter paused several feet behind a dump truck to get an unobstructed view.

One of the construction workers stepped forward to correct the speaker. ''There's only two bodies down there and one of 'em's a real tiny baby.''

Amy saw her mother go white. She began to sway unsteadily. ''Mom?''

There was a sudden grinding noise and the dump truck suddenly began to roll backward.

''Get back!''

Amy reached for her daughter and her mother. Her mother stumbled. Before she could pull them to safety, someone roughly shoved all of them to the asphalt, out of the path of the runaway truck. A man's large body, lying across her back, partly covered her.

''Stay still,'' a masculine voice rumbled in her ear.

Voices shouted. Someone screamed. And the truck bounced past, scant inches from where the man had flung them. Amy gripped her daughter's hand, fighting the adrenaline rush of fear.

There was a horrific sound as the truck's rear wheel hit the lip of the hole. The truck canted to one side, off balance. The heavy load groaned and shifted. There was a tortured cry of metal as something gave way and gravel began spewing everywhere.

A haze of dust swept over them. The sudden silence that followed was almost painful. The person on top of her pulled away. Amy rolled over and came eye-to-eye with the only man she had ever loved.

"Are you okay?" he asked. An incredulous expression suddenly swept his harsh features as recognition hit him. "Amy?"

"Hello, Jake."

"My God! What are you doing here?"

"Mommy?"

Amy sat up and tugged her daughter to her side. "I was taking my mother and my daughter to lunch."

Feeling sucker-punched, Jake rose to his feet and stared down at the face that had haunted his dreams for nine years. Amy hadn't changed a bit—and yet she had. She was older, of course, but more beautiful than ever. Her sea-green eyes still glowed with that vibrancy he remembered, only now there was a maturity that hadn't been there before. Her hair was gloriously long. It was silky, and lighter in color than he remembered, but one thing hadn't changed. Her mouth had always been made for kissing.

"Is anybody hurt?"

Jake tore his gaze from her face at the sound of the police chief's question. Hepplewhite and Officer Garvey had apparently made it out of the pit before the truck had half filled it full of gravel.

"I'll be damned. I think my leg's broke," Zeke announced, sounding stunned.

Jake turned back to Amy, assessing her for injuries. Other than smudges of dirt, she was fine. Amazingly, Zeke was the only one in the crowd who'd been struck by the truck. Several people had been hit by flying gravel, but no one was seriously hurt.

"What happened?" Hepplewhite demanded of the foreman.

"I don't know. Look out!"

Near the edge of the pit, the ground gave way beneath the weight of the truck. More of the gravel spilled into the hole.

"Get everybody back! Lee, secure the scene until I can get Osher and Jackstone over here," Hepplewhite ordered the other officer with him. "Now we've really got a mess."

"Do you want help?" Jake offered.

The police chief sized him up. "See if you can get these people inside the restaurant and keep them there until I can ask a few questions."

Jake nodded. He kept his gaze impersonal as he looked at the crowd, refusing to stare at the one person he wanted most to look at. "Everyone inside where it's safe," he said firmly in a tone that started people moving. "You and you—" he picked two of the construction workers "—carry Zeke inside and set him down in the bar until the ambulance arrives."

Zeke managed a smile. "I could use a beer," he announced. "For the pain."

"We should go home. My mother isn't well," Amy protested.

"Grandma?"

Jake squatted beside the frail woman he recognized as the mailman's wife. "Are you hurt?" he asked gently.

"It's her heart," Amy said quickly.

Jake glanced around and spotted one of his dishwashers lingering at the scene. "Billy, get inside and call for an ambulance."

Instantly, Amy's mother struggled to sit up. "I don't need an ambulance! I'm fine. I'm not an invalid."

"One of the workmen was injured," Jake said reassuringly. "We'll need the ambulance for him."

"Oh. Oh, of course."

Before she could protest, he lifted her into his arms and stood.

"I can walk."

"Of course you can, but surely you won't deprive me of a chance to carry such a beautiful woman to safety."

"Oh." She blushed a deep rosy pink. "I'd heard you were a charmer," Susan Thomas said. "Isn't he a charmer, Amy?"

Jake's eyes locked with Amy's. He saw a flash of remembered hurt before they turned to green chips of ice that sparkled like the crystals in her ears.

"Oh, yeah, he's a real charmer, Mom. Come on, Kelsey." She pulled her daughter tightly to her side and turned away without another word. Her skirt whirled almost defiantly about her shapely, graceful legs. The rush of remembered heat startled him. It had been years, but he could still feel those legs wrapped tightly around his body as they came together with incredible abandon.

"My daughter worries about me," Mrs. Thomas was saying. "I was recently diagnosed with a heart condition and my family thinks they have to pamper me."

Jake pulled his thoughts back to the here and now. "I don't blame them one bit. Are you certain you're all right?" She did appear pale, now that he really looked at her. Pale and badly frightened. Shadows of fear lurked in her eyes.

Well, who could blame her? She'd come for lunch, not to be flattened by a ten-ton truck.

Jake realized he'd gone soft. Before his last mission had gone sour and left him with injuries he was still trying to overcome, his reaction to what had just happened would have been quicker, more decisive. But those days were definitely gone, and if he didn't set this woman down soon, the whole town would realize just how far gone *he* was. He could feel the pull of weakened muscles and restored skin across his back. The bullet wound and the shrapnel from the exploding boat had left permanent damage that no amount of operations would ever restore. His shoulder was growing white-hot with the pain of holding even this woman's slight weight.

Ben Dwyer, his new bartender, met him at the restaurant door. Jake gave him a stern nod. "Get everyone back to work. Free drinks, but nothing alcoholic. Chief Hepplewhite wants us to keep everyone inside and able to answer questions."

"You got it."

Of necessity, Jake set Mrs. Thomas down at the table nearest the door. "I apologize for the excitement. I'll be right back." He didn't look at Amy who was sputtering protests as he left, but he could feel her gaze bore a hole through his back as he strode toward the rear of the restaurant and the stairs leading up to his private quarters.

Lifting the woman had been an incredibly stupid thing to do. The pain spread. He grit his teeth, hating the necessity of taking pills, but he wouldn't be able to function if he didn't get the spasm to pass quickly.

He focused his thoughts on Amy to get them off the pain in his back. This was turning into one heck of a day. First the bodies, then the truck accident. Naturally, Amy would have to pick today to drop into his life again. She always did have exquisite timing.

He'd thought he was prepared to see her again after all these years, but he'd been sadly mistaken. He'd known this day would eventually come when he'd made the decision to move to Fools Point, the town where she'd grown up. Deep in his heart, he'd hoped for the chance to see her again. But his secret fantasies hadn't prepared him for reality. Amy still had the power to touch something elemental inside him—something that only responded to her. What surprised him was that Amy was still upset after all these years.

Jake sighed. He'd never known Amy to hold a grudge, yet anger had radiated from every stiff line of her carriage as she'd walked ahead of him into the restaurant. He deserved that and more. He'd walked out on her and what they'd had because of his own insecurities. He'd been able to face death without flinching, yet he hadn't been able to face what she'd made him feel. Instead, he'd told himself he couldn't offer her the sort of life she ought to have and he'd left like a coward. Loving Amy had made him vulnerable, and a big, tough navy SEAL couldn't afford to be vulnerable that way.

What a self-centered jerk he'd been.

Over the years he'd wondered about Amy, if she was happy and well, if she'd found someone special to fill her life. He'd known she probably had, but for some dumb reason, he hadn't pictured her married with kids. Maybe part of him hadn't wanted to take the image that far.

Yet Amy had a daughter.

The knowledge ate at him. He hadn't really believed she'd been waiting for him all these years. Not after the way he'd left her.

Jake sighed. He took two pills, chased them down with a glass of water, and told himself to stop thinking about the pain. He was alive. Three of his men weren't.

He turned his thoughts away from the memory of a mission gone bad and tried to focus on the bodies under his parking lot. Who had put them there and why? He walked back downstairs slowly, knowing it was going to be a very long afternoon.

His guess proved correct. Jake was left with little time to think about Amy or anything else once the police descended on the Perrywrinkle and his customers.

AMY WATCHED JAKE move about the room and tried not to be too obvious. She ate her food with mechanical precision, barely listening to her mother and daughter. He still moved with an economy of motion, but the fluidity wasn't the same. There was a stiffness about him now. It was especially noticeable when he'd bent to retrieve a napkin that had slipped from an older woman's lap.

Had he been injured?

Had he hurt himself when he'd tackled her in an effort to protect them?

Did she care? she chastised herself mentally.

Unfortunately, that answer was yes. She shouldn't care now that she'd done what she'd set out to do. She'd shown Jake his gorgeous daughter and he'd barely even noticed. Yet she still couldn't take her eyes from him.

And that made her worse than a fool.

"Ladies, how was your lunch?"

Amy jumped, startled to find him beside her. He'd always done that, she remembered. He moved so silently that he was there before a person realized.

"Glorious," her mother responded with enthusiasm. "The food here is marvelous."

Amy nearly jumped again as her mother actually kicked her under the table.

"Yes. The meal was good," she admitted without looking up. In truth, she couldn't have said what she'd eaten. Her thoughts had never once been on the food.

"I liked the rolls best," Kelsey put in. "And the coconut pie."

Jake smiled. A genuine smile instead of the formal and distant ones she'd watched him use with others. Pain tugged at Amy's heart. Her daughter had that same smile.

"I'm glad to hear it."

"The entertainment was pretty interesting, as well,"

Susan Thomas put in, eyeing the police officers who were
still talking with a couple in the corner.

"Yes, well, I'm afraid I didn't have much control over
that part of your lunch, but I'm happy that everything
else met with your satisfaction."

He looked at Amy as he spoke and her cheeks immediately warmed under his penetrating stare. She'd forgotten that about him. How he could focus so intently on
a person they felt as though he were peering into their
very soul. She shook her head at the thought.

"Something wrong, Amy?"

Just hearing her name on his lips took her back to hot
summer nights and wildly fabulous sex. What was wrong
with her hormones for crying out loud?

"I'd like to pay the check."

"Lunch is on me. And I apologize for the incident
outside. We don't generally have runaway trucks in the
parking lot."

"Just bodies, hmm?"

He stared at her and her pulses leaped erratically.

"I'll be happy to have your dresses dry-cleaned if they
were damaged from your tumble."

"That isn't necessary. They'll wash."

"Glad to hear it. It would be a shame to ruin them."

Answering heat swept through her at his penetrating
look, but she knew she couldn't respond to the sensual
pull he still exerted.

"Whenever you're ready to leave, let me know and
I'll drive you home."

"We can walk," she stated firmly.

His eyes chastised her. He glanced at her mother. Amy
knew she was blushing again but she couldn't stop. Her
mother's gaze flicked from one to the other of them as
if she were watching a tennis match. Even Kelsey looked
interested.

"I said I'll drive you," he said softly.

"That would be lovely, dear," Susan said decisively. "So nice of you to offer. I feel so full I'm actually ready for a nap."

Jake turned the full force of his smile on her mother. "Then I've done my job."

"Quite well, I'd say. Ignore my daughter. She's being temperamental today for some reason."

"I hadn't noticed," he lied smoothly.

Susan laughed as if delighted. "Are you ready, Amy?"

"The police—"

"Have assured me that they are finished questioning you for now," Jake said smoothly. "Shall we go?"

"I knew I should have brought my car," Amy muttered beneath her breath.

"I'm sure Mr. Collins is a capable driver. Aren't you, dear?"

"So I've been told." He stared into Amy's eyes as if demanding that she remember.

"WHY DON'T YOU let me drive this time?" she purred, running her fingers across his lightly furred chest.

"Are you suggesting I didn't get you where you wanted to go?" he teased as he toyed with her breast.

"Oh, you're a capable driver, but now I want to show you what I can do."

AMY COULD FEEL searing heat ignite her face as the memory of their erotic lovemaking that day filled her head. She refused to look at him again.

Her parents' home was only down the street, yet it seemed to take forever to drive the short distance. She knew darn well her mother had conspired to put her in the passenger seat up front where she could all but feel Jake's nearness.

Her mother was matchmaking! That was all she needed. Her mother wouldn't be so quick off the mark if she knew who Jake really was. While Amy had never told her parents the identity of Kelsey's father, could her mother have guessed?

It would be surprising, actually, if her eagle-eyed mother didn't pick up on the likeness between Kelsey and Jake. Kelsey's coloring, her dark eyes and square little jaw—fortunately softened in her little-girl features—were so much like her father's that Amy had been certain Susan would see the obvious right away.

Or was Amy reading too much into things because she knew.

"'Bye, Mr. Collins. Thanks for lunch," Kelsey called, jumping from the car. "I'm going to call Sarah and tell her about the bodies!"

The resiliency of youth. Amy stepped from the car to help her mother, but the older woman was already out and moving spryly after her granddaughter.

"Yes, thank you, Mr. Collins. It was a most interesting afternoon," Susan agreed. "Are you coming, dear?"

"In a moment, Mom. You and Kelsey go ahead." Amy wasn't anxious to face the third degree she knew was coming as soon as she stepped inside the familiar house. She turned to Jake as soon as her mother and daughter were out of earshot.

"What are you doing here, Jake?"

"Running a restaurant," he offered mildly.

"That isn't what I mean and you know it."

His gaze darkened, running over her with sensual knowledge of exactly what was beneath her clothing. "You haven't changed, Amy."

"Oh, yes. Yes, I have. That look, those old lines, they won't work on me anymore, Jake."

"Too bad. I remember some very good lines that led to some wonderful times together."

That hurt. "Funny. All I remember is the way it ended. Stay away from me, Jake. I mean it."

He regarded her for a moment, then nodded. "Don't worry, I don't poach on other men's territory." His glance dropped to her hand where it was fisted on the roof of the car. "But then, I wouldn't be poaching, would I? You aren't wearing a ring."

For a minute Amy saw red. How dare he?

"Goodbye, Jake."

"Amy?" he called after her.

She told herself not to listen, but she stopped walking and barely refrained from turning back to him.

"For what it's worth, I'm sorry about the way things ended."

His voice was low, personal, intimate. Her stomach clenched right along with her fists.

"I've waited nine years to tell you that."

Amy didn't turn around. "You should have saved your breath." And she forced herself not to run as she strode away from Jake Collins and her past.

JAKE CLIMBED painfully back into the car and started the engine. He watched her daughter come running back outside, chattering away. Amy listened and nodded, putting a hand on the little girl's head. The two of them walked up the steps and onto the porch together.

A pain that had nothing to do with physical hurts lanced him more deeply than a cut. If he hadn't been so stupid, so egotistically certain he knew the right thing to do, that could have been their daughter. Kelsey had his coloring, he thought humorlessly. He wondered what her father looked like. She was a beautiful child, just as her mother was beautiful. He'd been the world's biggest fool nine years ago.

It wasn't until he walked inside the Perrywrinkle, lost in recriminations of the past, that it hit him. How old was the child? Seven? Eight?

Was it possible?

He calculated quickly.

More than possible.

Jake thought of what he knew about Amy. She'd been a virgin at twenty-two—and she'd loved him. Maybe it was ego talking, but he couldn't believe she would have gone from him to another man so quickly.

He'd always listened to his instincts and they were shouting now, loud and clear. If he wanted to see Kelsey's father all he needed was a mirror.

Why hadn't Amy told him? How *dare* she not have told him! Didn't she think he had the right to know? This was his child. His only child! She had no right to keep that a secret.

"Boss," Ben Dwyer said, walking up to him, "we've got a small problem. There are reporters in the bar to see you and Matt's looking for you. He says there's an old lady out by the construction site acting all weird and spacey—his words. He thinks she's the mayor's aunt."

Jake cursed under his breath. He wanted to turn around, go back to Amy and demand answers. But first he'd have to deal with this situation.

"Where's Matt now?"

"I don't know. He went back outside when I told him you weren't here. Is it true what they're saying?"

Jake waited.

Ben didn't flinch at his expression. Instead he went on calmly. "Some of the customers heard the cops talking. They said that someone deliberately released the brake and put that truck in reverse."

Jake stared at his bartender while the hairs on the back of his neck lifted. "I hadn't heard that," he said softly.

Jake went back outside, his mind churning. That explained the questions Hepplewhite's people were asking. He'd wondered why the police wanted to know if he'd seen anyone in or around the truck before it began to roll. He'd supposed it was an accident. If Ben was right, they were looking at an entirely different scenario.

Had someone deliberately tried to dump that load of gravel into the pit to cover the scene of a murder? Why bother? The bones had already been discovered. On the other hand, the gravel would compromise the crime scene, making it much harder for the forensic team to do its job.

Jake looked around as he neared the roped-off area. The truck still canted oddly over the hole. Gravel was everywhere and the crowd had grown. Cindy Lou Baranksi would not be happy if her aunt turned up on national television. Image was everything in an election year and the mayor's aunt was in the early stages of Alzheimer's or some form of dementia. Cindy Lou had the added responsibility of looking after her aunt. Gertrude Perry was generally monitored closely.

If he hadn't been so busy thinking about Amy when he returned, Jake would have spotted the older woman hanging around outside. He also would have noticed the network news van on the far side of the building.

Jake had no one to blame but himself for the past. But he needed to deal with the future right now. By the time he got to the end of the parking lot where the workers had exposed the horrible tomb, Gertrude Perry was gone.

No doubt one of the locals had run her home. Everyone knew old Ms. Perry. As a relative newcomer to town, Jake had quickly learned that Gertrude and her brother Marcus were direct descendents of the Perry family who had founded Fools Point. Marcus Perry had been the last to marry and have offspring. Only his daughter, Cindy Lou, had ever felt the need to keep up appearances for the sake of the family name. She was a decent mayor from what he could see. And it wasn't her fault people had started to refer to the town as Mystery Junction behind her back. Today's gruesome discovery would only add fuel to the already smoldering talk around town. Cindy Lou wouldn't want her family featured in that talk, but this *was* their old family homestead.

Police officials were still at the site. Chief Hepplewhite had called in the support of the Montgomery County Police. His six-man force couldn't possibly deal with this situation. The county police would deal with the evidence and probably assist with the investigation. But first, someone was going to have to move a ton of gravel.

Jake frowned. He scanned the crowd again, but his nephew Matt was nowhere to be seen. The time had come to do something about the youth. To the locals, Matt was nothing but a wild teen, constantly in trouble. To the aunt and uncle he had lived with since the death of his parents, he was an unwanted burden. But to Jake, he was the reason for the Perrywrinkle and Jake's presence in the small town of Fools Point.

Jake sighed and returned inside to face the reporters. The after-work crowd had descended by the time Jake finished, then the supper crowd began to arrive and mingle with the curious. The restaurant staff was kept hopping, especially him. He stewed, knowing there was nothing he could do about the question gnawing at his insides until things quieted down for the night and he could turn the bar over to Ben's capable hands.

The young man was working out even better than he'd expected. Solid, dependable—honest. Jake would bet his military pension that there was a story behind Ben's presence here in Fools Point. In time he'd learn what it was, but he wasn't thinking about that as he swallowed a couple of aspirins and, ignoring his car, set off down the path that would lead to the street and ultimately Amy's front door.

He strode briskly in the cool night air. Maple trees were just beginning to display their colorful fall cloaks. They still obscured most of the houses from the view of the street.

Overhead, the moon was dancing with the clouds so not much light filtered anywhere along his path.

Admittedly his senses had turned rusty in the past year and a half, but not so rusty that they'd shut down completely. Jake slowed his pace as he neared the house. Years of training kicked to life the moment he saw a dark figure dart from behind a tree to scamper surreptitiously behind the house.

Jake flattened himself against the nearest tree, doing his best to melt into the shadows. His white shirt and pale face would act like a beacon if the intruder looked in the right direction. Stealth was not easily accomplished in a business suit. Using the overgrown bushes for cover, he followed the dark figure around to the back of the house.

The feeble glow from inside the kitchen offered little illumination on the porch, but it was enough for Jake to see the figure begin working feverishly on the door.

Someone was attempting to break into the house where Amy and the little girl he was certain was his daughter lay unprotected.

Chapter Two

Amy fretted, knowing it was useless, but worried just the same. Her mother hadn't asked, and by late evening Amy felt she should have been pushing for answers to Amy's relationship with Jake Collins. That she hadn't was so out of character, Amy grew worried. Her mother must already suspect the truth.

When her parents had asked her about Kelsey's father all those years ago, she'd never mentioned Jake by name. She'd told them the simple truth—she'd foolishly fallen for a man she'd met in Annapolis. A man who hadn't been interested in being a father any more than he'd been interested in a long-term commitment. Being the sort of parents they were, they'd never pushed her to reveal more. She'd been grateful, because it had been so hard to think about Jake back then without crying.

Actually, not crying had never gotten as easy as it should have until she'd firmly locked away her thoughts of Jake.

Amy decided to approach her mother after Kelsey had gone to bed. Though she'd told her daughter pretty much the same story she'd told her parents, she'd always known the time would come when Kelsey would want more detailed information about her father. Amy didn't intend to lie. She just wasn't sure how to handle the situation now that the time appeared to have arrived.

Amy found her mother puttering in the kitchen, alone. Taking a deep breath, she decided to get it over with.

"About Jake—"

"Charming man. So gracious and kind."

"Yeah. Kind." So kind he couldn't bring himself to acknowledge his own child. "I guess you're wondering how I know him."

"Well, actually, dear, I was simply hoping you could put paid to the rumor about him being in the Mafia."

"Mother!"

"Well, it does seem ridiculous," she said, briskly wiping her hands and folding the dish towel.

"He was in the navy, not the Mafia."

"Good, dear. That's such a relief."

Her mother could be exasperating when she chose to be. And there was only one reason Amy could think of that would explain why she was choosing to be so obtuse about Jake. She suspected the truth. Amy needed to disabuse her mother of any idea she might be harboring about matchmaking.

"I met him that summer after I graduated college."

"When you were staying in Annapolis with your friend?"

The college friend she'd forgotten all about the night she was introduced to Jake. "Yes." She waited for the inevitable questions. Her mother couldn't fail to make that connection.

"I'm glad, dear."

"You are?"

"Yes, of course." Her mother pushed absently at a wisp of silvery hair. "I never did like the idea of the Mafia in Fools Point. You know, dear, I'm feeling awfully tired this evening. Would you mind if I turn in a little early?''

Amy gaped at her. While true that her parents had always respected her right to privacy, her mother wasn't even going to ask?

Then concern set in. ''Are you okay? You're not having any pain or anything, are you?''

''Who's having pain?'' her father demanded, coming into the kitchen on the end of her question.

''Now, Corny, don't go getting all upset. I just said I was tired. I'd like to go up to bed and read for a while but I didn't want our daughter to think I was ignoring her.''

''I wouldn't think that.'' But she was puzzled and very concerned. Her mother hadn't looked well since the incident outside the restaurant. If Amy hadn't been so caught up in her own dilemma she'd have realized that much sooner. The walk in that heat and then being thrown to the ground like that…

Cornelius Thomas laid a wrinkled hand on his wife's arm. ''That sounds like an excellent idea,'' he agreed tenderly. ''I just bought that new science fiction book R.J. and some of the others were talking about down at the general store. I'll come up with you and read, too. You don't mind, do you, Amy?''

''No. Of course not. You two go ahead. If you need anything, just call out.''

For the first time Amy accepted that her parents had aged a great deal in the years she'd been gone. They'd always been older than most of her friends' parents. Amy had been a surprise baby coming to them late in life. That fact had never bothered her until now.

''Good night, dear. Don't forget to check the locks before you come up, will you?''

''I won't forget.''

She kissed them good-night, then wandered aimlessly around the house she had always called home. Despite the newly installed satellite dish and its variety of stations, there was nothing on television to hold her interest. She flipped through the channels, trying not to wonder what Jake had been doing with himself all these years. Had he stayed in the military or had he gone on to do something else? It was hard to imagine him running a restaurant. She couldn't remember him cooking anything more than steaks on the grill when they'd been together.

Jake had changed in others ways, as well. He seemed stern now—more aloof and forbidding. No wonder the town thought he was a gangster. His facade placed a wall between him and the world at large. His eyes were watchful, but in their depths a person glimpsed a soul that had seen too much of the hard side of life.

Amy tried to shake off thoughts of Jake. But the feel of his body over hers this afternoon had brought about a resurgence of so many emotions.

Amy finally turned off the television and settled back on the couch with a book. Unfortunately, the novel couldn't hold her attention, either. Jake's face kept intruding.

He'd always been a private man until one really got to know him. And he'd always carried an air of arrogant competence. But where was the man she'd laughed with? Made love with?

It was hard not to remember his hands engulfing her small breasts, stroking and readying them for the pleasure his mouth could bring.

Amy closed the book with a snap. She was not going to think about that.

"Idiot!" She set the book on the coffee table. A romance novel couldn't compete with the reality of their past. It had been nine years since they'd parted, but his every touch lined her memory.

Amy stood and walked to the living-room window, gazing out over the porch without really seeing. She had to purge her recollections somehow. She had to—

A flicker of motion caught her attention. Had she just seen someone move from behind the maple tree on the curb to the cluster of pines in the front yard?

She strained to see, watching the dark yard intently. Should she turn on the porch light for a better view? Maybe she'd just imagined... No. Definitely not her imagination. Something or someone had just slipped from behind the tree to blend into the overgrown bushes that surrounded the porch.

Her pulse quickened. Eleven o'clock was definitely too late for neighborhood children to be playing hide-and-seek in her parents' front yard. Besides, the figure had been too tall for a young child.

Someone was up to no good. She curbed the instinct to step onto the porch and call out. Ten years ago she wouldn't have hesitated, but Fools Point was no longer the safe, quiet town she'd grown up in. Heck, the downtown area practically looked like a war zone. They were still repairing the damage to the buildings that psycho had blown up last month. And the renovations were barely under way from the fire that had destroyed most of the motel. No wonder she'd heard one of the locals refer to Fools Point as Mystery Junction in the restaurant today.

She'd better call the police. Chief Hepplewhite only lived a few doors down. That fact alone would practically guarantee her an instant response.

She headed for the kitchen.

Her mother kept a small night-light plugged into the

wall near the stove. The light offered enough illumination to show a shadow at the back door.

Her breath caught in her chest. Someone was on the back porch.

But they hadn't knocked.

Fear gripped her as she realized the person was using a knife to cut open the screen door. Someone was trying to break in.

Fear and anger swept her in equal measure. Her family didn't need this! She hit the switch, flooding the kitchen with light. The shadow fled, footsteps racing across the old wooden porch. As the person disappeared from view, Amy reached for the telephone hanging on the wall.

Before her shaking hand could punch in the first number, she heard heavy footsteps on the porch. He'd returned!

She choked off her scream as a fist pounded loudly on the back door.

"Amy! Let me in."

She nearly dropped the telephone. "Jake?"

Her knees were weak with reaction and her hand shook so bad she could barely unbolt the door. "What do you mean by scaring me half to death that way? Who do—"

Without warning, he enfolded her in his arms. Strong arms that had always offered safety and comfort—and unbelievable pleasure.

"Shh. It's okay. He took off. You're all right now. We need to call the police."

Amy pulled back. She'd allowed herself to snuggle into the familiar scent and feel that only Jake had ever evoked for her.

"What are you talking about?"

"Didn't you realize? Someone just tried to break into the house."

"That wasn't you out there?"

In the blink of an eye she glimpsed his hurt before his rigid mask returned.

"I was coming to talk to you when I saw someone sneak around the corner of your house. I wasn't sure what was going on so I followed. The person saw me when you turned on the light and took off. I was going to give chase until I saw you standing in the kitchen."

He hesitated. Once more she glimpsed pain behind his expression.

"I decided to make sure you were okay," he said.

"I'm sorry. I didn't realize there were two people out there. I only saw one."

"So did I." Jake regarded her without expression. "Do you want to call the police or shall I?"

"Is there any point? Whoever it was is long gone by now."

"You should still report the incident." His mask was back in place, his manner coolly aloof once more. "He might try breaking into someone else's house next."

"Yes. You're right. Okay. I just don't want my mother disturbed. She and Dad are pretty heavy sleepers but she isn't feeling well."

"She wasn't hurt this afternoon, was she?"

"No. Nothing like that. She's just tired."

Her gaze riveted on Jake's once dear face. This close, she saw that the years hadn't been kind. Deep lines bracketed his eyes and mouth. The sadness behind his dark, watchful eyes called to something in her soul.

"What are you doing here, Jake?"

"I came to ask you a question."

"I meant here in Fools Point."

His expression didn't change. "I decided to make my home here now."

"Why?"

"Does it matter?"

No emotions showed at all. She wanted to tell him that it did matter, but then he'd want to know why. Amy wasn't sure she had an answer for that particular question.

"What did you want to ask me?" she asked instead.

He moved close enough that she could reach out and touch him. Her heart sped up and her stomach muscles contracted in expectation.

"Is Kelsey my daughter?"

The world dissolved in icy shock to reform in blazing anger. "How dare you ask me that?"

"Is she?"

Hands gripped her shoulders, pinning her beneath his steady stare.

"You bastard. You never even read my letters, did you?"

Jake blinked. "What letters?"

She tugged free, moving away from him, wrapping her arms around her suddenly chilled body. How could he stand there and ask her that?

"I never got any letters from you, Amy."

"Right."

"I never lie, Amy."

She rounded on him angrily. "Well, if you didn't get them, then your brother-in-law is a bigger bastard than you are."

Jake flinched, but his gaze didn't waver.

"Ask him," she insisted. "I wrote you twice. Once when I found out I was pregnant, and once after Kelsey was born. I almost didn't send you the second letter since you never responded to the first one, but I figured you'd at least want to know if you had a daughter or a son."

Jake tried to quell the sick feeling in the pit of his stomach. He could only stare at her while her words flayed him with a pain much deeper than any physical wound.

"My brother-in-law is dead," he said softly. "He and my sister were killed in a plane crash almost eight years ago."

He watched her face crumple in consternation.

"I didn't know." Her hand lifted as if to offer him comfort, then abruptly fell to her side.

He rubbed his chin, trying to make sense of what she'd told him. "You gave Ronnie the letters to send to me? Why didn't you give them to Carrie?"

"Your sister wouldn't take my calls after you left. I wanted your address, but Ronnie wouldn't give it to me."

She tried to conceal her remembered hurt, but he knew. One more snippet of guilt to live with.

"Ronnie wasn't friendly, either," she went on more stoically. "I figured he and Carrie knew we'd broken up and they didn't want to get involved. While Ronnie wouldn't give me an address to write to you, he agreed I could send you a letter through him."

Jake's pain bit a little deeper. Jake had told Ronnie and Carrie he didn't want to talk to Amy. He'd never thought about the position he'd put them in. He hadn't told Amy how to reach him because he'd wanted to keep the breakup simple and as painless as possible. Amy wouldn't understand that he'd done it to spare her. He didn't understand it himself anymore. He could see Ronnie tossing out her letters thinking she was trying to cling to a dead relationship.

"You didn't tell Ronnie about the baby."

Her eyes snapped green fire. "It wasn't any of his business. Are you telling me he never sent you my letters?"

"I'm telling you I never got any letters from you, Amy," he said quietly. "I don't know if Ronnie didn't send them, or if they never caught up with me. I moved around a lot on my assignments overseas. Sometimes…well, mail didn't always catch up with me. I didn't learn about the plane crash until months after it happened. I swear to you, I never knew about Kelsey.''

He could see she wasn't sure whether to believe him or not. He didn't blame her. He'd had months lying in that hospital bed not so long ago regretting the choices he'd made. Especially the fact that he'd let her go—and the unforgivable way he'd gone about it.

''I'm sorry, Amy.''

''So am I.'' A sheen of tears hovered in her eyes. ''Now get out of here, Jake.''

The words fell like a blow. She followed them up with a knockout punch of calm deliberation. ''My duty was to let you know. I did my part. Goodbye, Jake.''

He deserved her anger and more. He shook his head, knowing he was going to have to hurt her even further.

''That isn't how it's going to work,'' he said mildly.

''Oh, yes. Yes, it is, Jake Collins. Kelsey is my daughter. I've raised her, cared for her and loved her since she was born. I don't need you and neither does she. Now get out of here.''

She immediately pressed 9-1-1 on the phone she held in her hand. Her eyes held his accusingly.

''This is Amy Thomas. I'd like to report an attempted break-in at my parents' house. *Someone*—'' she held his gaze steadily ''—cut the screen trying to get inside the back door.''

Her pain ate at him. He deserved her anger, but she had it wrong. He wasn't about to walk away now that he knew he had a daughter.

He was a father!

The unbelievable miracle would take some getting used to.

"The police are sending a car," Amy told him. "You can leave now."

"They'll want to talk to me."

"Maybe they will, but I don't," she said with quiet dignity.

The quiver of her lower lip was the giveaway. She was holding back tears.

"I'm not going to justify walking away nine years ago."

"Good. Don't."

"I couldn't if I tried," Jake said softly. "But I want you to believe one thing. If I had known about Kelsey I would have done everything in my power to take care of both of you."

Amy gave a ladylike snort. "I didn't need anyone to take care of me, Jake. I managed just fine on my own."

"Of course you did. You were always stronger than you thought you were." He glimpsed the reflection of flashing lights in the living-room windows. "The police are here. I'll speak to them, but this conversation isn't over."

"Yes, it is."

He walked past her through the house, heading for the front door. Officer Derek Jackstone was just mounting the porch steps.

"Officer," he greeted Jackstone.

"Hello, Mr. Collins. I didn't expect to see you here. We had a report of a prowler?"

Jake explained the little he'd seen, then nodded toward Amy who watched the exchange in silence. "I'll be at the Perrywrinkle if you need me for any reason."

"Thank you." Officer Jackstone stepped past him and Jake headed down the steps without looking back. "Ms. Thomas," he heard Jackstone greet Amy.

"Derek, you may wear a uniform now, but I'm still

the same Amy who sat next to you in biology,'' she told him.

Yes, she probably was, Jake thought. She was still the same Amy he'd fallen in love with nine years ago. And she was more out of reach now than she had been then. He sighed and wondered if it was too soon to take another pill for his back.

ONCE DEREK LEFT, Amy paced the house nervously, trying not to think about Jake or the past or anything else. The attempted break-in didn't disturb her as much as their conversation.

She didn't want to feel sorry for Jake. She didn't even want to believe him.

But she did.

Amy turned off the lights, double checked the doors and windows, and headed upstairs. Her parents must have fallen asleep early because even the flashing lights of the police car hadn't brought them downstairs to investigate.

Ronnie had never sent her letters to Jake. All this time she had thought he didn't care and Jake hadn't known the truth. Not that it changed anything. Jake was Kelsey's biological father, but he had no place in their lives. Amy had only wanted to show him what he'd given up.

Yet he hadn't given her up if he never knew of her existence.

Amy shook aside that thought. Walking away without any explanation was proof enough that he wasn't the sort of stable influence she wanted in Kelsey's life. One day they were lovers in every sense of the word, then next he'd left on a mission for the navy. When he'd returned, he'd announced he was being sent overseas—indefinitely. And he'd thanked her—*thanked her!*—for the past few months and left.

The hollow feeling returned along with the memory.

She'd been so desperately in love with him she would have followed him anywhere.

And in a way she had. She eyed her reflection as she finished brushing her teeth. After all this time she could finally admit to herself that the only reason she'd taken the translator's job was that she'd known they'd send her overseas on military contracts. Overseas, where Jake was.

But it hadn't mattered. She'd never seen Jake again.

"Spilled milk," she told her reflection. She and Kelsey didn't need Jake. They didn't need anyone.

She turned off the lights and slipped between the sheets of the big double bed, staring at the ceiling and listening to every creak the old house made. Had the house always made this much noise? It wasn't as if there was a lot of wind or anything tonight.

Finally she had to admit that she wasn't going to sleep anytime soon. While Derek Jackstone had assured her that the prowler had probably been some kid looking for easy money, Amy realized the incident had unnerved her more than she'd thought.

Even with Derek's promise that he would drive past the house frequently tonight, she was uneasy, jumping at every sound.

Though Jake's presence had distracted her right after the attempted break-in, she now began to wonder. Derek's explanation of some kid made no sense. Any local teens would know she was staying here with her parents. Why would they risk breaking into an occupied house when the living-room light had clearly been on? That made no sense.

What would have happened if Jake hadn't come by in time to scare the intruder away? Amy shuddered.

Resigned to a sleepless night, she got up and walked over to the window. No moonlight or streetlight broke the darkness. Not even the flicker of fireflies relieved the stillness. She watched intently while her thoughts roamed wildly.

And something moved in the shadows across the street.

She tried to calm the flutter of fear that captured her breath. She stared until her eyes ached with the effort. But she still couldn't decide if someone lurked in the shadows of the gnarled old maple tree or not.

FINGERS FISTED, the watcher stared at the old house. Anger flared at the unfairness of the whole thing. So much was at stake. Too many people knew the truth. People who could no longer be trusted to keep the secrets of the past. The parking lot had picked the worst possible time to collapse.

She was still the biggest danger of all, of course. If it hadn't been for the restaurateur's interference...but he had interfered and now the situation would require some thought. She'd been alerted to her danger.

At least the gravel spill would delay things for a while, but not indefinitely. Still, putting the truck in gear had been a stroke of genius, even if the laboratory tests would eventually reveal the truth. Chief Hepplewhite wasn't like his fatuous predecessor. He'd move on the crime scene with care...and unfortunate speed.

There was no choice. Fools Point would have to bear witness to a fatal accident. Possibly, an entire series of accidents. She wasn't the only danger—just the most immediate one.

Too bad the dump truck hadn't knocked her into the hole and buried her beside the others. All the problems would have been solved neatly then.

The next accidents would require careful planning and strategy. No more leaving things to chance. But in the end, all of them would be as dead as the bones in that old root cellar.

Chapter Three

"Chief Hepplewhite?" Amy said as she opened her front door. "I wasn't expecting you. Did you catch our intruder from last night?"

"I'm afraid not."

"Amy? Who is it, dear?" her mother called. "Oh, hello, John. Come on in. Amy, don't just stand there. Let John come inside and sit down. In fact, come on back to the kitchen. We were just sorting through some old photographs. How about a glass of iced tea? Did you catch our brazen housebreaker from last night? We went to bed early and never heard a thing. I couldn't believe it when Amy told us this morning. He totally destroyed the door screen."

Amy stepped back and allowed the officer entrance to the house. As her mother turned and led the way back to the kitchen, Hepplewhite motioned for Amy to precede him. "I'm afraid we didn't catch the person, Mrs. Thomas. Officer Jackstone said Mr. Collins chased him off."

Amy tried to hide a grimace. She didn't want her mother asking a lot of questions about Jake's part in the events of last night. The police chief took a seat at the table while her mother bustled around the kitchen setting out another glass of iced tea and a plate of cookies.

Self-consciously, Amy returned to her seat, setting aside the box of snapshots she'd been sorting with her mother. She pushed the photo albums to the center of the table, now glad that Kelsey had gone to school with one of the neighboring children today. The school year had begun before Amy could return to the States so she was home schooling Kelsey until she located a new job and more permanent housing arrangements for the two of them.

"I understand you never got a clear look at the intruder?" Chief Hepplewhite asked Amy.

Amy shook her head. "He was just a shape through the window."

"Good thing Mr. Collins stopped by then."

The words begged the question, and Amy was prepared. "Jake wanted to check on my mother to be sure she was okay after that incident at the restaurant yesterday."

"And I am so thankful that he did," Susan added, handing the police chief a tall glass of iced tea. "What with all the strange things going on in town anymore."

Hepplewhite thanked her, took a long swallow and sat back in his chair. "Please, sit down, Mrs. Thomas. Actually, that brings up another subject I'd like to discuss with you. We're trying to identify the bodies in that old root cellar."

Susan Thomas gripped the back of a chair.

"Mom?"

"How on earth would I know them?" she asked faintly.

"Sorry. I stated that badly. I didn't mean to imply that you knew them personally. We're canvassing everyone who's lived in Fools Point for a long time, trying to get some idea of who the woman and child could be."

Amy had risen to go to her mother, but Susan waved her back and sank heavily onto the chair.

"Maybe you'd better come back later, Chief," Amy said quickly. "Mom hasn't been feeling well and—"

Her mother shook her head. "I'm fine, dear. It's just such a shocking thing. Very upsetting."

"Yes," Hepplewhite agreed.

Amy perched on the edge of her chair, watching her mother closely.

Susan managed a wavery smile. "How can I help you, John?"

"I figure you and Cornelius probably know everybody in town."

Her mother rallied. "I would hope so. Corny's been delivering mail for over fifty years now."

Hepplewhite smiled, catching Amy off guard once again. She hadn't realized the chief was so much younger than he looked. With that shock of white hair and the lines bracketing his eyes, she'd originally thought him close to fifty. Now she revised her estimate down a good ten to fifteen years—maybe more. He was a nice-looking man with a lived-in face.

"Since I've only been in town three years, I have to rely on natives like you for information. We'd like to identify the woman and her child as quickly as possible."

Amy knew the chief didn't miss the way her mother's fingers tightened on the edge of the tabletop. But Susan Thomas managed a sad smile. "Of course. Their poor family. How can I help?"

"We're looking for anyone who might have been pregnant and suddenly went missing. Or someone who had an infant and disappeared."

Susan shook her head. "I'm afraid Fools Point has seen the birth of a lot of babies over the years, but I can't think of anyone who disappeared."

Amy straightened in her chair. The chief glanced at her and she worked to keep her expression as blank as possible while apprehension crawled up her spine.

Her mother was lying.

"Do you know of anyone, Amy?" he asked calmly, obviously not aware of her mother's perfidy.

"No." She thought quickly, wanting to divert his attention from her mother. "Not precisely. But back when I was in high school several women disappeared, including a girl who graduated the year before I did. Remember, Mom? The police were looking for a serial rapist, I think. Most of the victims were from Frederick County, but one of the girls that lived out at Hearts Keep—Gabriella, I think it was, also disappeared about that same time."

Hepplewhite shook his head. "I reviewed those cases and that one in particular when I took over as police chief. None of the missing women was known to be pregnant."

"Well, as to that I wouldn't be so sure. As I remember it, Gabriella was running with a pretty wild group at the time," Susan rallied to argue.

"Something to keep in mind, but I'm thinking we need to go back further than that," Hepplewhite said. "Based on the decomposition and the things I observed at the site, my guess is that those bodies were in that root cellar a lot longer than ten years."

Because she was so attuned to her mother, Amy caught the shudder that seemed to run through her body.

"Long enough to have been a runaway slave or something? I think the Perry house might have been part of the underground railway way back around the time of the Civil War."

"They aren't that old."

"How can you tell?" Amy asked.

"The clothing wasn't that old, for one thing. The medical examiner will make the actual determination. There are forensic tests that will give us a good idea when the mother and child died, and hopefully what they died of. With any luck, we can also get DNA samples, but we'll need something to compare them with."

Amy saw her mother close her eyes as if she were in pain. "Mom?"

"Sorry, dear." Susan's eyes fluttered open. "I just keep thinking of the poor relatives."

She was lying again. Amy was sure of it. Her mother's hand trembled where it rested against the table. Amy became all bristling concern.

"Mom, I think you should go upstairs and lie down."

"Yes, perhaps I should at that."

That response scared Amy more than anything else. What was going on?

Hepplewhite's expression became concerned. "Can I do anything to help?"

"No, no. I'll be fine. I just find it distressing to think of that poor woman and her child down there all this time. Was she... Do you think she was—" her mother swallowed hard "—murdered?"

Hepplewhite looked chagrined. "It's too early to say, Mrs. Thomas. I can tell you that I didn't see any obvious signs of trauma. I had a preliminary glance around before the truck slipped gears and Lee and I had to scramble for our lives, but forensics isn't really my field."

"Is that what happened with the truck?" Amy demanded, still trying to divert his attention from her mother. "It slipped out of gear?"

"It's one theory," he confirmed. "Did you see anyone around the truck before it began moving?"

"Your officer asked us that yesterday. The answer is

still no. We'd just gotten there. The truck was behind us.''

''Yes. You were almost directly in its path,'' he said neutrally.

''That's right. Jake threw us to the ground just in time.'' She saw her mother shudder. Apparently so did Chief Hepplewhite.

''I'm sorry again.''

Susan put a hand to her chest. ''You have a job to do. I understand, John. But I think...I wonder if you'd excuse me? I'm not feeling well right now.''

''Mom?'' Amy was on her feet instantly, but her mother waved her off.

''I just need to go up and rest for a few moments. If you'll both excuse me.''

''I am sorry,'' Hepplewhite apologized sincerely. ''I didn't mean—''

''It's not your fault.'' Susan patted his arm. ''I seem to have a weak stomach for this sort of thing. I promise, if I think of anything that would help, I'll let you know. Please stay and finish your iced tea.''

Amy stared uncertainly after her mother, torn between a desire to go after her and the need to stay with their uninvited guest and get some answers of her own.

Fear churned her stomach. Why was her mother lying to the police? What could she possibly know or suspect about the bodies in an abandoned root cellar?

''I didn't mean to distress your mother,'' the police chief said kindly.

''Mom hasn't been feeling well lately. She has a heart condition, you know. I think maybe you'd do better to talk with my father or someone like Miss Tooley at the post office. Or what about Mrs. Kitteridge at the general store? She usually knows all the local gossip.''

Chief Hepplewhite nodded. ''They're on my list. I

came here first because of what happened last night. The bodies are a high priority, but I also wanted to reassure you and your mother that we'd be keeping a closer eye on the neighborhood for the next few days. I doubt the person will come back, but I want you both to be alert.''

The serious expression in his eyes caused a hitch in her breathing. ''Officer Jackstone said it was probably some kid.''

Hepplewhite's lack of expression instantly aroused her earlier suspicions.

''I thought it odd that a kid would break into a house where the lights are on and someone obviously is not only home but still up.''

Hepplewhite regarded her shrewdly. After a moment he seemed to come to a decision. ''Do you plan to stay in Fools Point for a while?''

The sudden shift took her by surprise. ''I'm not sure yet. Why?''

''Frankly, Ms. Thomas, I doubt if this was an attempted burglary.''

Her stomach iced in alarm. ''A rapist?''

His shoulders lifted a fraction. ''We may never know for sure. I don't want to panic you, but I think it would be a good idea for you to be vigilant. It's possible someone saw you through the window, decided you were here alone and marked you as a victim.''

Amy shuddered. His logic made horrible sense. Much more sense than a neighborhood kid.

''It was probably a very good thing that Mr. Collins came by when he did.''

''Yes,'' she agreed faintly.

''Now, I don't want you to panic.''

''No panic, but my fear quotient just jumped several notches.''

He didn't smile at her weak attempt at humor. "Have you known Mr. Collins a long time?"

Amy nodded without thinking. "We met the summer I graduated from college. One of my roommates was friends with his sister."

Hepplewhite seemed to be filing that information away.

"You don't think Jake—"

"Not at all. But he does tend to keep to himself so I was a bit surprised to hear he was here last night."

Amy sought for a diversion. She really didn't want to discuss her relationship with Jake with the police chief. "Without sounding paranoid, I think you should know I thought someone was watching the house last night."

"Before or after the attempted break-in?"

"After." Briefly she described what she thought she'd seen. "I have to admit, I didn't get much sleep after that."

"You should have called us immediately."

"I might have been mistaken."

"Amy, our job is to check out suspicious activity. That's what we get paid for. Don't ever hesitate to call us."

"All right."

Hepplewhite's expression was grave. "Even petty thieves have been known to kill. If you see anything— and I mean anything at all unusual, day or night—call and let us do the confronting."

"Don't worry, you've convinced me."

"Your mother needs to be vigilant, as well. I'm sorry she's feeling poorly, but rapists don't care who the victim is. Rape isn't an act of sex. It's an act of violence. I'm going to have men drive by regularly. I don't like the idea that someone may be stalking you."

"I'm not real excited about the idea, either!"

"Pay attention at all times to your surroundings. It would be best if you stayed with others and didn't let yourself become isolated."

Truly frightened now, Amy's first thought was her daughter. "Do you think Kelsey is in danger?"

"Look, maybe this was just a fluke, but I'm even more concerned now that you told me someone may have been loitering out front after Officer Jackstone left."

"Maybe...maybe it was Jake."

"Why would you think that?"

"I didn't call you because I'd half convinced myself that Jake had come back to sort of keep an eye on us."

Hepplewhite said nothing and she found herself explaining more than she'd wanted to. "Jake and I were, uh, good friends a long time ago. Despite rumors to the contrary, Jake isn't involved in organized crime."

The lines beside his eyes crinkled in amusement. "I know."

"You checked him out?"

"It wasn't difficult. One of the locals, Noah Inglewood, recognized Mr. Collins as a Special Forces leader he had shared a mission with once. Mr. Collins has a rather impressive military record."

"Oh."

The chief stood and thanked her for her time and the iced tea. Silently, she walked him to the front door.

"Please apologize to your mother again, but try to warn her to be careful. That serial rapist you referred to earlier was never caught. I don't want to find out the hard way that he's returned to his old stomping grounds."

Amy shuddered. "You think this could be the same person who was in the area a few years ago?"

"No," he said firmly. "If, and I stress the if, the person last night was a would-be rapist, I suspect it was a matter of seizing what he saw as an opportunity."

"I understand."

"Stay alert. And if you can think of anything that would help us identify the woman and baby in the root cellar, let me know."

"There is one thing. Have you talked with the Perry family? The restaurant is the old Perry mansion, you know. The mayor's mother lived in the house until a few years ago."

He paused on the front porch and nodded. "I'm afraid Ms. Perry's mental faculties aren't sufficient to be reliable anymore. I plan to have a talk with her niece, the mayor, but—"

"What about her brother?"

Hepplewhite hesitated, his brow pleating. "Eugene?"

"Not the mayor's brother, I meant Ms. Perry's brother, the mayor's father. General Marcus Perry actually inherited the estate but he didn't live there once he joined the military. He and his wife, Millicent, had Cindy Lou and Eugene. I'm not sure where Eugene lives, but I know old Ms. Perry lived in the house until she started having problems. Of course, she was always a little—"

"Strange?"

Amy nearly smiled. "I was going to say reclusive. Her brother Marcus is…" She paused on the verge of calling the general strange. "I've met General Perry in the course of my duties for the military," she added quickly instead. And in every case Marcus Perry had stared at her with a disquieting expression. Amy had taken to avoiding any place where she might run into the man. "He would probably know when the root cellar was closed up."

"An excellent suggestion. Thank you. I'll ask Cindy Lou how to get in touch with her father."

"Good luck."

She closed the screen door behind him. After a moment, for the first time in memory, she locked it as she watched the officer stride to his waiting vehicle.

"IF I UNDERSTAND YOU correctly, Officer Garvey, someone tampered with that dump truck on purpose."

"I didn't say that, Mr. Collins."

The policeman's gaze swept the empty dining room. Shortly, the Perrywrinkle would open and the carefully laid tables would fill with the usual lunch crowd.

Jake tipped his head and raised his eyebrows. "Is there some indication that the truck had faulty gears?"

Lee Garvey smiled ruefully. "The state police are looking into that for us. I know you already answered this once, but I thought maybe after sleeping on the incident you might have remembered seeing someone near the truck before it began to roll backward."

"My attention was elsewhere at the time." On a woman with golden-brown hair and lips made for kissing. A woman who had haunted his memories for years and given life to his child.

A woman who hated him.

"You think someone deliberately put the truck in gear?" Jake asked.

"Not necessarily. It could have been a kid fooling around."

Instantly Jake came alert. His body tightened imperceptibly. "Matt was on the other side of the hole. I saw him myself right before I realized the truck was moving."

"I wasn't accusing anyone."

Perhaps not, but fifteen-year-old Matt Williams's reputation made that almost inevitable. Matt had been caught boosting vehicles for a car theft ring the FBI had broken up several weeks ago. An orphan, Matt had lived with his maternal aunt and her husband until he'd witnessed a murder and become a liability to the car thieves. To keep him silent, his aunt and uncle's house had been blown up—with Matt inside. The boy had been lucky enough to survive.

"I understand he's staying with you," Garvey said.

Jake tensed. In truth, he had no legal standing where Matt was concerned. Matt's paternal aunt and uncle were still his official guardians, but Dwight Kornbaum had confessed that he and Matt couldn't be in the same room without arguing. The boy was ruining his marriage and his life. Dwight was more than ready to turn Matt over to another relative.

"Matt is staying here so his schooling won't be interrupted while his aunt and uncle's house is being rebuilt," Jake said simply. "Catherine and Dwight are staying in D.C. with some friends who live close to where they work."

He didn't add that Matt acted as if the new arrangement didn't matter to him one way or another, but Jake recognized the signs of a boy who knew when he wasn't wanted.

During the time the Perrywrinkle was being gutted and refurbished, Jake had done his best to get to know the skittish boy and earn his trust. If Matt wondered why his relatives had come to this arrangement with Jake, he'd never asked, though Jake had presented several opportunities for him to do so. Matt trusted no one. Forging a bond with him took time and patience. Jake had plenty of both.

Since he'd come to stay with Jake, Matt had slowly begun to lose some of his initial wariness. Jake wasn't about to have that destroyed by a false accusation.

"He had nothing to do with the truck," Jake stated firmly.

"Hey, I believe you."

After a moment Jake inclined his head. "I thought the fact that Matt once stole your car might still…rankle." Especially since the policeman had left a gun in the car that was later used in a murder.

"You can stand down, Papa Bear," Lee said with an infectious grin. "I don't hold grudges. I'm looking for answers, not pointing fingers."

Jake decided it was hard not to like the affable policeman.

"The chief may have already asked you this, but did you know about the root cellar when you bought the estate?"

"No. There was a decaying gazebo close to that spot. I took some pictures of the grounds when I first purchased the land."

Lee's expression lit up. "May I see them?"

As they passed the bar, Ben waved at them from behind the large mahogany counter where he was inventorying stock. Jake inclined his head and led Lee up to his makeshift office. The upstairs was sparingly furnished in used pieces, many of which had come from the original estate. The attic was still filled with items the family hadn't wanted. Jake hadn't had time to go through it all.

Lee Garvey peered around curiously, but Jake offered neither an apology nor an explanation. The furniture might not be much, and he'd made no attempt at any homey features, but the place was clean and his files were neatly organized. Without hesitation, Jake pulled out the pictures he had taken shortly after buying the Perry estate.

"If you look closely, in this shot you can see the remains of the foundation for what I believe was the old servants' quarters. Right about here is where the parking lot caved in."

The picture clearly showed the gazebo inside the area

that must have been an outbuilding. The gazebo was nearly rubble from the same lack of care the rest of the grounds had received.

"As you can see, the outbuildings had all been torn down before I bought the estate."

"At least this explains why the root cellar was so far from the main house. It went with the servants' quarters and not the main house."

Jake said nothing.

"May I borrow these for a few days?" the officer asked.

"I have the negatives."

"Even better, thanks. I'll return them."

As the two headed for the stairs, Matt came running up to the second floor. "Hey, Jake!"

The teenager stopped dead when he saw the police officer. All trace of youthful exuberance faded from his expression. His features became wary and instantly defensive.

"Officer Garvey needed some pictures of the original grounds," Jake explained softly.

"Oh."

Surprisingly, the policeman showed his sensitivity by waving the negatives and smiling at Matt as he moved past him down the stairs. "Hi, Matt. Thanks again, Mr. Collins."

Matt followed the man's progress with an adult watchfulness that saddened Jake.

"What was your good news?" he asked the boy.

Matt watched the officer move out of sight before he turned back to Jake. Some of his earlier excitement returned. "I made a starting position with the soccer team."

Jake relaxed.

"The coach said I'm really fast on my feet."

Not surprising considering the life of crime he'd been heading toward, Jake mused silently.

"I have to keep my grades up to stay on the team, but the coach organized a mentoring program. If I have trouble in a particular area, he pairs me off with another student…"

Jake listened intently. Thankfully, a boy still lurked inside the street-smart young man. Matt was a bright kid. He needed a break and someone who cared. Jake planned to see to it he got both.

"Do you have time to eat lunch with me?" Matt asked. "It's okay if you don't."

"I'd like that," Jake said sincerely.

Matt beamed. "Since we only had a half day of school, I'm going to meet a couple of older guys at the school to get in some extra practice. Is that okay?" he added as an afterthought.

"'Older guys'?" Jake asked mildly.

"Two of 'em are seniors."

"Ah. Their advice should be invaluable."

"Yeah. The coach was gonna try and sneak away from the teacher meetings to come and give us a few pointers."

"Then we'd better see if we can get the cook to feed us quickly."

But when they reached the dining room, they found Officer Garvey still inside, talking with a large table of customers. Matt stiffened. Jake laid a supportive hand on the boy's shoulder.

General Marcus Perry, out of uniform but looking every inch his rank, sat at one of the large tables with his entire family. As far as Jake knew, it was the first time any of the Perrys had set foot inside their old family home since it had been converted.

Except Eugene. The general's son had started hanging

out in the bar with Thad Osher and a few of the other regulars in the evening.

The mayor was speaking animatedly while her aunt stared in pale-eyed confusion at the once-familiar room.

"Why's he still here?" Matt muttered.

Jake knew the boy was referring to Lee Garvey. "He needs to ask questions so they can identify the bodies."

"They're just skeletons."

Jake nodded. "I know." As they watched, the policeman took his leave. "I have to greet that table. Why don't you order us both a couple of burgers? Tina can serve us at table six."

"Okay. Can I order a milkshake?"

Jake's lips twitched. "Order two."

Matt grinned and raced off toward the kitchen. Jake donned his formal host persona and approached the table. While he'd never met the general in his military capacity, Marcus Perry had sat in on the hearing where Jake had been called in to testify against his son, Eugene. A prank had gone awry and the men involved had found themselves facing a disciplinary hearing. While there had been nothing personal in the testimony—Jake hadn't known Eugene—the man hadn't forgotten and Jake doubted the general had, either.

"Good afternoon. I trust everyone is enjoying their meal."

Cindy Lou Baranski smiled affably, but then, she was coming up for reelection soon, Jake remembered. Eugene glared at him with a sulky scowl. The general studied Jake with steely green eyes that held no trace of warmth, while his fashionably attractive wife smiled politely.

"The food is marvelous," the mayor gushed. "These rolls are to die for. It's remarkable how well this all turned out." She waved a hand at her surroundings.

Gertrude Perry peered at Jake in confusion. "Do I

know you?'' she demanded sharply. ''Where is my piano?''

Eugene snorted, but his sister patted her aunt's hand. ''It's at home, Aunt Gert. Remember? You live with me now.''

For a moment the cloud seemed to lift. ''Of course I remember.'' Gertrude Perry looked straight into the general's eyes. ''I told you this would never work. You wouldn't listen. You never listen. Now what are we going to do?''

The general came to attention without moving, though a muscle twitched in his jaw.

''What wouldn't work, Aunt Gert?''

''Gertrude, dear, you mustn't get upset again,'' Millicent Perry admonished in her proper Bostonian accent.

Gertrude ignored both women, but under her brother's quelling gaze, her eyes lost their focus. She peered at Jake uncertainly. ''Do I know you?''

Eugene barked a laugh and slouched back in his seat, ignoring the silent reprimand from his father. As far as Jake knew, Eugene hadn't held a job since leaving the military as soon as his term was up. Interestingly enough, Eugene never seemed to lack for funds.

''Enjoy your meal,'' Jake said. He joined Matt at table six, only to find the youngster staring at the group.

''I was talking to Arly out in the kitchen. He says they all showed up looking for old Ms. Perry.''

Matt bit into his hamburger and Jake lifted his. Matt's eyes flitted back to the other table.

''Arly says Ms. Perry keeps sneaking off to come over here and stare down the hole. I've seen her myself. She just stands there muttering. Arly figures Ms. Perry knows who the skeletons are.''

Jake surveyed the family. Eugene's expression was even more surly than before. Cindy Lou now sat in tight-lipped anger she appeared to be trying to hide. There was a brittle expression on Millicent Perry's face while the general leaned forward, obviously speaking to the others, his posture ramrod stiff. Only Gertrude remained unaffected by what was being said. She continued gazing about as if puzzled by her surroundings.

"Arly just might be right," Jake said mildly.

"Do you think she killed them and covered over the root cellar so they'd never be found?"

"Someone did."

Matt swallowed another bite, his eyes glittering with youthful excitement. "Yeah. Only, she's an old lady."

"She wasn't always old," Jake pointed out.

"I guess."

Time had a different meaning for a teenage boy, Jake thought. Actually, it hadn't been all that long ago that time had had a different meaning for him, too.

"How long do you figure they were down there, Jake? I mean, they were just bones, right?"

"Right." He swallowed some of his milkshake before answering. "I think they were down there a long time, Matt."

"So she could have killed them?"

"Anything's possible."

The speculation wasn't confined to Matt. The notoriety of the situation was doing wonders for business. People were coming by just for the curiosity factor. But they were staying for the food, Jake thought in satisfaction.

He ate slowly, not hungry, but welcoming a chance to spend time with Matt. The pinched, closed look was starting to fade from the boy's features, Jake noted in silent pleasure. Matt wasn't a bad kid, just rebellious and angry at the way fate had destroyed his world. Soon, Jake would have to sit him down for a long talk. Jake wasn't looking forward to that moment. It could ruin all the trust the two of them had built together.

Matt finished bolting his food and asked to be excused. Jake nodded and stood, as well. They were short-staffed this afternoon so he needed to get back to work.

Jake didn't get a chance to relax again until the lull between the lunch crowd and the evening crowd. By then his back was stiff. He was preparing to go upstairs in search of another muscle relaxant when Ben Dwyer burst into the kitchen.

The bartender was clearly agitated. "Boss, you'd better come. Some woman was hit by a car out in the parking lot."

"Arly, call an ambulance," Jake ordered, already moving toward the door.

"No need," Ben said. "A couple of Emergency Medical Technicians were there when it happened. They were just coming off duty. They're with her now."

Jake moved through the restaurant, mentally cursing the recent rains that had weakened the ground under the parking lot, and the person who had left the bodies in the root cellar in the first place. The restaurant didn't need all the curious onlookers who wandered over to the roped-off section for a quick look down. What they hoped to see, he had no idea, but it had only been a matter of time before someone got hurt.

The current commotion was practically right in front of the restaurant door. A cluster of people surrounded someone struggling to sit up. Jake caught a glimpse of golden-brown hair right before he heard her voice.

"I do not need to go to the hospital. What I need is for one of you to call the police."

Jake shouldered aside the beefy EMT who was reluctantly helping the woman to her feet.

"Amy?"

Relief flooded her features the moment she saw him. She came into his arms, as delicate as porcelain and smelling sweetly of some light, unidentifiable fragrance.

"Thank God," she said against his shirt.

He felt her trembling in his arms and he tightened his hold. "Are you all right? What happened?"

She seemed to gather herself before looking up into his eyes. Hers were cloudy with fear, but they showed no sign of pain that he could see.

"What happened?" he asked again more softly.

"I was coming to see you when someone tried to run me over."

Chapter Four

"Someone deliberately ran you down?" Jake demanded.

"I think so."

Conscious of their audience, Jake looked at the EMT. "Is she hurt anywhere beside the scrape on her arm?"

"I don't know, sir. She won't let us examine her."

"The only thing I hurt was my pride. I seem to be spending an inordinate amount of time on the asphalt of your parking lot and frankly, I'm not all that fond of parking lots."

"Your arm is bleeding."

"It's a scrape."

Jake remembered that set to her mouth. "Let's go inside." But before he could usher her away from the crowd, Chief Hepplewhite pulled up in a marked car. He strode over, his expression grim.

"I got a report of a hit-and-run."

"That would be me," Amy said wryly.

His gaze whipped toward her, assessing her with a glance before turning to the EMT. "Is she hurt?"

"No, I am not hurt. Why won't anyone listen to me? I was paying attention like you told me to. I heard the car coming up behind me. When I realized it wasn't going to stop I darted for that tree. The car barely brushed against me. It was enough to throw me off balance and

I scraped my arm on the tree. That's all. I was more startled than anything else.''

They had drawn a good-size crowd. Despite her calm manner, Amy trembled beneath his touch. She didn't pull away, but Jake wasn't sure she even knew his hand rested on her shoulder.

"Did you get a look at the driver?" Hepplewhite asked.

"No. I think it had dark tinted windows, but I'm not sure. Everything happened so fast."

"I saw it happen," one of the EMTs said. "Wes McGinnis, Chief. My partner and I were pulling in when a large black SUV came out of a parking space and seemed to go right for her. The driver was obviously drunk or not paying attention or something. I got the make, model and license plate." He rattled it off.

"Hey, wait a minute!" Eugene Perry suddenly hustled forward, pushing his way through the crowd. His face was ruddy, and he was wiping sweat from his forehead with a large handkerchief. "That's my car! I left it parked right over—" His pointing finger wavered over the empty space. "Somebody stole my car!"

"Did you see which direction the vehicle turned?" Hepplewhite asked the witness.

"South on Perry Road," McGinnis stated firmly.

"I'm going to take Amy inside," Jake announced. He didn't wait for approval, but turned Amy and led her indoors. The parking lot was filling with curious customers. He sensed her gratitude as he guided her through the restaurant to the upstairs bedroom he used as a living area.

Amy barely glanced around at the sparse, battered furnishings. She sank into the lumpy sofa with a relieved sigh. Jake returned with the first-aid kit and a wet washcloth.

"Let me have your arm."

"What are you doing?" she asked as he squatted beside her.

"I'm going to clean off that cut."

"I can do it."

Jake tilted his head. "Are you afraid to have me touch you?"

"Of course not."

She stuck out her arm as he'd known she would. Jake began to gently wash the scrape. Amy stared at a point on his shoulder while she sat stoically silent.

"Do I have dirt on my shirt?" he asked in quiet amusement.

"What? No." Her face flooded with color, but her gaze slid away from his. Relieved that his touch could still bother her after all this time, he moved slowly and deliberately, wiping away all traces of dirt and blood and then applying an antiseptic cream to the wounds with a tender, light touch.

Her skin was still as soft as he remembered while her muscle tone remained clearly defined. For such a slender woman, she had an athletic build. "Do you still swim and play tennis every day?"

"No."

His stroke became a light caress and she finally met his eyes.

"Don't."

Jake stopped.

"I need to leave."

"What's going on, Amy?" he asked quietly.

"Nothing's go... You mean, the accident? Probably what that man said. A drunk driver or a car thief. I just happened to be in the way."

Jake raised his eyebrows. "First last night, now this. Your popularity seems to be slipping."

She lifted her head in surprise at his deliberately light tone. After a moment her expression turned wry. "You left out the dump truck."

"So I did." He drank in her delicate features, afraid of the emotions stirring to life inside him. "I don't remember you being accident-prone."

"And I don't remember you wanting to own a restaurant."

Silence stretched between them. He studied the familiar tilt of her head and tried to tamp down a surge of desire. He admired her spunk. In fact, he admired a great many things about Amy. He always had.

"Will you give me an honest answer if I ask you something?" she questioned.

"I've never lied to you."

Her snort was dismissive. "Were you watching the house last night after the police left?"

The hairs on the back of his neck prickled in alarm. "No. Someone was watching the house?"

"Maybe. I can't be sure. I thought I saw someone across the street." She hesitated. Almost reluctantly she added, "The police don't think the man you chased off was a burglar."

Jake waited, watching fear edge the corners of her eyes.

"They think maybe…he could have been a rapist."

Anger and fear mixed in equal measure at the thought of someone stalking Amy. "We need to get you away from here," he said tightly.

"I just knew you were going to be difficult about this."

"Difficult? Amy, it's only common sense."

A sudden rap on the door frame startled both of them. Jake realized he'd lost his edge. He'd never even heard the approaching footsteps.

"Am I interrupting?"

"Chief Hepplewhite! No, come in."

Jake raised his eyebrows. Amy blushed.

Jake rose and faced the police chief. "Amy tells me she's being stalked."

"Wait a minute. What I said was—"

"I heard what you said," he insisted, turning back to her. "The person I chased off returned later last night to watch the house."

"We don't know it was the same person," Amy stated. "I'm not even totally sure there was a person. And if there was, he didn't try to get in again."

"Because he knew you were on guard," Jake argued. "He may have seen you in the window watching him."

Disconcerted, she bit at her lower lip. He'd forgotten that habit of hers.

"I did suggest you not go anywhere alone," the police chief said mildly.

"Amy never was very good at following orders," Jake told him.

"They weren't orders, it was a suggestion." She glared at Jake then turned to Hepplewhite. "I thought I'd be fine. I mean, it's broad daylight outside. There were people all around. I wanted to come over and talk with Jake before..." She glanced away, her embarrassment deepening.

"Before I came over to ask him any questions?" the police chief asked politely.

"Well, yes. I wanted to be the one to tell Jake what happened."

Jake cocked his head, aware that he was missing something here. "I suggested Amy go away for a while."

Amy glared in frustration. "We don't know that the intruder intended to rape anyone."

"Do you want to take that sort of chance? Where's Kelsey?" Jake asked abruptly.

"She went to school for the day with Mom's neighbor's daughter. Mrs. Cznery is going to pick them up afterward. Mom isn't feeling well and I thought she could use the break. Kelsey's a quiet child, but having us in the house is a strain. And don't worry, I didn't leave Mom home unprotected, either. Dad's there. He's trying to talk her into going to see the doctor."

"The only one who isn't protected is you," Jake said in annoyance.

"I'm not taking chances. Chief Hepplewhite said to be vigilant. I was extremely vigilant."

"You got hit by a car."

"Bumped. Look, Jake, we aren't even sure a threat actually exists. And why would a rapist suddenly try to run me over with a car?"

"I don't know."

"Exactly, it makes no senses. There is no reason for me to leave town. Besides, I don't have anywhere to go."

"You could stay here."

Silence screamed between them. He hadn't planned to say that, but somehow the words had slipped past his lips. Amy stared. He didn't have a clue what she was thinking, though he was aware of Hepplewhite watching silently.

"I... No. I couldn't stay here. I have Kelsey and my parents. I couldn't."

Hepplewhite cleared his throat. "You may want to reconsider that decision, Amy. We found the vehicle that hit you."

"Already?"

"It was abandoned in the church parking lot next door."

"Out of gas?" Jake asked, but knowing in his gut what the answer would be.

"No."

"Why would the person only drive it next door?" Amy asked.

"Because the driver obviously didn't want to leave your vicinity." Fear made his words come out sounding harsher than he'd intended. But he had to make her see the danger she was in. Jake watched her face pale in comprehension.

"Mr. Collins could be right, Amy. From the eyewitness accounts, the car veered off at the last moment. It's entirely possible the driver wanted to scare you."

"Retaliation for being scared off last night?" Jake asked.

"Maybe," Hepplewhite agreed.

"He could be downstairs right now. We wouldn't know."

Hepplewhite nodded. "I don't have the manpower to have her watched around the clock. Especially not with this other situation to deal with. I'm sorry."

"I understand."

"Well, I don't," Amy said. "There is still nothing to say the two events are even connected, am I right?"

Hepplewhite nodded reluctantly.

"Then be reasonable. I'll go home and talk with my parents, but my mother isn't feeling well. I don't want to leave unless I have to."

Hepplewhite's radio abruptly squawked. The words were indistinguishable to Jake, but Hepplewhite seemed to understand the message. "Copy that, Carolyn. I'll meet him outside." His gaze went from one to the other. "I need to go. I'll have the men continue to patrol your mother's place as often as possible, but I think you should reconsider, Amy. If you'll excuse me."

Jake watched him leave with a hollow feeling. "Amy, don't be stubborn."

"I'm not trying to be stubborn." She rose and faced him. "If you want the truth, I'm every bit as scared as Chief Hepplewhite wants me to be. I'll start looking for a place to live tomorrow, but I can't leave today."

"Does your mother have a spare room?"

"Yes. I'm using it."

"Want to share?"

The pulse point in her throat began to clamor against her skin. Her lips parted slightly and the green of her eyes deepened in color, making them look wider and more innocently tempting than ever before.

Jake took a step toward her. Amy raised her hand, palm toward him. Jake stopped moving.

"You said you'd never lie to me."

He knew before she said the words what was coming next.

"Tell me why you walked out on me all those years ago without an explanation."

Jake sighed. "Because I was a fool."

"That isn't an answer."

He inclined his head in agreement. "Do you remember my friend Brian and his wife, Jean?"

"Of course. He was your best friend. They had a couple of children."

"The oldest was three, the baby was only a year." He hesitated, but there was no easy way to say it. "Brian came back from his last mission in a coffin, Amy." Funny how it was still painful after all these years.

"Oh, Jake." She reached for him in an unconscious gesture of sympathy. "Why didn't you tell me?"

He shook his head, seeking the words that would explain his thoughts and his actions. "I went straight to Jean's place when I got back. She came apart completely. In the end, they had to sedate her. When I left, Brian's three-year-old was sobbing inconsolably because she didn't understand all the turmoil. Brian should have transferred out of our unit once he married and had children. It wasn't fair to his family.''

For a moment she absorbed his words, her expression going from sorrow to something he couldn't define. He felt the loss when she withdrew her hand.

''Are you telling me because Brian died, you turned tail on our relationship and ran?''

Her quietly spoken accusation caught him unprepared. And the barb bit all the more deeply because that was exactly what he'd done. ''I wouldn't have put it in those terms but—''

''There isn't any other way to put it.'' Amy shook her head. ''The big brave navy SEAL didn't want to be responsible for leaving a helpless little woman behind.''

Jake's jaw clenched hard enough to hurt. What had he thought she'd say? ''Thank you for being so noble''? He'd hurt her deeply and he didn't know if he could ever make it right.

''What I do for a living—did for a living,'' he corrected, ''was dangerous. We could be gone for months at a time, called up on a moment's notice. What you and I had between us was pretty intense, Amy. I couldn't afford our relationship to carry over into some of the situations I had to deal with.''

''So it came down to me or the navy, huh? And I lost.''

Jake cursed under his breath. ''I wanted to spare both of us.''

Her laugh was bitter. ''You make quite a martyr, Jake. All that deep brooding silence. Do you realize you've got half the town scared to death of you? The other half thinks you're a snob.''

Jake blinked.

''I never cared much for martyrs,'' she continued angrily. ''I always figured they were too busy feeling sorry for themselves to work up a viable solution to their problems. Thanks for confirming my assumption."

He was so stunned that she nearly made it through the door before he stopped her, a hand on her slender arm. He withdrew it when she grimaced and he realized he had grabbed her wound.

"I didn't want you to—"

"Suffer the way Brian's wife did?" she asked mock sweetly. "Let me tell you something, hero. You should have stuffed your nobility. I spent nine years wondering what I'd done so wrong that you could walk out without a backward glance."

"You didn't do anything wrong at all."

"Yes. I did. I got involved with you and all you wanted was a quick summer fling. You could have been up front and told me so from the start."

"In fairness, I don't think either of us was thinking about what we wanted beyond each other. I wanted you the moment we met and I didn't think past that until Brian died. Then it was like something in me short-circuited. He's suddenly dead, his family is grieving, they tell me I'm being reassigned overseas and you're waiting back at the apartment to take up where we left off. I knew I couldn't do that. I didn't know how to explain it."

"You panicked at the idea of commitment and you ran. See. Easy."

"Amy..." Knowing he deserved her condemnation didn't make it any easier. "I'm truly sorry."

"Good." She started for the stairs.

He spun her around, bringing her to a halt. "Where are you going?"

"Back to my mother's."

Her eyes crackled with fire. Jake felt his own anger rising in response. "You can't go alone. It isn't safe."

"So you say." She looked pointedly at his hand where it now rested on her wrist.

Jake ignored her look. "You have every right to be bitter, Amy."

"I'm not bitter. I'm angry. There's a difference."

He tipped his head to one side. "Not from where I'm standing."

She closed her eyes for a long second. When she opened them, the fire was gone, leaving behind a wealth of sadness. "Maybe you're right, Jake. Maybe I am bitter. We had something special once. At least I thought we did."

"Amy—"

"No, Jake. It's nine years too late for excuses that in my book don't justify your actions. You did the expedient thing and it worked."

Jake grimaced, thinking about Kelsey just as he knew she was doing. Before he could say anything, she plunged on.

"I didn't realize I harbored all that anger, but I'm glad I got to have my say."

"Believe it or not, so am I," he said softly.

"Then let me go, Jake."

He took a deep, calming breath. "I can't do that."

"Planning to turn on the charm now?" She shook her head. "It won't work. I've had nine years to grow up. You ought to try it sometime."

Beneath her scathing words lay the wound he'd inflicted. But she wasn't indifferent toward him. Right now Amy walked the fine line between love and hate. Could he get her to cross that line to his side once more? She might not want to be, but she was still aware of him as a man, and that gave him hope.

There'd been instant, physical chemistry between them from the moment they'd met. That same tension still hov-

ered between them. He slid his thumb over the palm of
her hand, rubbing in a subtle caress. Her gaze slid from
his. Beneath his fingers, he felt the erratic beat of her
pulse.

"Stop that."

She had always responded so quickly to light, sensual
touches.

"I'm not the same person I was, Jake."

"I know." He released her hand and touched her hair
lightly, trying to gauge her emotions. "You've matured
into a beautiful woman."

"One who is much smarter than the girl you used to
know. Let me go, Jake."

"Is that what you really want?"

"Yes."

She wasn't trying to pull away. She watched him with
a vulnerability that made him ashamed. He released her
and stepped back. Maybe he'd misread her emotions, after all. Maybe he'd only seen what he'd so desperately
wanted to see.

"We can't go back," he said softly.

"I'm glad you realize that."

"But we could go forward."

"Dream on, Jake."

"We have a child together. A beautiful little girl that
I knew nothing about."

Panic tightened her features. "You're not taking my
daughter from me, Jake."

"Never," he said quickly. "I wouldn't do that. But
since she's my only child, I would like to be part of her
life. If you'll let me."

"Jake! Hey, Jake!"

They turned as one to see Matt dash up the stairs and
come to an uncertain halt.

"Matt, meet Amy Thomas," Jake introduced.

"Uh, hi."

"This is Matt Williams. He lives with me."

"Hello, Matt," Amy greeted with a forced smile.

"Hi." The boy immediately turned anxious eyes on Jake. "The cops are downstairs. They want to talk to you."

"Someone tried to run Amy over in the parking lot," Jake said soothingly.

Trepidation disappeared instantly. "For real? You mean, on purpose?"

"He might have been drunk," Amy said, shooting Jake a warning look.

"Or he might have been the person who tried to break into your house last night."

"Hey! Jake told me about that. I think I met your daughter today. She's Sarah's friend. Kelsey, right? Mrs. Cznery gave me a lift back when she picked up Sarah's brother Tucker. He's one of the guys I was with," Matt added for Jake's benefit.

"Kelsey went to school with Sarah today," Amy said.

"Cute kid." Matt turned worried eyes to Jake. "The guys were talking... Did you know the cops are asking if anyone saw someone near the dump truck before it rolled toward the hole?"

Jake placed a reassuring hand on his shoulder. "They're covering all bets. They still don't know if the truck slipped out of gear or if someone was trying to rebury the evidence."

"Yeah?"

Jake squeezed the boy's shoulder in reassurance. "They know you're clear. Why don't you get a jump start on that English paper you have do this weekend while I go deal with the police. Then we'll have dinner together and you can tell me about your practice session."

Matt relaxed. He almost smiled. "Okay, Jake. Nice to meet you, Ms. Thomas."

"Same here, Matt."

"I'll drive you back to your mother's," Jake said as they started back downstairs. Amy hesitated but finally nodded.

As soon as they reached the ground level, Jake was called to the kitchen to handle a crisis. He steered her over to the bar. "Wait here for a moment. Ben? See that Ms. Thomas isn't disturbed," he said tersely.

The bartender waved and finished pouring a beer.

"Jake, for heaven's sake."

"I'll be right back."

Amy watched him disappear, her thoughts chaotic. She did not want to be attracted to Jake anymore. It was crazy. But her whole life had become crazy again the moment her mother mentioned Jake's name.

She'd been so certain that he loved her the way she'd loved him. That he'd walked out because he was afraid of commitment shouldn't have surprised her. But it did.

She'd always known Jake's quiet nature covered his emotions. Only in the privacy of their bedroom had he ever let down his guard, and even then, not completely. If only she had demanded answers nine years ago. In the end, it probably wouldn't have changed anything, but at least she wouldn't have spent all this time wondering what had gone wrong.

She wasn't ready to forgive Jake just yet. Maybe never. But they did have a daughter together. That was a bond that wouldn't go away. Could she put aside years of grief and recrimination for the sake of their daughter?

"You weren't hurt, were you?"

Startled, Amy turned to face the man who slid onto the bar stool next to where she stood.

"Eugene Perry," he introduced himself. "It was my car the creep stole."

Hastily, she shook the moist hand he thrust at her.

"No. I was just scraped."

"Good. Glad to hear it. My insurance company will be even happier. You're the Thomas girl, right? You and the major got a thing going?"

"Hey, Eugene," the bartender interrupted, coming over and saving her a response. "Thad Osher's looking for you. He's over there."

A beefy blond man in a police uniform was just sitting down at the other end of the bar. Eugene gave the bartender a scowl, but nodded at the other man. "Okay, thanks. I'll see you around, sweetheart." He swiveled off the stool and sauntered to the far end of the bar.

"Thanks for the rescue," Amy said to Ben.

"Eugene giving you a hard time?"

"Not yet."

"Good. He's pretty full of himself, but he's generally harmless."

"Who's harmless?" Jake demanded, coming up beside them.

"Eugene Perry."

Jake's gaze flashed to the far end of the bar. Eugene gave him a mocking salute and winked at Amy. Amy sensed the tension in Jake, though he didn't betray himself outwardly.

"If he gives anyone any trouble I want to know about it immediately," Jake told Ben quietly.

The young man looked surprised, but nodded. "I'll keep an eye on him."

"Did he say anything out of line?" Jake asked as he guided Amy outside.

"No. He wanted to know if I was okay."

Jake's jaw clenched.

"I gather you two know each other? He called you 'Major'."

"I testified against him at a military hearing some years ago. He was part of a group that pulled a prank where someone got hurt. I was one of the witnesses."

"Great. You do have a way of making friends."

Jake ignored the gibe. "If he approaches you again, let me know."

His protectiveness was a new side to Jake. Or was it possessiveness? He'd never acted possessive before. Funny, they'd lived together an entire summer, but they hadn't really known each other. Sexual chemistry had comprised the biggest part of their relationship, she realized.

From their first meeting her response to Jake had been incendiary. She had gone to bed with him that first night, drunk on his presence rather than the two beers she'd consumed. Other people had faded away and time stood still whenever they were together. Their conversations had been inconsequential. They'd lived and loved in a dream-spun cocoon that had shattered the instant reality touched it and them.

Her college roommate had tried to warn her to slow down. But Amy hadn't been listening to anyone but her heart that summer. When Jake walked out, she'd been devastated with no one to blame except herself.

Well, she wasn't twenty-two anymore. If her hormones were rioting again, she would take control. She didn't even want to *like* Jake anymore. She would not allow the mere touch of this man to send shivers of anticipation down her spine again.

But she still wanted him.

"I was thinking. Maybe if we hire you a body-guard…"

Amy came to a stop as they crossed the parking lot.

"Are you crazy? Even if I could afford one, I'm not going to hire a bodyguard."

Jake cocked his head. His mouth opened for a reply, but quickly shut again as General Marcus Perry strode toward them. For an instant Amy could have sworn she saw a flash of hatred in the general's expression when he recognized her, but it was gone before she could be sure.

"Have you seen my sister?" he asked Jake without preamble.

"No, sir. Is Ms. Perry missing again?"

The general regarded Jake as if he were some raw recruit who'd committed a major screw-up. "Cindy Lou failed to keep a tight watch. I thought Gertrude might have wandered back over here."

"I haven't seen her but I can have my staff—"

"I'll handle it, Major."

He strode toward the roped-off hole.

"He gives me the creeps," Amy said out loud before she could stop herself.

Jake regarded her curiously. "You know him?"

"I ran into him in the course of my job a few times." She shook her head in dismissal of the irritable general. "Jake, I need to get back home before Kelsey does. I don't want my family to hear about the hit-and-run from someone else."

Jake nodded.

They rode in silence to her parents' place where three cars were parked in the driveway. "Having a party?" Jake asked.

"If we are, nobody told me."

"I'll come in with you."

Jake was out of the car and coming around to her side before she could formulate an argument.

Inside the house, several neighbors were setting food on the dining room table, buffet style.

"Hello, Amy," Mrs. Cznery sang out. The woman's mouth dropped at the sight of Jake at Amy's side.

"What's going on?" Amy asked her mother's neighbor.

"Oh, uh, we were supposed to have a potluck meeting of the library committee," the flustered woman explained hurriedly. "But the power went out again so your mother kindly volunteered her place instead." Her timid gaze rested on Jake's still features. "Hello, Mr. Collins."

Jake inclined his head.

Susan Thomas rushed over to them. "Hello, dear. Mr. Collins, how nice to see you again. Would you like to join us?"

"I'm afraid I have to get back to the Perrywrinkle."

"Yes, of course."

"I thought you weren't feeling well," Amy said to her mother.

"Oh, I was fine after a short nap, dear."

Her mother did not look fine. There were circles beneath her eyes and a tenseness to her features. "Where's Kelsey?"

"The girls went to a movie. Mr. Cznery is picking them up on his way home from work. I hope you don't mind, but I told Donna Cznery that Sarah and Winchester could spend the night over here. She just had her carpets professionally cleaned. I can't imagine what that cost."

"Mother."

"Yes, dear, but it would be nice to hire someone to do mine, don't you think?"

"Amy," Jake interrupted, "I'd like to stay but I have to get back to the restaurant. I'll come back tonight after I close."

"That isn't necessary."

Reluctantly, her mother turned away as one of the neighbors asked her a question.

"Not even a stupid burglar or rapist would bother a house with the library committee, two eight-year-olds and Winchester in residence."

"Winchester?"

"Sarah's Great Dane."

"Ah. Then I'll call you."

He almost looked vulnerable. Probably her imagination. Nevertheless, she found herself nodding. "We do need to talk."

He lifted her chin and before she knew what he intended, kissed her lightly on the lips. "We will."

Her traitorous lips had wanted to cling. She'd had to forcefully still her hands to prevent them from reaching for him as her heart raced and her body came alive in a way she could barely remember.

In her peripheral vision she saw Mrs. Cznery's shocked expression. Belatedly, Amy realized Jake had just kissed her in full view of half the town gossips.

She would kill him, she decided as heat filled her face and Jake disappeared through the front door. No jury would convict her.

"Why, Amy," the head librarian said, "I didn't realize you knew our Mr. Collins so well."

She gritted her teeth and pasted a smile on her face. "We're friends. Mom, can I talk with you for a moment, please?"

Her mother looked up absently. "I'm afraid now isn't a good time, dear. Isn't that Kelsey coming in the door?"

Eventually, Amy came to the inescapable conclusion that her mother was avoiding her. This sudden burst of good citizenship wasn't unlike her mother, but the timing was a bit too convenient. She didn't suppose her mother had gone so far as to sabotage the circuit breaker at the library, but her mother did agree Kelsey could invite three more girls to spend the night. Obviously her mother was going out of her way to prevent any quiet time to speak with her daughter.

Amy had overheard several people discussing the bodies in the root cellar and noticed that each time her mother had found something to do elsewhere. Once Amy overheard someone speculating on her relationship with Jake. Amy had been glad when the meeting broke up and the house finally quieted down. Or as quiet as five giggling eight-year-olds could be.

Her parents retired upstairs early again, leaving Amy to maintain a silent vigil at her bedroom window. She'd tried reading, but couldn't concentrate. And it had nothing to do with the smell of popcorn, or the muted sounds that made their way up the stairs from the living room.

Amy nearly jumped a foot when the telephone rang. By the time she walked around her bed to answer it, her daughter had already picked up. She heard Kelsey saying hello over and over again. The buzz of conversation and a movie played in the background. Winchester woofed loudly.

"Must have been a wrong number," Kelsey said to someone as she replaced the receiver.

But Amy heard a distinct click in her ear as the silent caller finally hung up.

Chapter Five

Fear left Amy shaking.

Maybe it had been a wrong number. Or maybe it had been Jake. But what if it had been someone with something more sinister in mind? If only her parents had Caller ID. She could hardly call the police about a wrong number, but she wouldn't sleep a wink tonight.

The children were safe. They had to stay safe. After a moment she dialed information and got the phone number for the Perrywrinkle. The line rang a long time before it was answered. No wonder. It was nearly midnight.

"Hello?" a man's voice answered.

"Uh, this is Amy Thomas. Is Jake Collins there?"

"Yeah, sure. Hold on." The mouthpiece was roughly covered and she recognized Ben Dwyer calling Jake's name. "For you, Jake. Amy Thomas. I'm going to take off now, if that's okay."

"Good night, Ben," Jake said as the receiver switched hands. "Amy, what's wrong?"

The moment she heard his deep voice, her fears receded. All the conclusions she'd jumped to now felt foolish. "Jake, I'm sorry. I shouldn't have called."

"What's wrong, Amy?"

The calm, low tone soothed her as it always had. She managed a weak chuckle. "I let myself get spooked over nothing. I thought maybe you had just called here. Someone did, and Kelsey answered. The caller stayed on the line but didn't say anything."

She tried to relax her death grip on the telephone, but saying the words brought back the fear. Why hadn't the person said something? Or at least disconnected before Kelsey did? "It was probably a wrong number, like Kelsey said."

"I'll be right there."

Her heart pounded erratically. "You don't need to come over."

"Five minutes to get the rest of my staff out of here and be sure Matt is in and settled for the night."

"Jake, you don't..." His silence spoke louder than words. Amy realized no matter what lay between them, she'd welcome his presence right now. "Okay, but... could you come to the back door? I don't want to alarm the girls."

"Seven minutes total. And, Amy, I'm going to circle the house first."

"Oh."

"You did the right thing." He hung up before she could respond.

She felt foolish, but only slightly. Where her daughter was concerned, she would take no chances. It was gratifying to know that Jake felt the same way.

Amy headed downstairs. Her daughter waved at her from the living room, but Winchester was the only one to follow her out to the kitchen. The huge animal's head was chest-high on her. If a person didn't see his dopey expression, they could be forgiven for running in the opposite direction. His head was larger than hers. She wondered if Sarah's mother would consider renting the beast.

"Want to go for a walk?" she asked.

Winchester wagged his tail in agreement, placing everything in range in jeopardy.

"Sarah, I'm going to take Winchester out for a quick walk."

"Okay." The little girl called back from the other room, "His leash is in the kitchen somewhere."

Amy found the heavy leather leash and snapped the lead onto his massive collar. "Come on, fella, we're going outside. But take it slow, okay. I don't have a saddle."

She opened the back door and found Jake standing there with an expression of amusement on his face.

"I take it this is Winchester?"

The dog woofed approvingly and nearly tore the lead from her hand so he could sniff a greeting to the newcomer.

"Now I see why you said my coming over wasn't necessary," Jake said, humor threading his voice. "Only a fool would go up against an animal this size." He rubbed the dog behind the ear as Winchester nearly tugged her down the three stairs.

"Why don't you let me have the leash, Amy?"

"Gladly. Whoa, boy, whoa!"

Jake chuckled. The remembered sound tricked over her like a warm breeze.

"That's the first time I've heard you laugh in a long time."

She felt his gaze, but he didn't answer. In companionable silence, they let the dog circle the backyard until it selected a spot. Half of Amy's attention remained firmly on the house. The other half was entirely too aware of Jake and the fact that her hormones had come shockingly alive. The sultry night shrouded them in darkness, isolating them in a little pocket of quiet.

"How can it be this hot in September one day and then cold the next?" she asked to make conversation.

"Amy, do you have an ex-lover or someone who could be stalking you?"

Shocked by the unexpected question, Amy wished she could see Jake's face clearly. "Of course not."

"No scorned boyfriends or wanna-be boyfriends?"

"I have many friends, Jake. Some of them are even male. But I don't know anyone who would try to hurt or scare me like this. I wasn't even dating much in Belgium." Belatedly, it occurred to her that perhaps she shouldn't have offered him that information. "It's not that I didn't date, but my work kept me pretty busy."

"You never thought of getting married?" Jake asked.

"Of course I did. I was even engaged once."

"You were?"

"You don't have to sound so surprised. Lester was a good person. We had a lot in common."

"What went wrong?"

"Nothing, really." She hesitated and then decided there was no reason to hide the truth from Jake. "He wanted me to put Kelsey in boarding school."

Not until she sensed Jake relaxing did she realize how tense he was. What was he was thinking? Had she left herself too vulnerable with that admission?

"Lester wasn't comfortable with a ready-made family. We parted amiably when we realized it wasn't going to work," she added. "What about you?"

Jake stroked the Great Dane's head and let the animal lead the way back to the porch. Jake sank down on the middle step a bit stiffly, as if his back was bothering him, and began stroking the dog.

"You know I didn't leave you so I could run to some other woman, Amy."

"I don't *know* anything. One day you're going off on

assignment and everything is fine. Then you return and say it was fun, now, goodbye.''

Jake winced. ''The one thing completely right in our relationship was what we had in bed.''

''Not much to bond people together, is it?''

His shoulders lifted and fell, the movement barely discernable in the dark. ''Maybe not, but it produced Kelsey.''

Amy couldn't think of a response to that. ''Why did you leave the navy? You loved the military.''

In another person she would have thought his prolonged silence indicated he didn't want to talk about it. With Jake, she knew he was weighing options, deciding what to tell her. Finally he patted the step beside him. Amy joined him cautiously. Their thighs touched and their shoulders brushed, taking her back with a pang of longing so sharp she had to suck in a breath.

''A job went sour under my command. People died.''

His pain reached her. She laid a hand on his arm, felt his corded muscles bunch, and wished there was a way to comfort him.

''Your back. You were hurt.'' The stiffness in his movements made sense now.

''Yes.''

She realized that was all the explanation she was going to get. She knew Jake couldn't talk about his missions so she went after other information instead.

''Why a restaurant? Why Fools Point?''

Before Jake could answer, Winchester abruptly lifted his head. The dog's body stood alertly, staring toward the line of trees out back. Jake continued to stroke the animal, but he also tensed. He leaned in close enough to Amy for her to smell the coffee on his breath.

''Go inside,'' he said so quietly she had to strain to

hear him. "Do it slow and casual. Keep the girls away from the windows."

Panic smothered her mind. Anyone watching would never sense the urgency of his whispered words, but her mouth was dry. Kelsey was inside.

Amy came to her feet as if jerked upright on strings. "I'll bring us both out something to drink," she said, striving to sound normal. Her voice came out high and shrill. Winchester now pulled at the lead, his huge head craning toward the line of trees. "I'll be right back," Amy added.

She was terrified. Not for herself, but for Jake. Because she knew he was going to investigate whatever it was that held the dog's attention.

Please, God, let it be some innocent rabbit.

She walked into the kitchen and headed straight for the telephone. Taking the handset, she moved into the dining room where she could see the girls. Two were half asleep in their sleeping bags on the floor. The other three sprawled on various bits of furniture, watching the movie.

Chief Hepplewhite's home number was among those her mother had programmed into the speed-dial feature. Amy pressed the number.

"Hepplewhite," he answered on the first ring.

"This is Amy Thomas," she said in a whispered rush of words. "Jake's out back with Winchester, the Cznery's dog. There's someone in my backyard by the trees."

"I'm on my way. Keep the doors locked and keep away from the windows."

The phone clicked off in her ear. Did they both think she was stupid? After replacing the receiver, she returned to the dining room where she could watch the children as well as the front and back doors.

Minutes ticked by, each one interminably long.

Winchester let out a loud woof. Amy jerked. She waited for the sound to attract the girls or bring her parents downstairs. But the girls were lost in their movie and her parents must have been sound asleep.

A large shadow stepped onto the back porch. Her heart thudded against her chest wall.

"Amy?"

She ran to open the door for Jake. Winchester pushed his way in first, tongue lolling happily.

"Are you okay?" she demanded.

"I'm fine."

Beyond Jake she glimpsed three shadowy forms standing in the backyard.

"It was Gertrude Perry," Jake told her. "Winchester scared her to death. She was wandering around, muttering to herself. Fortunately, she recognized Chief Hepplewhite. She scolded him for being out of uniform," he added with a smile. "Officer Jackstone is going to run her home."

"That poor woman. This is a long way for her to wander at night." Her knees were weak with relief. "You know, from here she looks like a man."

He followed her stare thoughtfully. "Yes, she does, doesn't she? I didn't realize she was so tall."

"Her brother's a big man, too. In fact, the whole family is tall." She was babbling and she knew it. "Maybe Ms. Perry was the person I thought I saw last night. Does she wander around a lot at night?"

"I don't know, but that's a good question."

"Mom? Oh, hi, Mr. Collins," Kelsey said in greeting. "I thought I heard voices."

"I ran into Mr. Collins outside," Amy said quickly.

"Did you know there's a police car out front, Mom?"

"Yes. Ms. Perry wandered off again. Winchester

found her out back. If your movie is over, you girls need to turn off the television and get to sleep.''

"Not yet, Mom. Lisa brought over the whole Star Wars series and we haven't watched them all yet. We'll be really really quiet, I promise. You and Mr. Collins could come and watch with us if you'd like,'' she invited.

Jake smiled. With a lurch of emotion, Amy realized once again that he and his daughter shared the same smile.

"I'd like that, Kelsey. I'd like that very much.'' He hesitated, looking at Amy before he shook his head. "But it looks like I'll have to take a rain check tonight. Thanks for asking me, though.''

"You're welcome.''

Jake had wanted to stay. He'd obviously been waiting for her to give permission. "Oh. You can stay if you'd like,'' Amy said, flustered and uncertain.

"I'll come back another time.'' The words were a threat and a promise. "Sounds to me like I'd be seriously outnumbered in there,'' he said to the little girl with another smile.

Kelsey giggled up at him. "I'm having a sleep-over.''

"So your mother told me.''

"One more movie, Kelsey,'' Amy interjected quickly. "Then it's lights out.''

"Thanks, Mom. 'Bye, Mr. Collins!'' Kelsey disappeared on the run as if afraid her mother would change her mind.

"You wanted to stay,'' Amy said.

"I'd like to get to know my daughter,'' Jake said softly. "But tonight probably isn't the best time to start. She looks like you,'' he added unexpectedly.

"Funny, I was just thinking that she looks like you. I'm sorry, Jake. I didn't realize until too late that you were waiting for me to give permission.''

Jake leaned against the refrigerator, looking so sexy her pulses skipped a beat. Now that the tension had left his face, he looked less remote—more like the Jake she remembered than the cool stranger she'd met at the restaurant.

"She doesn't know I'm her father, does she?"

"No! No," she said more calmly. "When she asked a few years ago, I told her I fell in love with a man who wasn't ready to be a father."

Jake winced. "What was her response?"

"She wanted to know if he'd be ready soon."

The hesitantly spoken words settled over them, leaving silence in their wake. Jake closed his eyes.

"Did you notice? She has your smile," Amy added quickly.

"You think so?" He opened his eyes and looked momentarily disconcerted, then sadly pleased.

Amy tried to marshal her floundering emotions. "Why did you stay outside tonight, Jake? What if it hadn't been old Ms. Perry in the trees? What if it had been some nut with a gun?"

"Then I would have taken it away from him."

The words weren't spoken casually. Jake meant exactly what he said. There was a calm certainty about him that was both reassuring and troubling.

Jake came away from the refrigerator and winced. Amy wondered how badly he'd been hurt in that last mission, but she was afraid to ask for some reason. Thinking of Jake lying in some hospital in pain disturbed her on many levels.

"Were you worried about me, Amy?"

"Of course I was worried."

"I had Winchester."

"Fat lot of good that monster would have done you. In case you haven't noticed, Winchester doesn't have a mean bone in his body. A rabbit would be in danger of being licked to death.''

Jake's chuckle warmed a smile out of her. He started toward her with deliberate precision.

''What are you doing? Why are you looking at me like that?''

''At the risk of getting my face slapped, I'd like to try an experiment.''

''No. Jake, you are not going to kiss me again. Do you realize what you did today? We're going to be an item all over town tomorrow because of that kiss you gave me in front of everyone.''

''That wasn't a kiss.''

''It certainly was a kiss.''

She could have moved back. She could have turned her head. Instead she held her ground and found herself where she'd only dreamed of being—in Jake's arms once more.

His breath fanned her lips. With aching slowness, he lowered his head and his lips brushed hers. She tasted the coffee he'd drunk recently, smelled the light subtle scent of his cologne, felt the fabric of his summer-weight suit beneath her hand.

He watched her through heavy-lidded eyes that filled with a quiet yearning. A yearning her body responded to immediately. It had been so very long.

Her heart raced as her lips parted the tiniest bit. He took his time, touching her hair lightly, brushing her cheek with his knuckle. And when she thought she'd collapse from the wanting, his mouth settled over hers.

The world dropped away as he kissed with an urgency that stirred her soul.

Coherent thought disappeared. Her body reacted with no input from her scattered mind. She kissed him back with a sensual hunger she hadn't known she was capable of.

It was like coming home.

His mouth plundered hers and she greedily demanded more.

Some tiny thread of rational thought realized she was now pressed against the kitchen wall. Her arms circled his neck to bring him closer.

When had his leg worked its way between hers, pressing excitingly against a need that was almost overwhelming? Her breasts flattened against his suit as she tried to get even closer. Passion enveloped her. Their mouths fused and their tongues dueled. She would never get enough of Jake.

And somewhere nearby a child giggled.

Jake lifted his head, breaking the sensual haze that engulfed them. They heard the fading noise of smothered giggles retreating.

"Oh, no."

He released her and stepped back. The stirringly sensual look on his face was slow to fade. Amy felt boneless, rattled, needy.

"That," he said, moving toward the door, "was a kiss. Get some rest."

"You have to be joking."

He smiled and she could feel the heat of that smile clear to her toes. This smile looked nothing at all like one of her daughter's.

"You'll be safe tonight. The police will cruise past here every fifteen minutes or so. We'll talk in the morning. Lock the door behind me."

Bemused, almost lethargic, she watched him go, staring after him long after he'd disappeared from sight. "Mom?" Kelsey stood watching her from the doorway leading to the dining room. "Were you really kissing Mr. Collins?"

"Does that bother you?" Her lips still tingled from his kiss.

Kelsey weighed the question. Finally she shook her head. "No. I like him."

Unfortunately, so did Amy—far more than she should given their past.

"He's lots better than Lester," Kelsey announced.

He wasn't even the same species as Lester.

What was she thinking?

"Want to come watch the movie with us, Mom?"

The very last thing she wanted to do.

"It's got Harrison Ford," Kelsey cajoled.

Harrison Ford was no match for the living, breathing Jake Collins. "Sure. Why not?" She certainly wasn't going to get any sleep tonight.

THIS WAS GETTING too dangerous. The woman must die. She would cause irreparable harm if something wasn't done. She might be confused, but she wasn't stupid. How much longer before she said the wrong thing to the right person and they started putting it all together? So many lives would be ruined. It wasn't fair. After all these years it was intolerable. It couldn't be allowed to happen. She had to die. Soon.

JAKE LAY ON HIS BACK, staring at the dark ceiling overhead.

Matt had been going to bed when he came in. The boy had eyed him with an impish grin and said good-night. Right before he closed his bedroom door Matt had added, "That shade of lipstick looks good on you."

Jake had wiped the back of his hand over his lips before he remembered that Amy hadn't been wearing lipstick. The boy was too knowledgeable for his own good, but Jake found himself smiling anyhow. He'd come to know Matt pretty well. That had been Matt's way of saying he approved of Amy.

So did Jake.

He'd made a terrible mistake nine years ago and it had cost him dearly. It didn't matter that Ronnie had never forwarded her letters. Jake knew it had been his responsibility to check on Amy. They'd forgotten protection several times. Not surprising considering that when he touched Amy he forgot almost everything.

That hadn't changed. No other woman had ever held this sort of power over him.

He'd run scared. He'd seized on Brian's death like an anchor in a desperate attempt to regain the impersonal sense of control he seemed to lose around Amy. She'd become too important to him and he hadn't known how to handle all the feelings she stirred inside of him.

But a man could grow and change. He wanted to know his daughter and become a real part of her life. He didn't want to seek Amy's permission to sit and watch a movie with Kelsey and her friends. He wanted to know his child, to know what made her smile and what made her sad. He wanted to watch her grow and change into a beautiful woman like her mother.

He wanted a family.

The scary thought coalesced in his mind. Wasn't that why he had come after Matt when he learned about the boy?

Jake had spent years learning patience and discipline. He had always dealt with life by setting goals. Love and marriage hadn't been one of them when they'd first met. He couldn't undo the past, but he could create a new future. He would marry Amy, adopt Matt, gain the trust of his newly discovered daughter, and unite them all as a real family.

He wouldn't let it matter that he didn't have any first-hand experience with a real family. He knew what one should be like. And he'd already proved he wasn't so bad as a parent. He was making strides with Matt every single day.

He would approach the situation as if it were a military campaign. Know the enemy. Seek out their strengths and weaknesses. Plot a strategy that would lead to the goal.

He'd made a good start tonight. That kiss with Amy had certainly opened both their eyes.

Amy was stronger and more lovely than ever. Maturity hadn't destroyed the aura of goodness that was the basis of her character. She was an open, warm, giving person—traits he'd always envied. And the very factors that had sent him running nine years ago. He didn't know how to be any of those things. He was quietly self-contained. He'd had to be to survive. Self-preservation was a tough lesson to learn and even harder to unlearn.

With Amy, he'd sensed that he could push past the boundary that kept him reserved and aloof from the world, but he'd been afraid to take that step.

Jake closed his eyes and shifted to a more comfortable position. A family. *His* family. The unattainable had just become possible. Tomorrow he would set about finding the person terrorizing Amy. Then he'd secure his future.

JAKE'S MORNING STARTED with delivery problems, followed by the arrival of the police.

"Sorry to bother you so early, Mr. Collins," Chief Hepplewhite said. "I wanted to let you know they finished removing the bodies, but we'd like you to hold off filling in the hole just yet."

"Did you discover anything?"

"Some jewelry that may prove helpful. The woman was wearing what appears to be an expensive sapphire necklace."

"Guess that rules out a servant," Jake said. "Any idea how long the bodies were down there?"

"The medical examiner estimates between twenty-five and forty years. He'll know better after he has a chance to examine them more closely," Hepplewhite replied.

"Murdered?"

"It's too early to say. We aren't ruling it out, which is why we'd like you to keep the area open a little longer. You may have noticed that gossip spreads in this town ahead of the wind. I'm sure you and your people overhear a lot of the conversations that go on in here. I'm not asking you to deliberately spy on anyone, but if you hear anything that might be of help…"

"I'll tell my staff to keep their ears open."

The police chief hesitated.

"Is there something else?" Jake asked.

Hepplewhite nodded. "When I asked Amy's mother about the bodies, Susan became highly agitated."

"Some people are uncomfortable discussing subjects like that."

"It was more than that. I'm pretty sure Susan Thomas knows something. I think Amy sensed it, as well."

"Are you asking me to pump Amy for information?"

"No. Not exactly."

"What, exactly?"

"You have an impressive military record, Major."

Jake managed to not react. "Just mister. I'm retired now."

"Noah Inglewood recognized you a few months back."

Jake waited patiently. He'd recognized the other man

as well. Jake had been working for the CIA when they'd first met. Noah hadn't.

"Amy arrived in Fools Point on Thursday. On Friday we discovered the bodies. Almost immediately, she and her mother are nearly run over by a dump truck full of gravel."

Jake's insides chilled. "I thought you believed that was an accident, or that it was done in some misguided effort to cover up the crime scene."

"The latter maybe, but not the former. There was nothing wrong with the truck. Someone sent that truck rolling into the crowd on purpose. Amy was directly in its path."

"So were a lot of people," he managed to say mildly.

"But none of them had an attempted break-in the very next night. Nor was anyone else hit by a car outside this restaurant the following day."

"Where's the connection, Chief? Twenty-five years ago Amy would have been four or five years old. Forty years ago she wasn't even born."

"But her mother was."

The words lay between them, pregnant with all sorts of possibilities.

"Susan Thomas was with Amy that morning. It was her house someone attempted to break into. Unless I'm reading her all wrong, Amy's mother is frightened."

"What about the car that nearly hit Amy? Amy and her mother don't look at all alike."

"No, but it made a rather effective warning for silence, don't you think?"

Jake forced himself to breathe evenly.

"I don't want another dead body," Hepplewhite said. "This town has seen enough craziness already. If Susan Thomas does know something, Amy could also be at risk."

"What about the Perrys? They're the ones who owned the estate."

"Do you know General Perry?"

"By reputation, primarily."

Hepplewhite waited. Jake found himself almost smiling.

"I gave minor testimony against his son at a military hearing once. I can imagine you aren't getting much co-operation there. The general is up for a second star. The last thing he'll want is his name attached to some old scandal."

"So you have a history with the family, as well."

"Not really. I never had occasion to speak with either of them personally until the other day. The sale of the estate was handled through lawyers."

Hepplewhite nodded thoughtfully. "According to General Perry, the servants' quarters were abandoned more than forty years ago. The area was used for storage until it fell into disrepair. Apparently Gertrude Perry wasn't much for maintenance."

"No," Jake agreed, thinking of all the repairs he'd needed to make on the property.

"The general claimed his sister had all the outbuildings torn down when she became afraid teenagers or vagabonds would start using them. He says they didn't even know there was a root cellar."

"Who demolished the structures?"

"He doesn't remember. Gertrude handled the razing and erected the gazebo."

"And you can hardly question her."

"I gave it a try. Gertrude became highly agitated and Cindy Lou and the general's wife insisted I stop."

"What about financial records? That sort of work isn't cheap."

Hepplewhite shrugged. "He said they'd look for old records."

"So you're stymied."

"The dead woman had extensive dental work. We might be able to trace her through that if she was reported as a missing person."

"Have you talked to Amy's father?"

"Yes. Corny's harder to read than his wife. He remembers when the buildings were torn down, but no one seems to remember who did the work. And so far, no one can remember a pregnant woman or a mother and newborn who went missing."

"Maybe some construction worker seized an opportunity to get rid of his wife and child," Jake suggested.

"We're checking. In the meantime…"

"If I learn anything, I'll let you know."

Hepplewhite nodded.

Jake called Amy as soon as the officer left, but she and Kelsey had gone shopping and weren't expected back until late afternoon. As he headed back to the kitchen, Jake saw Matt's aunt and uncle being seated in the main dining room.

"Catherine, Dwight," Jake greeted as he reached their table.

"Hello, Jake." Dwight Kornbaum stood and quickly offered his hand. The palm was damp.

"Could you—would you have time to join us for a few minutes?" Catherine asked, fidgeting with the rings on her finger.

"Of course. Is something wrong?"

"Matt around?" Dwight asked.

"No. He's over at the soccer field with a group of friends."

"Good. I'm going to be blunt and come right to the point."

"Dwight," Catherine protested halfheartedly.

Dwight ignored her. "I've got a job offer in New Jersey. I plan to accept. Is there any chance you'd be willing to make this guardianship permanent?"

"It's not that we don't care about Matt," Catherine hastened to add, "but he seems to be settling in here..." *With you,* went unsaid.

"Have you told him yet who you are?" Dwight asked.

"Not yet," Jake responded. "If Matt is agreeable, I'd be happy to have him stay with me permanently."

The couple visibly relaxed and Jake tried not to be quite as obvious.

"Good, good," Dwight said with false joviality. "You seem to have a knack with the boy. He and I never got along all that well. If you need financial help...I mean, he *is* family and all."

"That won't be necessary," Jake assured the man coldly. "I'm his family, too."

"Er, yes. Right. You just keep it in mind. Chester Margolius can draw up the paperwork for us. He's old, but he's the only lawyer in Fools Point and he's got an office right there on Main Street. There shouldn't be any problem. This is just a formality, after all."

Jake nodded, noting that Catherine looked both relieved and unhappy.

"We tried," she said softly. "It just wasn't working. For any of us."

He felt sorry for the woman. Matt had been her brother's only child just as he was Jake's sister's only child. "I know, Catherine. I would have taken him from the start, had I known."

But Jake knew that was partially a lie. Four years ago he'd been no more ready to give up his career and take on a family than he had been when he'd walked out on

Amy. His priorities didn't change until he danced with death and came out alive.

"Matt and I understand each other. I'll talk with him this afternoon. I need to tell him who I really am anyhow. I don't think he'll be upset with the change."

"Thank you, Jake," Catherine said with a timid smile.

"I'll let you know what the lawyer has to say," Dwight put in quickly.

"Do that. If you'll excuse me, I'm needed elsewhere."

"Oh. Yes, of course."

Jake left the couple with mixed emotions. The overriding one was satisfaction. He was certain Catherine had tried to mother the boy, but he was equally sure that Dwight and Matt would never have come to terms. Dwight's resentment of the boy was too obvious.

Amy, on the other hand, would never let Matt feel unwanted.

Jake nearly smiled at the thought. He was one step closer to his goal.

Arly lifted his head as Jake stepped into the kitchen. "They're talking about severe thunderstorms tonight," the chef said. "The generator needs a quick check."

Jake nodded. Rain would put an end to the unseasonably hot weather, but storms meant the potential loss of electric power. They cooked with gas, but the refrigerators and freezers needed to be kept running, so Jake went out back to check the condition of the powerful generator he'd had installed.

And all the while he planned how to go about telling Matt he was his uncle. And why he had kept this fact a secret.

Chapter Six

Amy paced the floor irritably. Her parents had gone out with friends and there had been no opportunity to talk with them alone. All day she'd fielded questions from Kelsey about the past. She'd nearly told her daughter the truth, but she wanted to talk with Jake first.

Kelsey was begging to stay in Fools Point. She and Sarah had quickly become inseparable. But there were no apartments nearby and Amy didn't have the money to buy a house. Nor did she want to continue living with her parents. A visit was one thing, but she couldn't stay there indefinitely.

Their discussion had led to an argument that ended the day on a sad note. Kelsey fled upstairs to call Sarah, while Amy headed for the basement to catch up on their laundry and think about the future—and Jake. What would she do if he wanted to resume their relationship?

Maybe a better question was, how would she handle things if he didn't want to spend time with her? She would never again allow their relationship to become as intense as it had been nine years ago. But if last night had served no other purpose, it had shown her that where Jake was concerned, her body had a mind of its own. She still wanted him. Denying it was pointless. Could she have an affair with him?

The idea was both titillating and scary. Carrying on an affair with Jake would be difficult. Plus, she had her daughter to think about. How would Kelsey feel when she told her who Jake really was?

How had life become so convoluted? She wished he would call, but she knew he'd have to wait until the restaurant closed for the night.

Scenarios played out in her head as she waited for the dryer to stop. She folded clothing and headed upstairs. Halfway up, she realized the house was suspiciously quiet. Kelsey was probably still on the telephone, but it was getting late. She knocked on her daughter's bedroom door and got no answer.

"Kelsey?"

The knob turned beneath her fingers. The phone lay on the rumpled bed. Kelsey wasn't in the room.

"Kelsey?"

The house was entirely too quiet. Mindless waves of fear crashed in on her. Where was her daughter?

"Kelsey!"

She wouldn't have gone outside at this hour. It was late. There was a storm coming. And they'd had a long, frank discussion this afternoon about the dangers of someone prowling around outside. Kelsey wouldn't have opened the door to a stranger. Besides, Amy would have heard if someone had knocked on the door or rang the bell. But what if someone had forced their way in? She'd been lost in thought downstairs with the two heavy machines running. How much noise would the scuffle of a young girl make?

Amy dropped the pile of clothing and ran from room to room, calling her daughter frantically while alarm bubbled up inside her. There was no answer. Downstairs, she found the front door unlocked. It didn't appear that anyone had forced the door open, but apprehension made her ill. She stepped outside onto the porch. Maybe Kelsey had run next door for some reason.

"Kelsey?"

The wind went from a rustle to a sudden gust. Her voice drifted away helplessly.

Reason halted her mindless plunge down the front steps. She ran back inside and grabbed the cordless phone. Her fingers were shaking so hard she had to dial twice, but Donna Cznery answered the telephone right away.

"Donna? I'm sorry to bother you so late, but is Kelsey over there?"

"Why, no. She and Sarah were talking until I told them it was time for bed. Is something wrong?"

"I can't find Kelsey. Could you...may I talk with Sarah for a moment?"

"I'll get her."

Donna's obvious concern only added to Amy's growing sense of urgency. While waiting for Sarah to come on the line, she ran upstairs to search for a note or something that would tell her where her daughter had gone. Nothing. She stepped into the hall and the door to the attic drew her eye. The door was slightly ajar.

Dread landed on her chest. There was no reason for that door to be ajar. Her mother usually kept it locked. Amy reached for the knob. An unexpectedly severe gust of wind shook the house.

"Kelsey?" she called.

"Hello?"

Sarah's voice in her ear made her pause. "Sarah, do you know where Kelsey is?"

"No, Ms. Thomas."

Amy recognized a childish hesitation. "Sarah, this is important. When did Kelsey hang up with you?"

"Ha-half an hour ago."

"Do you know what she intended to do?"

"Well…"

"Please, Sarah. I can't find her. I'm frightened that something has happened to her."

Wind buffeted the house. The rain would come at any second.

"Did you look in the attic?" Sarah asked hesitantly.

"I'm looking now." She opened the door and turned on the light. Even with the two bare bulbs overhead for illumination, the attic would be a dark, dusty cavern.

Amy mounted the steps. The attic was empty. Most of the items stored up here belonged to her. There was no place for anyone to hide.

"She isn't up here." Amy took a deep breath to stem the rising terror. "Why was she in the attic, Sarah?"

But she already knew the answer because her gaze had come to rest on the filing cabinet where she stored her important papers. The top drawer was no longer shut tightly. It should have been. Amy had only been up here once since she'd come home. She'd put away their passports—and their birth certificates.

New panic blanketed her.

"I think…she said she was going to look for her birth certificate," Sarah said hesitantly.

Amy's hands reached for the drawer. She didn't really need to look inside to know that Kelsey had found what she was seeking. The file had been up front, clearly marked.

The birth certificate was also clearly marked.

Amy had named Kelsey's father.

Her frantic search turned up what she'd already known she'd find. The birth certificate was gone.

Blood pounded in her ears. Thunder crashed overhead. She should have told Kelsey the truth this afternoon. Her daughter shouldn't have discovered the facts this way.

"Thank you, Sarah." She pressed the button to disconnect the telephone and plunged back downstairs. Kelsey had gone to Jake.

JAKE LOOKED UP at the first crack of thunder. Thankfully the crowds had thinned. He was counting the hours until he could talk to Amy. They had a lot to discuss.

Matt was upstairs trying to get his English paper written so he could play soccer with his new friends in the morning. Jake hadn't yet told Matt about his aunt and uncle's visit. The afternoon and evening crowds had been larger than normal and they hadn't had any private time together. He hated to wait until morning, but talking over breakfast had become something of a morning ritual between them. Jake had found it a warm, comfortable way to start the day. He'd either tell him at breakfast or arrange to be free when Matt came home from school tomorrow afternoon.

As he strode through the hall to check on the kitchen, the front door opened on a gust of wind-driven rain. He turned to see a sodden figure hesitate inside the door.

"Amy?"

She lifted her head at the sound of his voice and ran past the startled hostess. Her hair was plastered to her head. She wasn't wearing a coat and her thin, cotton shirt was soaking wet, clearly outlining every curve. But it was the panic lining her face that caused his body to tighten in alarm.

"Jake! Where's Kelsey?"

Apprehension filled him. "I haven't seen her."

"She has to be here. She has to."

He grabbed Amy by the shoulders, aware they were clearly visible to the bar patrons as well as some of the diners. Her entire body shook and he didn't think it was from the cold rain. He pulled her over to the relative seclusion of the staircase. "What happened?"

She shuddered and gazed up at him with tear-filled eyes. "Kelsey found her birth certificate. She knows you're her father."

Amy had listed him as the father!

"We had an argument. I left her upstairs on the phone with Sarah. I went to the basement to do some laundry. When I came upstairs she was gone. She isn't in the house, I looked. Sarah doesn't know where she is. She had to have come here! Where else would she go?"

Amy's fear was contagious. He blocked his emotions, sealing them off for later. "Are you absolutely sure she isn't in the house?"

"I checked everywhere." Tears slipped down her cheeks. "I called Donna Cznery and she isn't over there. Where else could she be?"

More than anything in the world, he wished he had an answer for that.

"Come on." He led the way upstairs to his office and reached for the telephone. Drawn by their unexpected arrival, Matt left his room and stood uncertainly in the doorway as Jake connected with the Fools Point police dispatcher.

"This is Jake Collins," he said. "I need to report a missing child."

One fist pressed to her mouth, Amy stood forlornly, her other hand clenched tightly at her side.

"Ms. Thomas," Matt said, "Kelsey's missing?"

Amy nodded blankly, her eyes fixed on Jake.

Jake quickly explained the situation without any wasted words and hung up. "Chief Hepplewhite is on his way. I'll go outside and look around."

She reached for him with hands of ice. "I'll come with you. Please don't ask me to sit and wait."

"All right. Let me get you a sweatshirt and a jacket. You're freezing."

"I'll get her one of mine," Matt offered. "It'll be a better fit."

Jake gave the boy a grateful nod, even as he enfolded Amy against his chest. Her sobs tore at him.

"If anything happens to her...I couldn't bear it, Jake. I couldn't!"

"Shh. We'll find her. Maybe she took cover from the storm."

Amy lifted her head, but her expression of hope disappeared as fast as it came. "There's no place to go between Mom's house and here."

"She may not have come directly here, Amy. She might have wanted to walk and think first."

"Here, Ms. Thomas," Matt said, handing her an over-size sweatshirt. "Let me get my shoes and I'll go with you," he told Jake.

On the verge of saying no, Jake reconsidered. At fifteen Matt had a maturity far beyond his years. "I can use another pair of eyes," he agreed. "Amy, change into this while I go see if Officer Osher is still in the bar."

He wasn't, but Jake recognized many of the other locals. Quickly, he pulled his bartender aside and explained that Kelsey was missing and he might need to organize a search party. Ben Dwyer nodded, his features concerned.

The storm hit with a frenzy. Rain flew in their faces when they stepped outside. Their flashlights were nearly useless. Still, the three of them headed for the path the girl would probably have used. Jake's gut tightened unbearably as Matt raced on ahead and aimed his beam at the loosely covered pit where the bodies had been.

"Doesn't look like these boards were moved," he said. Though he sensed Amy's horror, Jake had to agree.

They were turning toward the path when he saw the police car pull into the parking lot. A second car was on its tail.

"Amy, we should go and talk to Hepplewhite."

"I'm going down the path," Matt shouted.

Jake waved acknowledgment and led Amy back to the front of the restaurant. He was pleased that Amy was able to hold her emotions in check. Tersely, she explained exactly what had happened, including what was on the birth certificate. Jake kept his arm around her shoulders while his own anxiety increased.

Hepplewhite immediately summoned help. In minutes, Montgomery County police officers and detectives pulled into the lot. A sweeping search began in earnest while the storm roared overhead, eliminating any clues Kelsey might have left behind.

"Ms. Thomas," Hepplewhite said, "you need to go back to the house in case she comes back or calls."

"But I have to find her!"

"Amy, we should let your parents know what's happening," Jake told her softly.

"Oh, God."

"I'll take her back to the house," Jake promised. "Would you let Matt know? He was going to backtrack along the path to the house."

Hepplewhite nodded.

"Come on, Amy. I'll tell Arly what's going on so he can lock up and we'll get my car and go."

"Mine's out front," she said almost dully.

In the end, they took hers and returned to her parents', their eyes sweeping the deserted streets.

Susan and Cornelius had come home. They were stunned and horrified by the news of Kelsey's disappearance. Susan Thomas looked ready to collapse, but she refused to go upstairs. Instead, she stood by anxiously while police checked the house for clues or signs of a disturbance. Amy answered questions over and over again until she thought she would scream. Donna Cznery arrived, no doubt drawn by the police cars out front.

Grateful to have Amy occupied, Jake pulled Hepplewhite aside. "What do you think?"

"She's what? Eight? Angry with her mother. Most likely she ran off to give her mom a scare. In that case, she'll show up pretty soon."

Jake didn't think so. Admittedly, he didn't know the child, but he knew Amy. He couldn't believe her daughter would behave in that fashion.

Their daughter.

"What if she doesn't? What if this has something to do with the person we saw creeping around the house?"

Hepplewhite's jaw set in a hard line. "We aren't ruling out anything at this point. Including kidnapping."

Fear was an old friend, but Jake discovered this was different. He'd never had a daughter before and that made a world of difference.

"This storm's going to complicate things," Hepplewhite said. "We won't be able to use the helicopter."

"What about a ransom call?"

Their gazes locked. Jake knew Hepplewhite was thinking the same as him. There would be no ransom call. This wouldn't be that sort of kidnapping.

Had anyone known of his relationship to Kelsey, it might have been a possibility. Jake had money, thanks to some lucky investments and a substantial inheritance from his parents, and he'd made some enemies over the years. But...

"Anybody know she was your daughter?"

"I just found out myself," he admitted.

Hepplewhite didn't say anything else. There wasn't anything else to say. Amy and her parents had no money.

If Kelsey had been taken by a pervert and the searchers didn't turn her up soon, they probably wouldn't find her alive.

"I need to help with the search," Jake said.

"I'm sorry. We're going to need to ask you more questions. Besides, you'll be more help staying here."

Jake followed the police chief's gaze and saw Amy standing alone, her arms wrapped tightly about her body. Quickly, he went to her, pulling her unresisting form against his chest.

The night moved forward with agonizing slowness. Matt arrived, wet and worried. "Nothing, Jake. I didn't see any signs that she'd even gone that way. I'm sorry, Ms. Thomas."

Amy tried for a smile and failed. "Thanks for trying."

"I talked to Arly and Ben," Matt told him. "They were going to stay and keep an eye on things in case she goes to the restaurant."

"You want to head back and try for some sleep?" Jake asked.

"I'd rather stay here with you."

Jake stared into eyes that were much too old for the boy's years. "I'd like that, too," he assured the boy.

At some point the elder Thomases were allowed upstairs to lay down. The neighbors went home, promising to return in the morning. Amy fell into a fitful doze on the couch, while detectives set up a phone tap. Jake found himself sharing hot chocolate and cookies in the kitchen with Matt.

"The police think it was some deranged weirdo, don't they?" Matt asked.

Jake nodded, fighting a silent battle against a building rage and anguish. The detectives who'd arrived had questioned him at length. Tomorrow the questioning would continue, but fortunately, every minute of Jake's time this evening could be accounted for. He'd been in plain view of staff and patrons all evening. He knew the police always looked closely at those nearest a victim and he was glad they wouldn't have to waste too much time looking at him.

"Jake...I, uh, I heard one of the cops say you were Kelsey's dad."

He met Matt's question head-on. "Amy and I knew each other a long time ago, but I didn't know about Kelsey until the other day."

"So you are her dad? For real?"

Jake wasn't so blinded by his own worry that he couldn't read between the lines to see Matt's insecurity.

He nodded. "I planned to tell you about this and some other things you need to know over breakfast, but I guess it had better be now. Your aunt and uncle came to see me yesterday."

All expression left Matt's face.

"I asked them for permission to retain full guardianship over you."

The boy blinked. His lips parted, but he didn't make a sound.

"That's if it's okay with you," Jake added.

"Yeah! Yeah, I'd like that. But...I mean...what about Ms. Thomas? I mean if the two of you are going to get together—"

"My plan is to unite us all as one family."

Matt's face fell. Jake knew what he was thinking. Matt had already tried being part of a family unit and it hadn't worked out.

"Matt, this isn't how I planned to tell you, but your mother was my sister."

His head jerked up and his eyes opened wide. "You mean you're the uncle no one could find? Oh, man. I knew your last name was the same as my mom's maiden name, but Collins is pretty common. After all these years I figured you were dead.''

''I was overseas on assignment. I didn't learn about the plane crash until a long time after it happened. I thought you were dead, as well.''

''Or you'd have come running to help the poor little orphan, too?'' Matt suddenly sneered.

''I'd have come, Matt.''

The boy swore. ''Sure you would have. I must be stupid or something. I never put it together. That's why you were being nice to me and all.''

Jake grabbed his arm to keep the boy from leaving. ''You're far from stupid, Matt. If I was nice, it was because I like you.''

''Sure. So much you didn't even tell me who you were. Why not?''

Matt's look of betrayal was one more nick on his soul. With an effort, Jake put a lock on his emotions and released his grip on the boy's arm.

''Do you remember how we met?''

Matt flushed. He'd been trying to steal Jake's car out in front of the Bide-Awhile Motel when Jake first arrived in town.

''I didn't know who you were then, Matt, but I recognized a kindred spirit when I met one.''

''You didn't call the cops,'' Matt grudgingly agreed.

''No.''

''You offered me a job. But you didn't tell me you were my uncle,'' he accused.

''If you'd been some happy, contented teenager, I'd have knocked on the door to your aunt and uncle's place and introduced myself. Instead I discovered a young man who reminded me of myself so much it was scary.''

''You used to steal cars?'' Matt sneered defensively.

''Nope. I found other ways to cause trouble.''

"Yeah?" Matt scoffed.

"I was kicked out of three boarding schools before my parents sent me to a military academy. I'll tell you about it someday if you want details."

Matt stared at him, anger, resentment, betrayal all mixed in the features that watched him so closely.

"Try putting yourself in my place, Matt. I couldn't just blurt out, 'Hello, my name's Jake and I'm your long-lost forgotten uncle.' You would have viewed me as another adult relative here to put demands on you."

Matt flushed again, but he didn't lower his gaze. Jake was heartened to see he was listening, trying to assimilate the information.

"And since I'm being completely honest, I have to tell you, I wasn't sure what I wanted from you when I first decided to look you up. You were my sister's kid. The only relative I have left alive. I wanted to see what you were like."

Matt toyed with his cup. "What about when we became friends? Why didn't you tell me after I moved in with you?"

"You wouldn't even talk to me in the hospital, remember? You'd witnessed a murder and almost got killed. You were so alienated by all the adults demanding things of you I wasn't about to put any more pressure on you."

Matt had been sullen, angry and frightened, all with good reason. It had taken weeks to build back the fragile trust they'd established after Jake had first arrived in town.

"We were friends. I didn't want to lose that. I still don't. I'm not much of an uncle, Matt. I don't have much experience with family," he said softly. "Your mom and I had live-in nannies from my earliest memories. I don't remember my parents ever touching us unless there was a specific reason. When we were old enough, we were shipped off to separate boarding schools. Your mother and I barely knew each other—and we didn't know our parents at all.''

A floorboard creaked. Someone stood in the dining room, just out of sight. Jake sensed it was Amy rather than the detective who was still moving about in the other room.

''Why'd they have kids in the first place if they didn't want you?'' Matt asked skeptically.

''Good question,'' Jake responded wryly.

''I remember Mom was always trying to do stuff with them, get them to come over and stuff. They didn't touch me, either. I didn't like them much.'' He looked guilty for that admission.

Jake set down his mug and nodded. ''Neither did I.''

''Yeah? Really? Mom and Dad used to argue about them. Dad used to tell her she couldn't teach old dogs new tricks. I didn't understand.''

''Your mom wanted to show them what they'd missed when we were growing up. Carrie adored you. She was determined to create the family we never had. I chose another route. The military became my family.''

Matt studied him silently.

''The summer I met Amy was the first time I was stationed locally. In fact, it was through a party at your mom's house that I met Amy. Your mom was good friends with Amy's college roommate.''

Matt suddenly perked up. ''You know, I think—I almost remember meeting you.''

''You were pretty young. I was only over at your house a couple of times.''

''But you wore a uniform. I remember that. And you sat in that big chair of Dad's. I remember you had a soft voice, and you do. It's sorta like Mom's, only deeper of course.''

Jake almost smiled. "I'm glad you remember. I'm afraid little kids were a lot like aliens to me back then. I was a little afraid of you, I think."

"Yeah? For real? You brought me a toy."

"A radio-controlled ship," Jake agreed. "Carrie wouldn't let you have it because it was too old for you."

Matt nodding excitedly. "But Dad and I snuck it out of the house and played with it on some water in the park."

They regarded each other quietly for a moment, different memories holding them both captive to the past. Jake wasn't sure if Amy was still listening, but he thought she was.

"No matter what happens, Matt, you and I share a bond we can't break. More importantly, we've become friends." He stared at the boy until Matt nodded. "God knows, I may be no good at this parenting thing." He thought of his daughter out there somewhere in the night and had to force back the impotent rage that threatened to consume him. "But for as long as you're willing to put up with me, I'd like us to be a team."

"But what about…? I mean…if you decide to get married or something? Dwight didn't like having me around all the time."

Jake scowled. "Dwight and your grandparents would have liked each other."

After a moment Matt slowly began to smile. The smile turned into a full-fledged grin. "Yeah, they would have, wouldn't they?"

Before the moment faded completely, Jake turned serious. "Thanks for your help tonight. It meant a lot."

"Well, yeah. Heck, I didn't do much. I mean Kelsey's a cute little kid. She doesn't deserve to have something bad happen to her. Do you think we'll find her Jake?'' He hesitated. "I guess I should call you 'Uncle Jake' now, huh?''

"Let's stick with Jake, if that's okay with you.'' It elevated Matt to equal status. Jake knew how important that was if he was to maintain the fragile web of trust he'd created between them.

"Yeah. Great.''

"And yes, we're going to find Kelsey.'' He stated the words forcefully. "In fact, we ought to follow everyone else's example and try to catch a couple of hours of sleep before the search teams start again. Morning is only a few hours away and we're going to need to be alert.''

"I'll go back over to the Perrywrinkle.''

"Wait until morning, Matt. Maybe the rain will have stopped by then.''

"You can go up and lay down on my bed,'' Amy offered, finally stepping into the room.

Her eyes were shadowed by worry and fear, her features pinched and drawn. Jake would have done anything to ease her anguish.

"That's okay, Ms. Thomas,'' Matt replied. "I'll just sack out on the recliner in the other room, if that's all right. You ought to go upstairs and try to rest. We're gonna find her, you know.''

Amy smiled wanly and touched his arm. With a silent look of sympathy for Jake, Matt disappeared into the dining room.

Jake wanted to go to Amy, but instead he rose and moved to the cupboard to pull down another cup.

"Matt's right, you know. You should try to rest, but I don't imagine you can sleep any better than I can. As long as I'm making free use of your mother's kitchen, may I offer you a cup of hot chocolate?''

"No. Nothing. Thanks.''

He put the cup down and waited.

"I heard what you said…when you were talking to Matt." She hesitated, her eyes filled with pain. "Would you have wanted Kelsey—if you had known?"

Jake faced her, waited for her eyes to meet his. He willed her to believe the truth of his words. "With every fiber of my being. I would have been scared to death, make no mistake about it. But she was part of us, Amy. That means something to me. This will sound trite, but you were the best thing that ever happened to me. Letting you go really was the hardest thing I ever did. If I had known about our daughter…"

She came into his arms, tears coursing down her cheeks. Jake held her tightly. He thought about the past, about all the years he'd lost, about an eight-year-old girl who'd never known a father's love. And for the first time since he'd been Kelsey's age, he let his own tears fall, as well.

THE MORNING BROUGHT detectives with more questions, fresh teams of searchers, the media, and well-meaning neighbors bearing food. Amy felt under siege. Everyone wanted something from her and all she could think about was her daughter.

The man introduced as Agent Alex Coughlin was someone she recognized from high school. His bad-boy image had changed so much that Alex now worked for the FBI. While his presence in that capacity was unofficial, Amy welcomed any and all help that would find her daughter. The detectives and their incessant questions were driving her crazy. She knew they were only doing their job, but it was wearing.

She and Jake had managed to snatch a catnap on the couch last night. She'd awakened in his arms, her left side completely numb where it was pinned against his side. She hadn't expected to sleep at all, unlike Matt who had lain back in her dad's recliner and gone straight to sleep.

Jake and Matt had gone back to the Perrywrinkle for fresh clothing, and she suspected medication for Jake's back. He moved stiffly, lines of pain overshadowed by his obvious concern for Kelsey.

The day was gloomy. A light rain fell almost steadily, seeping below the collars of the searchers and making everyone miserable. But no one quit.

Amy almost welcomed the numbness that settled over her after Jake and Matt were finally allowed to join the team checking the woods and undeveloped land out behind the house. She protested being left behind, but everyone insisted she needed to remain at the house in case Kelsey called.

A helicopter was brought in, however it developed some sort of electrical problem and had to leave before it could do much more than make a few passes. Despite the rain, a team of search dogs arrived.

Amy and her parents declined to be interviewed by the media. A reporter and photographer from the *Fools Point Ledger* had gotten inside by bringing food and promising not to take pictures without permission.

Donna Cznery had taken command of the kitchen. Food poured in from concerned neighbors. Amy sat with an untouched cup of tea and spoke mechanically to everyone. All she wanted to do was join Jake and Matt. The waiting was eating her alive. She needed to do something physical instead of sitting here as if she were holding a wake. Her daughter was out there somewhere. She wanted to be out searching.

Thoughts of Kelsey were a living ache inside her. She tried not to think about all the horror stories she'd heard over the years, but her mind probed at them like a sore.

General Perry's deep voice jerked her out of her reverie. Cindy Lou and Millicent Perry were setting casserole dishes on the heavily laden dining room table under Donna's direction. Her parents carried on a low-voiced conversation with the general.

Her mother looked as pale as death itself. Amy made her way over to them, but her father's stiffness and the cold stare he directed at the general made her pause. She could almost touch the undercurrent of animosity between the two men. What on earth?

As a postman for more than fifty years, her father knew everyone in town, but she couldn't remember him ever having any personal dealings with the Perry family.

"Daddy?" Before she could formulate a question, Cindy Lou Baranski was there holding out a couple of plates.

"Mrs. Thomas, Mr. Thomas, please, try to eat something. You really must keep up your strength. For your daughter as well as your granddaughter's sake."

With the media present, the honorable mayor wasn't about to miss an opportunity to prove what a strong community leader she was, Amy thought snidely.

Before she could take that uncharitable thought any further, Millicent Perry stepped between Amy and her parents. "My dear, your mother looks positively ghastly." She thrust a plate of food into Amy's hands. "She really must eat before she collapses."

Millicent Perry as a ministering angel would have been amusing under other circumstances, but in this case the woman was right.

"I had one of those people clear off the kitchen table," Millicent said. "Why don't you try to get your parents to join you before the searchers break for lunch?"

Amy was shocked to realize it was nearly noon. Her

parents did need to eat something. Especially her mother. "Thank you. Mom, Dad, come with me. Please?"

"The casserole is hot. I hope no one is allergic to mushrooms. No? Good."

Amy led her parents to the kitchen table and sat down. Drinks appeared. Plates of sweets were set in the center of the table. Silverware was provided. Everyone wanted to help.

Amy wished they'd all disappear.

She pretended to eat without putting a morsel in her own mouth, all the while coaxing her parents. Her dad ate quickly and mechanically while her mother chewed more slowly. Amy would have to ask Chief Hepplewhite or someone if they could get Dr. Martin to stop by. Her mother's pallor was bad.

Time had become distorted. At times it melted away while other times it crawled with unbearable slowness. Why hadn't there been any word?

Amy gazed around absently and came to a halt at the sight of Eugene Perry leaning against the back door. He was stuffing what appeared to be a flask in his pocket. Their glances met. A shudder of dislike coursed right through her. Eugene winked at her. Amy's fingers tightened around her fork.

Where had Eugene been last night when her daughter disappeared?

As if he heard her thought, he straightened. His expression changed to one of brooding dislike.

Seconds later, Jake appeared, unzipping his sopping jacket.

Amy didn't remember getting up. She didn't remember crossing the room. But she was in his arms, her eyes searching his before they filled with tears and quickly dropped to his shirtfront while she strove to contain their release.

"We'll find her," he said quietly in her ear.

She looked up and saw the lines of fatigue that bracketed his eyes and mouth. "It's been over twelve hours."

"And she's a resilient, resourceful girl."

"You don't even know her."

"No," he said sadly, "but I know her mother."

"Oh, Jake, I didn't mean—"

He pulled her head down against his chest, his fingers tangling in her hair. "I know. I know, sweetheart."

She took comfort from the soothing beat of his heart against her ear. She could smell the damp of his rain-slicked jacket, and she slid her arms around him, holding him despite their audience.

"I can't stay here, Jake," she whispered against his chest. "I need to be doing something. Anything."

"Let me get something to eat and I'll talk with the chief."

"I'll fix you a plate."

"Thanks." He gazed at her sadly and offered a weak smile. "I'll pass on whatever that food was that you were playing with if you don't mind."

She almost smiled. "Mrs. Perry's casserole. Tell them you're allergic to mushrooms. It'll get you off the hook."

"Thanks for the warning. Have you eaten anything?"

"I can't. I just…can't."

"Come on."

She knew every eye watched them, but Amy was past caring. Matt joined them long enough to pile his plate with food. She noticed he also avoided the casserole dish.

Another search team was being given instructions. Eugene Perry was among the group. She tugged on Jake's arm. "They shouldn't let him join them. I think he's been drinking. He's got a flask. I wouldn't trust any area he searches."

Jake's eyes narrowed. Without a word he rose and

went over to speak with Officer Lee Garvey. Lee listened and nodded. Jake returned to the kitchen table. "Officer Garvey will take care of it," he told her.

Amy felt Eugene staring at them and wondered if he'd heard what was said. She didn't care. The thought that her daughter's life could be in that man's hands frightened her.

Miraculously, the explosion of people began to dissipate. The general and his entourage left and there was a sudden lull that left Amy, her parents and Matt and Jake alone in the kitchen.

"Amy, there's something I need to tell you," her father began. "I've been keeping this secret for many years and—"

Susan grabbed her husband's arm, her face paling even further. "No! Corny, no! You mustn't!"

Beads of sweat were on both their foreheads. Amy's anxiety found a new channel. What sort of secret could her parents be keeping? Obviously one that terrified her mother, and because of that, Amy, as well.

"Susan, the time has come. We need to tell Amy the truth."

"Not now. We can't do this now!"

"We have to. You know we do."

"Whatever it is, can't it wait, Dad?" Her mother's fear was contagious. Amy didn't want to know whatever it was her father felt compelled to reveal now, of all times.

Susan Thomas clutched her stomach. Her features pleated in pain. "I'm going to be ill," she said weakly. And she suited action to her words.

"Mom!"

Amy sprang from her chair as her mother began to retch violently. Jake rose, as well, grabbing a clean dish towel from the drawer. Without warning, her father gripped his abdomen. "I'm going to be sick, too," he said in surprise.

"Mom? Oh, my God." Horrified, Amy held her mother while the older woman's face beaded with sweat. Her breathing became labored and her moans tore at Amy. A glance at her father showed that he was undergoing the same thing. And then the first convulsion hit.

"Jake!"

"Get an ambulance," Jake ordered above the sudden chaos.

She clutched Jake as panic smothered her. "I don't understand. What's happening?"

"I'm not sure, but I think they've been poisoned."

Chapter Seven

The scene became utter chaos. The house that had seemed too empty only minutes ago, now swelled with people.

As the paramedics worked to stabilize her parents, someone came running in to say they had three more people out front who were violently ill.

"Check the food on their plates," Jake told Chief Hepplewhite as he continued holding Amy. "I think this is food poisoning. I've seen it before, and this looks very similar. You'll need samples for testing."

The chief nodded and a moment later turned to them with a frown. "Someone already rinsed their plates."

"Who?"

"No one remembers. Do you know what they were eating?" Hepplewhite asked Amy.

She dragged her eyes from the gurneys her parents were being placed on. "I...think so. Some of it, anyhow."

"Better get samples of everything," Jake advised. "Especially anything with mayonnaise or mushrooms."

Hepplewhite headed for the dining room table.

"We're taking your parents to the hospital now, Ms. Thomas," the ambulance driver told her.

"Wait! I'll come with you."

"Sorry, there isn't room."

"We'll meet you there," Jake told him, and turned to Amy. "Your mom will need her purse and insurance cards."

"Yes. You're right. I'll be right back."

Jake surveyed the crowd. Eugene Perry stood on the back porch talking with Officer Thad Osher and another of the bar crowd. Ben Dwyer was in the living room talking with someone Jake couldn't see. He'd left Arly running the restaurant, but Jake had ordered the bar closed while the search teams were working.

"You said you've seen this before?" Hepplewhite asked, coming up beside Jake.

"I attended a military function once where several people ate a salad with mushrooms. They became ill a few hours later. Two of them died. I haven't eaten mushrooms since."

Hepplewhite nodded grimly. "You think that's what happened here?"

Jake hesitated. "Maybe. Amy's father was about to reveal a secret. His wife became highly agitated. She begged him not to say anything. The timing couldn't have been neater if it had been planned."

"Any idea what the secret was?"

"No, but he implied he'd been keeping it a long time."

Amy ran up, looking frantic, a purse slung over her shoulder. "We need to go, Jake!"

"I'll phone Dr. Martin and ask her to meet your parents at the hospital," Hepplewhite promised.

Amy's eyes misted. "Thank you."

Jake guided her outside, past the field of reporters and camera crews, only coming to a stop when he realized his car was no longer parked where he'd left it. When he and Matt had run over to the Perrywrinkle earlier to change clothes, Jake had driven back. A van now occupied his parking space.

Matt! He hadn't seen the boy since before Amy's parents became ill. He tried to dismiss the nagging thought that Matt had taken his car, but it wouldn't go away. Matt had a history of stealing cars and it would have taken his sort of audacity to steal a car under the watchful eyes of so much media and the police.

Without breaking stride he led Amy toward her car instead. "Do you have your keys, Amy?"

Wordlessly, she fished them from her purse and handed them to him. The police had to clear a path for them out of the driveway and onto the street.

"Okay?"

Amy managed a tight nod. Her hands were clenched so tightly together they looked painful. He covered them with one hand as he drove.

"What's going on, Jake? I don't understand any of this. Mom was terrified of whatever it was Dad wanted to tell me. And I keep thinking back to how upset she was when Chief Hepplewhite first tried to question her."

Amy's eyes were wide with a spill of emotions. He only wished he had some comfort to offer.

"Mom's been avoiding me since they found those bodies. Now Kelsey is missing. On top of that, someone may or may not be stalking me, and my parents are dying of food poisoning. I wish I had stayed overseas!"

Jake squeezed her hands. "Do you think your parents know who the bodies are?"

"I don't want to believe that, Jake. If they knew, why didn't they tell Chief Hepplewhite? But then, what is my mother so afraid of? And where is Kelsey?"

Jake hesitated. "I'm wondering if someone took Kelsey to insure your parents didn't reveal what they know."

For a long moment there was silence. Jake glanced at her and found her staring straight ahead.

"You think Kelsey is still alive?"

"Yes," he said firmly. "Don't start doubting now, Amy."

"I'm trying to be realistic. If some monster took my child—"

"Some monster did take our child. And we're going to get her back."

Amy closed her eyes. He glimpsed her anguish and shared her pain in ways she would never know.

"There won't be any ransom call, will there?" she asked after a moment of silence.

"Not likely."

He had to take the wheel in both hands as he turned off the highway and headed for the hospital.

"Thank you. For not lying," she added. Her voice quavered and she clenched her hands together in front of her. "Do you think… Will my parents make it?"

Jake let out a his breath on a sigh. "I don't know, Amy. It depends on what the poison was, how much they ingested, and the state of their overall health."

An ambulance sped past them, sirens wailing. Amy shuddered as he turned into the emergency parking lot. Rain began falling again. While it had stopped briefly around noon, the leaden sky showed no signs of being finished. There was a brisk wind building.

What was happening to their daughter? Was Kelsey warm and dry? Was she hungry? Hurt? Jake turned off that line of thoughts as counter-productive.

They got out of the car and made a run for the emergency entrance. The automatic doors parted and the familiar scents and sounds took Jake back to his own long months of healing. Inside there was standing room only—the day-long rainstorm had led to traffic accidents and other problems.

Amy suddenly whirled on him. "Jake? Where's Matt? Do you know what he ate? He didn't eat—?"

That Amy could think of Matt now, in the midst of her own crisis, touched him. "The casserole? No. Like me, he doesn't care for mushrooms nor potato salad and those are the two most likely culprits I saw on the buffet."

"But where is he? I don't remember seeing him when we left."

Jake kept his expression blank. "I'm not sure."

His tone must have alerted her, though he'd tried to keep the worry from his voice. Amy had enough to deal with.

"What's wrong?"

He felt like a traitor, but this was Amy. "My car is missing."

For a moment she looked puzzled. "Matt's not old enough to drive, is he?"

"Not legally."

"What does that mean?"

Jake sighed. "Matt used to steal cars, Amy."

Her mouth opened and closed without a sound. They were waiting to talk with the busy receptionist when a woman in a white lab coat appeared and gazed about the room. Belatedly, Jake recognized Dr. Leslie Martin.

"Over here, Amy." He steered her toward the doors boldly proclaiming No Admittance.

"Amy?" the doctor asked.

"Hello, Leslie."

"I heard you were back in town. I'm sorry we have to meet under these conditions."

"How are my parents?"

The woman studied Amy, looked to Jake, and returned

her focus to Amy as if satisfied. "I'm not going to lie to you. They're in a bad way. They've both slipped into a coma. We're pumping their stomachs and running tests to determine the toxin, but age is against them, as is your mother's heart condition."

Amy covered her face with her hands for a moment. "I need to see them."

"They won't know you're there, Amy."

"I still need to see them."

"Okay. I'll let you see them as soon as they're more stable."

The afternoon dragged into evening, but not before several other victims were admitted. The police came and went, taking them aside to ask more questions. Amy answered as if in a fog. Her parents were admitted into Intensive Care and Amy and Jake moved to a new but only slightly less-crowded waiting room.

When Amy was finally allowed a brief visit, Jake headed for a pay phone and called the restaurant to see if Matt had returned. Arly came on the line, gruffly assuring Jake that all was well.

"I'm not worried about business, but have you seen Matt?"

"I thought he was with you. He hasn't been back since the two of you were here this morning. I heard they called off the search until tomorrow."

That was news to Jake.

"I can handle the restaurant for you again tomorrow if you want."

"It's your day off."

"Makes no matter to me."

"Thanks, Arly. I was going to close it, but if you're willing to run things, go ahead. I'd appreciate that." He knew the older man needed the paycheck.

He hung up to find Dr. Martin striding toward him. "How are they doing?" Jake asked.

"Not good. I understand they haven't found Amy's daughter yet?"

His gut clenched. The fear was never far from the back of his mind. Grimly, Jake shook his head. "They called off the search for tonight."

"I'll write Amy a prescription to help her sleep. There's a pharmacy next door. You can get it filled while you wait."

"She won't take anything."

"Try. She's going to need her strength."

Jake understood the silent message. Amy's parents would probably not make it. "How long before we know anything?"

Leslie Martin shrugged sadly. She scrawled a hasty prescription and handed it to Jake. "I've got eleven cases so far. Her parents are by far the worst."

"Botulism or mushrooms?"

"We're running tests. Take Amy home and try to have her get some rest."

"I'll try."

THEY SWUNG BY the Perrywrinkle on the way home. Amy felt numb, standing there while Jake talked with his staff.

The employees were sympathetic and supportive, but no one had seen Matt. Jake left a note for the boy and went upstairs to get something, insisting he would drive her home. But as they stepped back outside the restaurant into the blustery night air, Jake abruptly came to attention. "Wait here."

Before Amy could protest, he was running toward the covered, roped-off pit. Only then did she notice the lone figure standing there, clothing whipping about her body as she stared past the police tape. Gertrude Perry. Amy ran after Jake, frightened without knowing why.

Jake slowed to a cautious walk before he reached the figure. Coming up behind him, Amy could see that old Ms. Perry stood in the dark, mumbling to herself.

''Ms. Perry,'' Jake said quietly.

''No good. Knew it was no good.''

''Miss Perry?''

The old woman turned, blinking rain from her eyes. ''Whore,'' she said distinctly.

Amy came to a halt not sure if the words were directed at her or were part of the woman's crazy soliloquy.

''Have to protect the child.''

Amy's heart began to pound a new rhythm. Did she mean Kelsey?

''What child is that?'' Jake asked, still in that soft, quiet tone.

''Knew it was no good. Now look what they've done.''

''Who?''

''Have to protect the baby,'' she said, becoming more strident. ''You can't hide your sins. I knew it was no good. Poor dead baby.''

Amy stepped forward. ''Kelsey? You mean, Kelsey?''

Jake frowned at her, but Gertrude Perry peered through the rain in confusion. ''Do I know you?''

''I'm Amy. Amy Thomas. Do you know where Kelsey is?''

''Who?''

Jake stilled Amy with the touch of his hand.

''Can you protect the baby, Ms. Perry?'' he asked softly.

Birdlike eyes stared at him. For a moment, Amy thought the older woman almost looked lucid. A crafty expression crossed her features before the clarity faded and she began mumbling again.

"Ruin and scandal."

The woman shuddered. Amy realized the poor old lady was only wearing a thin sweater over her blouse and pants. Her wet clothing whipped helplessly about her body in the strong breeze. The temperatures had dropped substantially and she was soaking wet. Mud caked her shoes and coated her wide-legged slacks.

"Come on, Ms. Perry," Jake said quietly. "We're going inside now."

"Okay."

They made it to the front entrance when a car pulled up, splashing all of them with water as it hit a wide puddle.

General Marcus Perry threw open the sedan door and stepped out. "There you are."

Gertrude Perry cringed.

"We've been looking everywhere for you, dear," Millicent Perry added, coming around the car. "Come with me. Cindy Lou will draw you a nice hot bath. You'll like that, won't you?"

"Mustn't disgrace the family name," Gertrude said, surprising everyone by her mimicry of Millicent's Bostonian accent.

Millicent recovered her shock quickly. "That's exactly right, Gertrude. Come with me."

"Sorry if she was a bother," the general said. "We're going to have her committed. She's gotten too much for Cindy Lou to control."

Amy stepped forward. "She's been talking about trying to protect the baby. I need to know if she means Kelsey."

General Perry shook his head, his steely eyes looking at her with distaste. "It doesn't mean a thing. Most of the stuff that comes out of her mouth is nothing but gibberish anymore. I'm sorry she upset you." He didn't sound the least bit sorry. "But my sister can't help you. Excuse me."

"No," she said to the disappearing car. "I will not excuse you." She knew Jake stared at her. "Gertrude Perry knows something about those bodies."

"Yes," he agreed. "Unfortunately, the general is right. The woman is clearly incompetent."

"Maybe so, but I'm sure she was talking about Kelsey when she said she wanted to protect the baby."

"Amy, she might have meant the infant who died in the root cellar."

"I don't think so," Amy said stubbornly. "Haven't you noticed? She has moments when she seems to know and understand exactly what she's saying."

Jake stroked her cheek. "Let's get out of the rain."

She walked with Jake to her car. Gertrude Perry was the key, Amy was sure of it. Amy would have to find a way to prevent them from locking Gertrude Perry away until they could try to get information from her.

As they pulled into her parents' driveway, she stared at the house where she'd grown up. The crowds were gone, most of the police were gone. But someone was moving around inside. Probably the detective who was monitoring the phone system. Rain continued falling, which suited Amy's mood perfectly. She didn't want to go inside and talk to any more police or well-meaning neighbors.

"We should let Chief Hepplewhite know about Matt."

"He'll be okay," Jake said flatly.

Jake's features were broodingly forbidding. Anyone would think he didn't care about Matt from his tone and his expression. But she knew better. Jake cared deeply. He tended to store his hurts inside where no one could see. Matt's disappearance had hurt him.

As if reading at least some of her thoughts Jake shook

his head. "Don't worry about him, Amy. Matt has a habit of running away when things get to him."

"You're angry."

"Let's go inside."

He got out of the car and came around and opened her door. Amy didn't move. She looked up at his tight features. "He's only a boy, Jake."

"He's more capable than you know. And he's angry with me right now."

"I don't think so. An angry child wouldn't have spent the morning with you and the search party. What if he didn't run off, Jake? What if the same thing that happened to Kelsey happened to Matt?"

Jake hesitated. Slowly, he shook his head. "It didn't."

"You don't know that. What if he saw something or heard something this morning that he shouldn't have?"

"You're grasping at straws."

"Am I? What if my parents were poisoned on purpose, Jake?"

For a long moment he stood there, the light rain plastering his hair to his head and running down his face. "Could we have this conversation inside—out of the rain?" he asked finally.

"I want to talk with Chief Hepplewhite."

In answer, Jake started back around the car. Amy climbed out quickly. "Come on. He lives next to the Cznery's. It'll be quicker to walk."

"We'll get soaked."

"We're already soaked."

She set off across the lawn. Ignoring the handicap ramp, she ran up the three steps onto the porch. The chief answered the door seconds later. He was still wearing his uniform, but now his shirt was unbuttoned and his hair stood in disarray as if he'd been finger-combing it.

"Amy? Mr. Collins. What's wrong? Have you heard from Kelsey?"

"No. Now Matt's missing," Amy told him.

His gaze went straight to Jake who inclined his head in affirmation.

"Think he took off again?" the chief asked Jake.

"It's possible," Jake said. "We had a talk last night. I told him a few things that may have upset him."

"Nonsense!" Amy reprimanded. "He wasn't upset. He spent the morning searching. I think he saw or heard something he shouldn't have."

"Why don't you both come inside?" The chief stepped aside and they entered the dark house. A television set glowed in the dimly lit living room. A woman in a wheelchair neither moved nor acknowledged their presence. Amy's mother had told her Mrs. Hepplewhite couldn't speak or move, but no one knew why. Even in a nosy town like Fools Point, no one had apparently gotten up the gumption to ask the chief what had happened to her. Gossip centered on the fact that he cared for her with nursing help that came in periodically during the day and evening.

"We didn't mean to interrupt you. I can see you're off duty."

"My job means I'm never off duty. Come on back to the kitchen."

It was the only room in the house that wasn't totally depressing, Amy decided. And that was probably because the lights gleamed dully. The remains of a frozen dinner sat beside a bag of potato chips and the daily newspaper.

"You were eating."

"I finished. May I offer you something?"

"No," Amy said. "We ate at the hospital."

Hepplewhite looked sheepish. "I'm afraid we didn't

leave a whole lot of food over at your place. We packed everything to be tested."

Amy shuddered. "That's okay."

"Sit down and tell me what you think Matt saw." He pulled clean dish towels from a drawer and handed them each one.

Amy gratefully wiped at her wet face. "I'm not sure, but consider the timing. Matt was in the living room eating when…when my parents became ill. No one remembers seeing him after that."

"He might have become ill, as well." Hepplewhite looked at Jake.

"My car's gone," he told the policeman without inflection.

"Do you want me to report it?"

Jake hesitated. Amy realized both men were trying to protect the boy. She reached for Jake's hand, offering silent support. He looked startled, then grateful. He clasped her fingers, engulfing them in a firm, warm grip.

"Why don't we wait and see?" Jake suggested.

"Chief Hepplewhite," Amy said quickly, "I don't know what this has to do with Kelsey and Matt's disappearance, but I think my parents know who the bodies in the root cellar are. Dad said he had a secret. I think it had to do with those bodies. And I think the Perrys know who they are, too. At least, Gertrude Perry does, and I wouldn't be at all surprised about the general, as well."

Hepplewhite leaned against the kitchen counter. His deceptively relaxed pose reminded her of Jake. The two men looked nothing alike, but their mannerisms were similar. Amy would bet the chief was ex-military, too.

"Dad doesn't like the general. The feeling is obviously mutual. I watched them at the house today. The animosity is visible. You know my dad. He gets along with everybody. And my mother's afraid of him."

"Your dad?" the chief asked.

"The general! She acted scared to death of him."

"He's a rather imposing figure, Amy."

"So are you and Jake, but they aren't afraid of you two. I know it isn't proof of anything, but I saw the way the general looked at my dad. He was warning him. And it was right after that Dad said he wanted to tell me something. Dad doesn't take well to threats, Chief. Then tonight the general and his wife practically dragged poor old Ms. Perry into the car. She was talking about ruin and scandal. You have to question her! She may know where Kelsey is!"

Jake squeezed her hand. "We found her standing next to the root cellar."

Hepplewhite frowned, his fingers drumming restlessly on the edge of the counter. "I think you may be right about what your parents and Gertrude Perry may know, but questioning her is futile, Amy."

"But we have to find Kelsey. And Matt. What if they're together? What if someone took them to warn my parents into silence?"

"I'd say the ptomaine poisoning is going to do that effectively." He hesitated as if considering his next words carefully. "Look, I'm going to tell you two something off the record. This hasn't been released yet, but those bodies have been down in that root cellar approximately thirty years. The M.E. thinks the woman may have bled to death giving birth. She was wrapped in a sheet and was probably carried down there after she died. The medical examiner believes the infant died at birth as well—probably strangled on the umbilical chord."

"That poor woman," Amy said.

"Yeah."

"Amy's mother would have been pregnant with Amy about thirty years ago," Jake mused.

Hepplewhite nodded. "Exactly. I think the two women knew each other. Maybe they used the same doctor. Leslie went through her dad's old records. Your mother wasn't one of his patients back then."

"Mom said I was born at home."

"Did she use a midwife?"

"I don't know."

"Interesting tie-in," Jake offered.

Hepplewhite nodded again.

"But if the woman in the root cellar wasn't murdered," Amy said, "why put her there? Why didn't someone call for a doctor?"

"That's the mystery," Hepplewhite agreed. "Someone either let that woman bleed to death, or they found her after the fact and didn't want anyone to know. We're looking at the Perry family for missing relatives."

"Opens up some interesting possibilities," Jake said.

"Yes. As I said before, we should be able to get an ID if she was listed as a missing person anywhere. Besides the dental records, pictures of the jewelry she was wearing will go out to the media."

"So we don't need to harass poor Miss Perry?" Jake asked.

Hepplewhite shook his head. "Sooner or later, we'll get an ID"

"Then the poisonings and the break-in and...and Kelsey's disappearance?"

"I'm sorry, Amy. It looks like coincidence. In fact, it appears Cindy Lou made the suspect casserole. She's going to be mortified when this hits the news media. In the morning, we'll be asking her where she purchased her mushrooms."

Amy's gaze went to Jake. She saw the same choked fear there that she was experiencing. If the kidnapping was unrelated to the bodies in the root cellar, the odds that Kelsey was still alive dropped dramatically.

Jake stood abruptly. "Come on. Tomorrow's going to be a long day. Let's let Chief Hepplewhite get some rest."

"I'll be over first thing in the morning," Hepplewhite promised. "And I'll have my men keep an unofficial watch for your car, Mr. Collins."

Jake nodded. They refused the offer of an umbrella and walked back to Amy's house in silence. At the front door, he paused. "Take one of those pills the doctor prescribed."

"No. The hospital might call. I don't want to be groggy. Jake...would you...could you stay the night? Please. I don't want to be alone."

"The police—"

"Are strangers." His reluctance hurt, but she was past caring. She would beg if she had to.

"Let me call the restaurant and be sure Matt didn't come home."

Amy opened the front door. "There's a phone in my bedroom."

JAKE WOULD BE ANGRY with him.

Matt felt pretty angry at himself. He was wet clear through, cold and desperately hungry and thirsty. Jake's car was stuck in the mud and he'd lost the old lady a long time ago.

It wasn't that he was scared, exactly, but Matt was far more at home in the city than the creepy old woods that seemed to go on forever. He'd been lost for a long time now. If only he'd stayed near the main road he wouldn't have gotten lost. But he couldn't after his foot had gotten stuck in the mud that passed for a road. He'd pulled his foot right out of his shoe and spent several long, frustrating minutes retrieving it. He decided then and there that the spongy grass was far better than the road. He should have gone back the way he'd come but he wanted to see where the old woman had gone. The problem was, in the dark, he'd wandered too far from the road and hadn't been able to find it again.

He wished he hadn't acted so impulsively. If only he'd stopped and told Jake what he'd seen. But then he would have lost her. Besides, Jake had his hands full with everyone starting to throw up and all. Ms. Thomas needed Jake. And Matt had been so certain he was right.

He paused against a pine tree to rest. He longed to turn on the flashlight again but the batteries were going. Besides, there was nothing to see except more trees.

He'd thought—he'd hoped—he was going to be a hero and make Jake proud. Instead, he'd really screwed up.

Again.

He started walking once more, so tired he wasn't sure how he was going to keep going. He'd already walked forever. He stopped and rubbed the water out of his eyes. A clearing up ahead had a building of some sort. Probably a cabin or a shed or something. Matt didn't care. It would be out of the rain and that was all that mattered at the moment. Maybe there'd even be someone inside with some food and a way to call Jake.

He lurched forward, half running until it dawned on him that caution might be advisable. That crazy old lady was out here somewhere. He slowed his pace and even took the time to circle the building. Definitely a cabin. It was too big to be a shed. But who'd want a cabin way out here? People were nuts. Deeply rutted tire tracks outside the building proved that someone had recently used the place.

Matt thought about the old woman and his excitement returned. If nothing else, the tire tracks would lead to a road and a road meant people and rescue. But first, he'd better check out the cabin. Maybe there'd be something to eat inside. And he could sit down for a minute out of this soaking rain and the cold wind.

There were no lights coming from any of the windows. He peered inside but couldn't see anything. The window was locked so he tried another one. Finally, convinced the cabin must be empty, he walked quietly onto the wooden porch. Muddy footprints led in and out of the main door. Small footprints, like maybe a kid or an old woman would make.

To his shock, the door handle turned freely under his hand. Slowly, Matt opened the door and waited. There was no sound from inside, but a fluttery feeling made him hesitate just the same. The place looked empty, but it didn't feel empty. He couldn't have said why.

Matt pulled out the flashlight. At first it wouldn't come on at all, but he gave it a hard rap with the heel of his hand and it produced a dim, wavery light.

The living room and kitchen were empty, but there were two other doors. Matt hesitated at the sight of the muddy footprints leading back and forth to the first door. His heart beat frantically. He remembered the last time he'd tried to follow someone into a dark building. That time it had been a barn and he'd nearly been killed.

But he had to know.

He crept forward silently. His hand shook as he reached for the door handle. It, too, turned beneath his fingers. Slowly, he inched the door open, ready to run at the first sound of anything at all. Silence. Very cautiously, he stepped inside what appeared to be a bedroom.

He turned the flashlight on the bed and saw a huddled form lying as still as death.

Chapter Eight

Amy spooned against his body, making sleep totally impossible. Her subtle scent, the feel of her warm body, left Jake struggling with too many memories of happy nights when they'd shared a bed and each other. She would never know how much he deeply regretted the past and all those wasted years. He never had been any good at expressing his feelings.

He'd hesitated before removing his shirt, not sure how she'd react to the scars on his back, but he needn't have worried. She moved like a somnambulist. Her attention and thoughts centered on the children and the fate of her parents.

He'd pulled off his shoes and socks and slipped into bed with his pants on. Not because of false modesty, but because he was aware of the detectives stationed in the house downstairs. If something happened, he wanted to be ready to go at a moment's notice.

Amy had disappeared into the bathroom and returned in an oversize T-shirt. The outlines of her bra and panties were clearly visible. She'd always liked to sleep in loose shirts, he remembered. But back when they were together, she'd worn nothing beneath them.

Despite the memories and his desire for Amy, going to bed with her now was about friendship and need, not

sex. If she'd come to bed stark naked he wouldn't have
touched her. Of course, he would have been a blithering
idiot by morning. He was already too aware of her and
how much he still wanted her. He made certain she
wasn't aware of the proof of that desire.

Though she lay perfectly still beside him, he knew she
wasn't sleeping any more than he was. When she started
to weep silently, he pulled her closer, laying his face
against her clean-smelling hair. While she cried, he shed
his own mental tears for Amy and the daughter he might
never get a chance to know. After a while she turned
toward him, resting her damp cheek against his chest. Her
breath was warm and subtly reassuring against his bare
skin.

"Jake?"

His name was the smallest of whispers. He squeezed
her gently to let her know he was awake.

"Will that toxicology test show if more than one poison was present?"

Jake realized he'd inhaled and forgotten to release his
breath. Slowly, he exhaled, stirring her hair. "Yes.
Why?"

"You'll think I'm reaching."

He stroked her cheek with the back of his knuckle.
"Then let me reach with you."

She raised her face. Tentatively she placed her hand
on his jaw, rubbing the stubble he should have shaved
before getting into bed with her. He'd lived alone so long
he hadn't even thought about it.

"My parents are so sick."

Her voice broke and his heart ached for her. Having
Kelsey go missing was more than enough horror for one
person to deal with. But having her parents at death's
door, as well...

"They're much sicker than anyone else. I know

they're older and their health plays a factor, but…I don't want to lie here thinking some pervert grabbed our daughter. I'd rather believe that crazy old Ms. Perry was trying to tell us something.''

She lifted up on one elbow. Her face was a mask of pain. And while he wanted to console her, he wasn't going to offer her false hope.

''There were a lot of people moving around the food table and in the kitchen,'' she continued before he could say anything. ''How hard would it have been to directly contaminate their food or drink?''

Jake was used to the organized chaos of a working kitchen. The scene in the Thomas house today hadn't been anything like that. People had milled about everywhere, getting in one another's way as they tried to be helpful.

''Easy enough, assuming you knew which plates and glasses were theirs,'' he conceded.

''Cindy Lou fixed all of us a plate. My parents were standing beside General Perry when she came over and insisted we eat. I thought she did it because of the reporter and cameraman from the *Ledger*.''

''And now you don't?''

''The mushroom dish came from her.''

''We don't know—''

''And it was her mother, Millicent Perry, who insisted we move into the kitchen. Or maybe that was Cindy Lou, too… It's hard to remember the sequence exactly, but I know Millicent was helping, putting drinks and cookies on the table. I even noticed Gertrude Perry hovering around the food table in the dining room. And Eugene…remember when I said I thought he'd been drinking? What if that wasn't a flask of whiskey he was putting inside his pocket? What if it was something he added to my parents' drinks?''

He heard the frantic desperation in her voice. Jake wasn't enamored of the Perry family, either, but Amy was talking conspiracy theory here. He, too, desperately wanted their daughter to be alive and unharmed, but there was no proof to tie in the Perrys.

"And what if Matt saw one of them do it?"

Her last question scattered his carefully marshaled logic to the winds.

Amy waited.

"If Matt saw something suspicious," he said slowly, "I'd like to believe he would have come and told me."

"That assumes he understood what he saw," Amy pointed out. "But what if he didn't? What if he saw something incriminating without realizing what he saw? The general disappeared right after his daughter approached me. In fact, the entire family vanished shortly after my parents sat down. And so did Matt," she added triumphantly.

"Except Eugene."

"Okay, except Eugene."

There was a chilling sort of logic to what Amy was saying. "Eugene and Cindy Lou would have been children thirty years ago," he pointed out.

She sat up completely, pushing back the hair that fell forward into her eyes. "Sure, but the mayor is up for reelection. Can you imagine what a scandal would do to Cindy Lou's image?"

"That isn't exactly a reason to poison someone."

"Maybe. But what if that woman in the root cellar didn't die in childbirth? What if she was murdered by the general or his sister? And what if Cindy Lou found out? Her family thinks they are safe. After all, thirty years is a long time. But now suddenly the bodies come to light. Forensic evidence has made tremendous strides. You heard what Chief Hepplewhite said. Sooner or later the police will discover who that woman and her baby are. And the family name is all important to the Perrys.''

''The chief said the victims died in childbirth.''

''He *thought* they died in childbirth. They haven't released their findings yet, and who's to say they can't be refuted?''

''That's a big stretch, Amy.''

''It's a theory,'' she insisted stubbornly.

He, too, sat up against the headboard, but his back protested the too quick movement. He'd taken enough medication for one day. Jake ignored the twinge of pain while trying to decide how best to couch his next words.

''You're doing it again,'' she said.

''Doing what?''

''Stop holding back on me, Jake! You always did that. Tell me flat-out what you're really thinking. Am I crazy?''

''You aren't crazy. People have been known to kill for all sorts of unfathomable and stupid reasons. I'm not saying your theory is impossible. One or all of the Perrys *may* actually have conspired to kill your parents to keep them silent about the death of a woman and her baby that happened thirty years ago. But—''

''But it sounds ridiculous when you say it like that.'' She slumped back beside him against the headboard.

Jake lifted a shoulder. ''You want to assume someone took Kelsey to use as leverage against your parents, right?''

Her fingers clenched the pillowcase. ''I can't help it. I can't stand thinking some sex offender pulled her from the house while I was downstairs.'' Her voice broke on a sob and she shuddered. ''My parents are dying, Jake, and I feel so helpless. I can't make the thoughts stop churning.''

He stroked her arm, sharing her pain. ''I know, I can't,

either. But even if your theory is right, the minute your parents die, Kelsey becomes a liability to someone.''

Amy fisted a handful of sheet. ''But they'd keep her alive until they knew for sure my parents were dead.''

Jake didn't answer with words. He covered her hand, lightly stroking the soft skin.

''I knew you'd think I was being stupid!''

''I don't think you're being stupid. In fact, first thing in the morning we're going to ask Hepplewhite what the lab results were.''

Hope animated her face. ''Even if there wasn't a second poison, bad mushrooms could have been added on purpose.''

''The problem is, we need a tie between the Perry family, the bodies in the root cellar and your parents.''

Amy suddenly scrambled off the bed. ''Maybe we can find one.''

''How?''

''Pictures.''

Jake cocked his head in silent question.

''The other day, Mom and I sat down to organize all her photographs. She has dozens, but only a few are in albums. We were going through my baby pictures. There were pictures of her and my dad holding me as an infant. Maybe there are pictures of Mom when she was pregnant with me.''

Her excitement, along with the faint possibility, stirred his interest. ''And maybe some of the pregnant women she knew back then?''

''It's worth a try. Are you tired?''

''I don't think either of us is going to sleep much tonight.''

''They're in her bedroom. Wait here. I'll bring them in and we can spread them out on the bed.''

He turned on the light as she ran down the hall. Her

resiliency was amazing. She was clinging to the thinnest of straws with a tenacity he admired.

Jake got out of bed to help as Amy returned, her arms laden with albums and shoe boxes of loose photographs. One of her mother's cats finally came out of hiding to watch from the hall as they spread the items out and settled back on the bed together.

"Remind me in the morning to have Hepplewhite initiate a search for my car," Jake said.

Amy's head jerked up sharply.

"If you're right, Matt could be in trouble, too."

Speechless, Amy stared at him. Jake was always self-contained. His facial expressions were difficult to read at the best of times. Yet she would have sworn he watched her now with a yearning she could almost feel.

"Are these in any order?" he asked, dropping his gaze to pick up the nearest album.

"N-no."

"Okay, tell me who you recognize."

Sitting beside Jake now was much harder than lying next to him had been. Where she'd been consumed with grief and worry earlier, taking some comfort from his presence, now her mind became aware of Jake the man she had once loved.

His chest was bare. As he opened the first book she had a sudden memory of the night he had let her lick chocolate icing from that chest. They'd brought ready-made icing and Graham crackers to bed and she'd accidentally brushed some icing on his chest. He'd been so shocked when she'd leaned over and licked it off with her tongue. But his shock hadn't lasted long. In fact he'd insisted on—

"Something wrong?"

"What?"

"Amy, if you're too tired for this tonight—"

"No! No, I'm sorry. My mind was wandering."

She knew she was blushing and she looked away. What was wrong with her? Kelsey was out there somewhere waiting for help and she was having carnal thoughts about Jake.

She was tired and scared, yet completely aware of the dangerously appealing look of the stubble on Jake's face. Her gaze strayed to the remarkably flat planes of his stomach and the thin line of hair that arrowed down to disappear under the edge of his waistband. Without a belt, those dress pants had a tendency to ride low on his hips.

"My parents waited a long time to have me," she said quickly opening a book at random. She had to concentrate! "Leslie Martin's father was the only doctor in Fools Point. Mom and Dad married late in life and old Dr. Martin diagnosed Mom with a medical condition that made it highly improbable she would ever conceive. That's why she stopped going to him. Fertility clinics didn't exist the way they do today. Dr. Martin recommended a gynecologist for a second opinion. I don't remember if Mom said she saw him or not, but I do remember her saying she and my father never expected to have a child."

She shut out the vision of her parents lying in a hospital bed surrounded by machines hooked into tubes. They had to live. They had to!

"Mom said she was shocked and ecstatic when she realized she was pregnant with me," she forced herself to continue.

"Your mother uses Leslie Martin now, doesn't she?"

"Yes. After Leslie took over the practice Mom started going to her for routine things, but to this day, she uses a specialist in Germantown for her female exams."

"Is this a picture of your mom and dad?" Jake asked, lifting a photograph.

"Yes. That must have been taken while she was pregnant with me. See how round her stomach is under that dress?"

"Good. Let's see if we can find another one around that same time."

But that photo seemed to be the only one that showed her mother expecting. As they sorted through the pictures, Amy's depression deepened. They were looking for a possibly nonexistent needle in a haystack—blindfolded. What had made her think this would accomplish anything at all? She didn't recognize most of the people. Her grandparents on both sides had been dead before she was born and her father's two brothers died together in a construction accident when she was small. She wouldn't have known any of them if her mother hadn't pointed them out the other day.

"I can't figure out who you resemble," Jake said abruptly.

"Dad always claimed it was the milkman."

"Got a picture of him in here?"

Jake paused to pore over some pictures of Amy as a young child. While his interest gave her a warm feeling, she had to remind him to pay attention to their goal. But when they came to a series of pictures of Kelsey as a baby, both of them lost all track of their original purpose.

"She was beautiful, Amy. She looks just like you." He fished for one of her earlier baby pictures and held the two side-by-side. "No one would ever doubt she was your child."

Her eyes filled with fresh tears. She blinked them back. She must be strong. If there was a clue in this mass of photographs, it was up to her to find it.

"She definitely has your smile and your chin."

"Think so?" he asked, looking pleased.

"But she has a mind of her own."

"I think," he said softly, "she comes by that one from both sides of the family."

"Are you saying I'm obstreperous?"

"Not me, I can't even pronounce it. But if it means stubborn…" He smiled kindly and her world shifted.

Something in the comfort level of the room changed. Amy found herself once more acutely aware that this was Jake. A man whose body she had once known as intimately as her own. A man who was alone with her in a bed more undressed than not. A man she still wanted.

"I think…maybe we've looked at enough pictures tonight," Jake said abruptly.

"We haven't even started on that other box."

"It's late, Amy."

Funny how they could hold a conversation on two levels at once. "You're right."

He got out of bed and turned away to begin scooping up pictures. Amy gasped.

He spun back to her alertly. "What?"

"Your back!"

"Oh. Sorry. I'll put a shirt on."

"Don't." She scrambled off the bed, reaching for him, holding him in place. His muscles corded with tension.

"You always hide from me, Jake. You always did. As soon as things get personal, you take cover behind that formal facade you've perfected over the years. Your back is a mess. Talk to me. Tell me what happened."

His shoulder lifted in that almost-insolent shrug of his. "A mission went bad."

But his negligent attitude couldn't cover the pain that underscored that simple statement. Amy knew without being told that Jake felt responsible for the failure of that mission.

"Some of these are burn scars."

"The boat exploded."

"Oh, Jake."

"Being thrown into the cold water probably saved my sorry hide. I can't tell you any details, Amy. Not because I'm trying to shut you out, but security—"

"I don't want to know secrets." She moved to stand where she could see his back. Lightly, she traced a long, nasty gash that disappeared beneath his waistband. "This wasn't due to fire."

"No," he agreed warily.

"You were shot?"

"Amy, it doesn't matter."

"It does matter!" she said fiercely. "This is so deep. You must have been in terrible pain."

He winced and she knew he still was.

"I was lucky."

"I don't think so. You didn't just walk away from this mission."

"No." Almost reluctantly he added, "I almost didn't walk away at all. But I was one of the lucky ones. I made it back."

She slid her arms around him, pressing her face against his back, unable to speak. The scars were deep and ugly. And the pain they represented scared her. With his family dead, who had been there to hold him when he lay in the hospital recovering?

"Amy, it was a long time ago."

He'd taken that gentle tone with her again. Angry at the way he continued to shut her out, she let him go and came around to face him. "Really? The skin is still healing. You have to be in a lot of pain. I've seen you wincing when you thought no one was looking. Talk to me, Jake."

Nine years ago she never could have pushed him this

way. Nine years ago she knew little about Jake beyond the fact that he was an incredible lover. Thanks to the conversation she'd overheard him having with Matt, she had new insight into this intensely private man. Jake didn't know how to open up with people. It was up to her to teach him.

Her hands cupped his face. She pulled his head down so she could cover his lips with her own. They met the expected resistance as she traced his lips with her tongue. He always held back, but not this time. Boldly, she sought entrance to his mouth.

For a moment she thought he'd pull away. Every muscle in his body seemed to tighten.

Suddenly he crushed her against his chest. His mouth opened over hers. He kissed her fiercely, with a passion that stunned her even as her body exalted.

The kiss shattered any misconceptions that he might not want her. She felt the stir of his arousal against her thigh through the flimsy T-shirt. Beneath the sheer bra, her nipples answered that challenge, tightening as she rubbed against his chest. She squirmed in an effort to get even closer. The stubble of his jaw abraded her skin. It should have hurt, but instead it added another layer of excitement. His mouth claimed her. Branded her. Thrilled her beyond all reason.

Amy sought to meet that challenge with one of her own. She greedily kissed him back, letting him know she wanted him every bit as much. Her restless fingers smoothed and skimmed over each ugly scar and ridge on his back. Jake made a low sound of satisfaction that sent ripples of longing through her abdomen. As his lips moved over her neck and down, her fingertip sought one of his nipples, gently flicking it. Finally she pulled back from his seeking lips to tongue it lightly.

"Amy!"

Her name was a growl of intense pleasure at the back of his throat. Her hand stole lower, seeking the bulge straining against the zipper of his pants.

Jake made a soft sound. His hand reached down, covering hers. For a moment, he held her pressed against that ridge before dragging her hand to his mouth and kissing it, turning it over to lightly brush the palm with his tongue.

"Jake!"

"We have to stop, Amy."

Her body sang with need and a longing so sharp it was almost painful. "Why? Why do we have to stop? We're two consenting adults. We—"

He cupped her head, pulling her mouth to his in a molten kiss that set fire to every jangled nerve in her body.

"We can't do this," he said raggedly, "because I don't have any protection, Amy."

His words and their ramifications doused the blaze of her need effectively. If they made love now, there could be a child. Another child like Kelsey. How could she have forgotten about her daughter or her parents even for a moment?

"Do you?"

She stared at him blankly. "What?"

"Have anything? Are you protected?"

"No." She wanted to hit something. What sort of parent could even think about sex when their child was missing?

He smoothed the hair from her face and kissed her forehead. Amy allowed him to tug her against his chest where the pounding of his heart mated with hers.

"I'm sorry," he whispered after a few minutes. "I didn't mean to start something—"

Amy snapped back, struggling to contain her anger. "Do you enjoy being a martyr?"

"What?"

"*I* started that. Not you. You don't always have to be in control, Jake. You don't always have to shoulder the blame. It's okay to need and want and share. That's how relationships are supposed to work. I want you. Just now, I wanted you. My daughter is missing. My parents may be dying. Yet I wanted you. I've always wanted you."

His eyes closed and opened quickly, but not before she saw the pain. Her vision blurred.

"Jake...I...I'm sorry." She swallowed hard. "But please don't push me out. Not now. Not when I really need you."

"What do you want me to say, Amy? Do you want to take the risk? You could get pregnant again."

The thought was electrifying.

She wanted another child, she realized. Jake's child.

"Sweetheart, I don't think—"

"You're right," she told him. "We can't do this."

Jake rolled away from her.

"As much as I'd love to have another child... You're doing it again," she told him.

"Doing what?"

"Hiding behind that wall of yours. Can't you ever relax, Jake? At least unbend enough for me to understand what you're thinking."

He ran a hand through his hair in frustration. "I can try, Amy, but I'm afraid I haven't had much practice at relationships."

"I know. We'll work on it. Together."

His eyes darkened. Something stirred in the depths. Something unexpected.

"Will you marry me?"

Amy's heart stumbled. For a moment she couldn't

catch a breath. Her mind was a blank and her heart began racing. "What did you say?"

"Marry me."

The words came out of nowhere. Nine years ago she would have done anything to hear those words. Now they left her speechless.

"We can make it work, Amy."

"I can't...I don't..."

"I know. My timing stinks. But think about it, Amy. After we find Kelsey and Matt I'll ask you again. I'd like to give Kelsey a brother or sister."

The naked hunger in his eyes was almost her undoing. She barely stopped herself from reaching for him again.

"I don't have any experience to draw on, but I'd try to be a good husband and father. I already know you're a terrific mother. Maybe you could teach me what I need to know about being a parent."

Her heart somersaulted in her chest.

"We know the sexual chemistry still works, Amy. In fact, if it worked any better, the fire department would be here right about now."

But what about love? He had never once told her that he loved her. And she needed that with every breath in her body.

"Think about it, all right?"

As if she'd be able to do anything else.

THE SITUATION had gone from bad to worse. There had to be a way to contain the damage. Careful planning and strategy. The woman wasn't the fool she'd appeared to be. Getting to her now was going to require decisive maneuvering. She'd protected herself quite well.

But strong defenses were nothing when faced with a determined assault. The silence of the house was jarred when the clock struck the hour. Late. Very late. The barrel of the gun gleamed on the polished wood desk. Such a simple tool. Efficient. Ugly. Necessary.

The woman would die tomorrow. Then the children. The police already suspected a child molester had the girl. Let them go right on believing that.

Regrets were useless. Planning and strategy, that was what was required. Keeping the police busy and focused was essential.

The bullets slid easily into the chamber, one right after another.

KELSEY RUBBED AT her hands where the handcuffs had chaffed her skin without taking her eyes from Matt. He was pretty sure she had no serious injuries, and was thankful for that. She was scared and tired and hungry, but as far as he could tell, she wasn't hurt.

Once he finally got her free of the handcuffs that had chained her to the bed, his euphoria at finding her quickly had dissolved right along with another heavy downpour that effectively trapped them inside in the dark. Explaining to the anxious girl why they couldn't just go charging outside was difficult.

"Bears?" she'd asked wide-eyed.

"Possibly. It's pitch black out there and it's raining. All sorts of animals may be roaming around. We wouldn't hear them or see them until they were right on top of us. We'll just have to wait until morning."

"But what if she comes back?"

Matt knew Kelsey referred to old Miss Perry. "She won't come back until morning." At least he hoped that was the case.

Despite the small fire he'd managed to light after rummaging around, he was cold and damp and thoroughly miserable. The old woman had brought food from the Thomas house and left it within Kelsey's reach. While it wasn't very appetizing, he talked Kelsey into eating some with him. Everything except the yucky casserole with the mushrooms inside. He pushed that out of the way and Kelsey didn't object. There was a can of soda that they split and some tepid water in a plastic bottle. Matt wished he was back at the Perrywrinkle with Arly.

He looked at the girl's grimy face and the hope and trust he saw there made him nod with a certainty he was far from feeling.

"Piece of cake. We just follow the tire tracks to the road. I've got a car," he said importantly. "It's stuck in the mud right now, but maybe somehow with your help we can get it unstuck and get back to town. If nothing else, by now Jake knows I took his car so the cops are probably looking for it and me."

"Jake's my father, you know. His name's on my birth certificate."

"I know. He's my uncle." And that knowledge had finally settled on him. At first he'd been upset, not sure how to handle the information. But now the fact pleased him enormously. He only wished Jake had been able to come for him right away after the accident, but Matt understood. The important thing was that Jake had finally come for him at all. And Jake really wanted him. Jake didn't treat him like a burden or some stupid kid he had to tolerate.

"You know what," he told the girl, "that makes us cousins."

Her eyes widened. "I've never had a cousin before."

"Yeah? Me neither."

She nestled closer despite his wet clothes. "Do you live with my dad at the restaurant?"

"Uh-huh."

"I wanted to ask him…you know…why he never came to see me or my mom."

"I don't think he knew about you, Kelsey. Why don't you ask him when we see him?"

"But what if old Ms. Perry comes back and catches us?"

"We can outrun an old lady."

"I don't know, Matt. She moves pretty fast."

"Nah. She just caught you off guard, that's all."

"Well, yeah, but she's stronger than she looks. I couldn't get away once she grabbed me."

"Don't worry about it, *cuz.* There's two of us now, and we aren't going to let her grab us this time. As soon as the rain stops, we go. If we hear a car coming before then, we run into the woods."

"What if we get lost?"

"We won't get lost." Matt had learned his lesson. This time he'd keep the road in sight at all times.

They huddled together as the night dragged on. Sometimes they talked, sometimes they didn't. For a little girl, she was pretty brave. Matt decided he liked the idea of being an older cousin. He'd keep the kid safe and bring her back to Jake and her mother.

Though he intended to stay awake, at some point he must have dozed off. Matt woke to a gray morning and a heavy dense fog that gave the woods a nasty, spooky look.

"Kelsey? Wake up. It's time to go."

"Is it morning? It still looks dark out there."

"Yeah. It's foggy. But at least it isn't raining anymore. What do you think? You ready to get out of here?"

"Yes!"

"Grab that apple and the orange. I'll carry the blanket."

"What are we bringing that stuff for?"

"Breakfast. And the blanket is in case it starts raining again. Come on."

Rain had completely saturated the ground. Yesterday the walking had been difficult. Today it was all but impossible. Matt knew they couldn't even walk close to the rutted track because the mud would suck at their feet. And cutting through the woods was becoming more of a problem because the dense fog made it hard to see more than a few feet ahead.

He was beginning to think he had made a mistake trying to lead Kelsey out. He was having trouble keeping the road in sight and they were barely making any progress at all. Kelsey's shorter legs meant he had to go even slower to accommodate her. She continued to surprise him by not complaining even once. He knew she had to be as miserable as he was, yet she was doing her best to keep up.

They walked a long way. Farther than he thought they'd have to go. Matt wondered if this was a different road than the one he'd come in on. Maybe they wouldn't even find Jake's car. Maybe they were going in the wrong direction, deeper into the woods.

Suddenly he heard voices. Kelsey heard them, too, because she came to a complete stop and looked up at him for advice. Matt motioned her to be silent. Voices might mean rescue, but Matt had learned caution the hard way.

He led Kelsey closer to the sound, but not so close that they wouldn't have an avenue of escape if the voices up ahead weren't friendly.

Shapes formed in the fog. Two cars. Had someone else gotten stuck or had someone found Jake's car and stopped to help? And then he saw a third car. The first one was Jake's. He wasn't close enough to recognize the other two.

"What good is a family name?" a voice suddenly shrieked. "I won't let you kill the baby."

The other voice was lower. Deeper. But Matt couldn't

tell if it was a woman's or a man's. He couldn't see the people yet. Heck, he could barely make out the cars. Then he saw the two ghostly shapes standing so close together it was as if they were one person.

Suddenly there was a shot. The sound was shockingly out of place in the quiet of the forest.

Kelsey jumped. As one of the figures collapsed, she gasped. Matt was already turning her away. Instinctively he knew they'd been heard.

Another shot rang out. Bark sprayed from a tree to the side of them. The gunman was shooting at them! Matt had to get Kelsey away from here.

"Run, Kelsey!"

Matt grabbed her arm and they plunged into the woods.

Chapter Nine

"We're widening the search today," Hepplewhite told Jake and Amy as he stood in her mother's living room the following morning. The rescue team was marshaling to continue their efforts.

"We'll concentrate on the woods and the cabins on the other side of Fools Point near Rover's Campgrounds as well as over near Trouble Lake."

"But Kelsey wouldn't have wandered all that far. Oh." She looked to Jake, dry-eyed even though tears burned in the back of her throat. Jake had squeezed his own eyes shut. His hand rested against her back, communicating the fine tremor than ran through his body.

"I've also posted a lookout for your car and for Matt," Hepplewhite told Jake gently.

Jake nodded his thanks and opened his eyes, but his expression was dark and forbidding.

"Would you like to go out with the group near the lake?" Hepplewhite asked Jake.

"Yes," Amy replied instantly.

"Amy—"

"Don't tell me to sit and wait for a phone call that we both know isn't going to come. I can't do that anymore, Chief. I've answered every question any of you could come up with. Now I need to be taking an active role."

"Your parents—"

"Are in critical condition." She swallowed hard. "There is nothing I can do to help them. But I can join one of the search teams and I intend to do just that. My daughter is out there somewhere. I have to try and find her!"

Her voice broke and her eyes burned with tears of frustration. She was grateful for the reassuring hand Jake kept against the small of her back.

"Amy's coming with me," Jake told the chief.

Hepplewhite searched her face. Amy was acutely aware of the whisker burns that makeup couldn't hide, but she didn't flinch. The entire town probably already knew Jake had spent the night in her bed. She wasn't ashamed of that or the fact that by now everyone must also be speculating about Jake being Amy's father.

Hepplewhite finally nodded. Amy released a sigh. She'd been prepared for more of a battle. That he caved in so quickly confirmed her worst fear. They weren't looking for her daughter any longer. They were looking for her body.

"I'll check on that toxicology report," Hepplewhite promised. "I'm sure it's in. I just haven't made it to the office yet today. Officer Jackstone's going to head up the teams over by Trouble Lake. Report to him and I'll give you a holler if we hear anything."

"Excuse me, Chief Hepplewhite?"

General Perry stood in her mother's faded living room with a forbidding expression in his angry green eyes. He gave an almost imperceptible nod of acknowledgment in Amy's direction, but he kept his focus on the chief of police.

"Forgive the interruption, but we seem to have mis-placed my sister again."

"General Perry—"

"I'm afraid it's urgent this time." He hesitated, looking distinctly angry and surprisingly uncomfortable. "I own several personal weapons including a .38 revolver. It seems to be missing, as well."

A chill raced up Amy's back. She sensed a new alertness in Jake's stance while Chief Hepplewhite barely blinked. "You have some reason to think your sister took the gun?"

"I can't imagine why she would. But...we've searched the house both for her and the gun. A few minutes ago we realized Cindy Lou's car is missing, as well."

Hepplewhite frowned. "Would Gertrude have taken the car?"

"As far as I know, she hasn't driven in years. But given her current mental state...there's no sign that the house was broken into. As near as we can tell she left the house last night or early this morning after taking my weapon from the gun safe."

Amy looked at Jake, but he was listening intently with that inscrutable lack of expression that Amy found so infuriating. If Gertrude Perry had their daughter and now she had a weapon...

"Was the gun loaded?" Hepplewhite asked.

"I'm afraid bullets are also missing."

Hepplewhite rocked back on his heels. "Do you have any idea where she might have gone?" he asked.

"None. She's taken to wandering all over town lately. We've searched everywhere we can think of. I thought perhaps the restaurant, but Cindy Lou's car wasn't in the parking lot. The young man who works there assures me they haven't seen my sister."

"Any idea what she was wearing?"

"Uh, no. Perhaps Cindy Lou would be able to tell you, but she and my wife are out looking for Gertrude."

"All right, let me get this on the air," he began, speaking into his radio.

Amy jumped when Jake nudged her. "Let's go." He inclined his head toward Hepplewhite who nodded as if the two men had exchanged words instead of glances.

General Perry watched them through angry narrowed eyes and Amy tried not to let her distaste for the man show. The general gave her the creeps. Something about the way he looked at her made her want to shrink and slink away. She lifted her chin and strode boldly after Jake.

The media had returned, she saw in dismay. Jake shielded her as much as possible. They wouldn't get many good photos today anyhow because of the heavy fog that blanketed the area. Besides, they'd have a new feeding frenzy as soon as they heard about Gertrude Perry and the missing gun.

When Jake braked for the only traffic light in town, Amy laid a hand on his arm. "The Perrys used to have a cabin somewhere back in the woods near Rover's Campgrounds."

Jake ignored the green light. He studied her face and she tried to keep her anxiety from showing.

"Do you know where?"

"Not precisely."

"Hepplewhite said they are going to search that area today."

"It's a big woods."

"It's a dirt-and-gravel road back in there, isn't it?" Jake asked thoughtfully. "I'm not sure this little car would make it after all this rain."

Amy simply looked at him.

"You think Gertrude took Kelsey there?"

"It's a possibility we should consider," Amy faltered.

"If they get the helicopter up this afternoon," Jake

began, "that infrared imaging package they have will tell us if anyone is alive in the woods."

He flinched, and she knew it was over his choice of the word "alive."

"I know, Jake, but they don't know if the helicopter will be able to go up today and...I mean, this might sound stupid, but remember when we found Ms. Perry in your parking lot?"

Jake waited patiently while she fumbled with half-formed images and thoughts. "Her feet and her pants were caked with mud."

"It had rained earlier."

"But your parking lot isn't muddy. Even the path from my house up to yours wouldn't have accounted for that amount of mud. When I heard she was missing I remembered the cabin. It would make an awfully good place to hide someone, wouldn't it?"

Jake drummed his fingers against the steering wheel. He'd borrowed a razor from her this morning, but the blade had been dull, leaving patches of stubble. She longed to reach out and touch his face, so she clasped her hands together to keep them still.

"You should have mentioned this to Hepplewhite."

"Can't we take a quick look first?"

"Okay. We'll swing by the road and see how passable it looks."

Amy settled back, her inner demon temporarily satisfied. The weather people had predicted the fog would burn off by midmorning. It hadn't. While much of it had thinned, there were still pockets of thick fog. Amy knew this had delayed the search operation considerably.

Because they'd lain awake most of the night, she and Jake had overslept once they had finally fallen asleep. Jake's unexpected proposal had made sleep all but impossible, even though she'd drawn enormous comfort from his presence. The two of them had lain there lost in the chaos of their thoughts when what they had wanted was to be lost in each other.

Dr. Martin had woken them when she called with a progress report on Amy's parents. Or more correctly, a lack-of-progress report since both of them were still considered critical and nothing had really changed.

Amy had talked with her mother's cardiologist as well as the attending physician and the floor nurse. All were cautiously hopeful.

Amy tried to concentrate on what she could do rather than the things she couldn't change. Her parents were tough. They would survive. They had to survive. Amy had to find her daughter. She *had* to find Kelsey.

According to the dashboard clock it was moving toward noon and fog still pooled over the low-lying areas. The road leading to Rover's Campgrounds started out wide and heavily graveled at the mouth, but a short way down, it split into two roads and the gravel petered out. So did most of the road. The track became a dangerously narrow muddy swamp and the lingering fog gave everything an eerie look that prickled the back of her neck.

"Amy, this isn't good. We need to stop before we get stuck."

"But someone's been up and down this road recently. You can see the tracks."

"What I can see is that we're going to get stuck or rip out your undercarriage. We need a four-wheel drive to go any farther. We'll have to turn around somehow and see if we can borrow a heavier vehicle."

Amy was about to protest when her car suddenly plunged into an unseen pothole and became mired in a sucking pit of mud. Jake looked resigned rather than upset as he coaxed the little car, rocking it back and forth. Amy clenched her hands together. She was about to suggest he get out and push when suddenly the car lurched forward, somehow finding traction.

Jake steered it off the path, practically running them into the tree line. "There isn't enough room to turn around. I'll have to try and back out."

"Wait! Jake! There's a car up ahead."

Jake stopped. He peered through the windshield. "I don't see anything."

"I caught a glimpse of it a second ago."

"We can't go any farther, Amy."

"I know, but what if someone else is stuck? Maybe it's Ms. Perry."

Jake hesitated. He seemed to be weighing her words against the reality of their situation. Finally he nodded. "Wait here while I check it out."

"No, wait! I'll come with you."

"Amy—"

"Please, Jake. Don't make me sit here by myself."

She couldn't explain the frantic fluttering somewhere in the middle of her stomach. The strangeness of it all was definitely acerbated by the gloomy surroundings.

Trees overhung the road like grasping unearthly wraiths. The road was dark enough to be suitable for any horror film ever made. And to add to the atmosphere, the smell of freshly churned earth was pungent.

With a nod, Jake got out of the car and shut the door so gently it didn't make a sound. He felt the wrongness, too, she was sure of it. The woods were still and silent. Obviously, the search teams hadn't started over here yet. But where were the bird sounds? She'd even settle for an insect or two.

Amy tried to follow Jake's quiet lead, but her side of the car had mashed all sorts of plants and small bushes and she barely had enough space to climb out.

Probably poison ivy, she thought with grim humor.

Good thing Jake had reminded her to wear boots and dress warmly this morning. The rain had dropped the temperature a good thirty degrees. While not really cold, the dampness had a way of seeping into a person's bones.

Jake studied the churned-up mud. Then he studied the woods on both sides. He turned to her as she came up beside him.

"I think we should hike out and come back with a search team."

"What about the car?"

"We'll leave it."

His voice was so low she found herself whispering in response. "Okay, but shouldn't we check out that other car first? What if someone is hurt?"

Jake hesitated, clearly torn. "On one condition. If I tell you to do something, you do it immediately. Don't ask questions, don't look to see why I'm giving the order, just do what I tell you. I want your word on this, Amy."

She nearly asked why. The question was on the tip of her tongue, but she settled for a nod instead. This was a side to Jake she had never seen before. He seemed bigger, harder—more dangerous. This was the man who had commanded a special forces unit.

"Stay behind me," he directed. "At the first sign of trouble run back to the car, get inside, get down, and lock the doors. Understand?"

"Yes." She nearly added "Sir."

Mud sucked at their feet. The holes they made were promptly filled with fresh ooze. Amy realized she was moving forward hunkered over. She wondered if Jake knew he was practically crouching as he cautiously inched forward.

Her thoughts came to a screeching halt as they rounded the curve. Two cars, not one, and signs that there had once been a third car. The first vehicle nearly blocked the road completely. The frantic signs of the struggle to free it from the mud were clearly visible.

Jake's car!

Amy almost spoke out loud, but a subtle motion of his hand kept her silent. He was tensely alert. Fear crawled inside her. Jake approached the nearest vehicle and scanned the insides without touching anything. He paused for a long second by the driver's window. His training showed in the silent, careful way he moved. She felt like an elephant fumbling through a glass showroom in comparison.

Jake finished his examination before checking his car the same way—looking without touching anything. Amy wondered what he was looking for. She wondered where the drivers of the two cars could have gone.

Near the front bumper, Jake stopped abruptly. Even with his jacket on, she saw his muscles bunch. He reached out and touched a dark stain on the side of his car with a fingertip. He looked at his finger and abruptly straightened, his gaze swinging to the trees surrounding them.

Amy finally saw what he'd already seen. There were splotches of blood all over the front fender of his car.

Her heart beat so loud she couldn't hear over its pounding.

"Back to the car," Jake whispered. "Now."

Amy didn't need encouragement. She turned and plunged through the sticky mud, running in her mind, even if her body couldn't quite manage the feat.

She tried to tell herself Matt had hit a deer. But there was no carcass and no Matt. Who had been driving the second car? Was it the mayor's missing car?

Jake suddenly grabbed her by the shoulders. "Stop! Head for the woods. Behind us."

He didn't give her time to hesitate. He half pulled, half

shoved her in this new direction. Amy stumbled and nearly fell. Jake was there, supporting her as he dragged her deeper into the gloomy woods.

Frightened and out of breath, she plunged on until Jake paused, turning to search behind them.

"Listen to me," he said softly. "I want you to stay right here. Don't come out unless I call you. If you hear any shots—"

"Shots!"

"—work your way back toward the main road and try to flag down a cop. Understand?"

No, she wanted to shout. Instead, under his penetrating gaze she nodded mutely. He kissed her forehead and disappeared, becoming part of the woods and the mist that seemed to close in around her.

JAKE CURSED HIMSELF for a fool. He'd known the situation felt wrong yet he hadn't listened to his instincts. As if that wasn't bad enough, he'd nearly let Amy get all the way back to her car before he'd noticed the hood was ajar.

They weren't alone in the woods.

Jake wasted little time on self-recriminations. He needed to identify the target and either circumvent or eliminate it. There was a slim chance Matt was out there somewhere, but he couldn't dwell on that right now, either. He tried not to think about the blood and what it symbolized. He prayed it hadn't come from one of the kids.

The marks in the mud would have told him a lot if there had been time to study them, but his first priority was to protect Amy.

He'd recognized the second car as the mayor's. If the general was to be believed, Gertrude was somewhere nearby. But was she the victim or the murderer?

Jake worked his way back to the road until he could see Amy's car. The hood definitely wasn't shut tight. Even more alarming, Jake realized that whoever was out there had a serious advantage. They were armed and all they had to do was go a few yards back. An exposed field guaranteed that if he and Amy tried to hike out the way they'd come in, they would find themselves exposed without cover or protection. Whoever was out here only had to sit back and wait them out.

For the first time in his life, he saw a reason to own a cell phone. He could have help here in minutes if he or Amy had one. But they didn't.

With his training and patience, Jake could have waited the other person out or gone after him as he longed to do. But Amy wouldn't be able to stay put long enough. The best thing was to get Amy away from here and bring back reinforcements.

He was guessing her car had been disabled, which meant they'd have to hike out through the woods. Since he wasn't all that familiar with this area, he needed to find out if Amy knew of any shortcuts or if they were in for as long a hike as he suspected.

When he deemed he'd stretched Amy's tolerance far enough without spotting anyone, Jake squirmed back to the spot where he'd left her. She was crouched against the bole of a tree, a stout branch clutched firmly in both hands.

"Amy."

She whirled at the sound of her name, the branch raised threateningly. "Jake!"

"Shh. We can't go back the way we came. Do you know these woods?"

"Not really. I know there should be cabins up ahead someplace."

"Any of them have phones?"

"I don't think so. Trouble Lake is somewhere in that direction," she whispered, gesturing with the branch.

Jake nearly smiled. "That way," he corrected, taking the stick from her hand.

"Are you sure?"

"Positive."

Amy shrugged. "I wasn't a Girl Scout."

"Neither was I. Come on."

"Where are we going?"

"I'm probably going to regret this, but I thought we'd have a look at a couple of those cabins." A low warning growl of thunder made them both glance at the gray sky.

"Do you think Kelsey—"

"Shh. Stay close to me."

"I won't even give your shadow room."

"I don't think that will be an issue," he told her with a lift of his lips. "No sun."

Her eyes smiled back at him. He was relieved to see his gentle teasing had had the desired effect. He didn't want her so tense she couldn't function. Jake kept them moving north in a line he hoped was parallel to the road. Without good visuals, this was far from easy. He blessed his military training while wishing he was armed for a mission.

There were two more rumbles of thunder before they came upon a clearing. There he discovered the road must snake all through the woods because they were suddenly only feet from it once again. And out of the mist, a cabin rose, dark and silent and ominous.

"Jake!"

"Shh. Not a sound. Get down behind this stump and wait here. Don't move until I tell you."

He could almost hear her protest, but he gave her high marks for knowing when not to voice them. There was a rustle of sound overhead. Jake looked up as the first raindrops began to fall. Great. Exactly what they needed. More rain.

Muddy tire tracks had churned up the soil in front of the cabin. Mud had been tracked onto the porch, which meant the cabin had been recently used—and by more than one person.

There was no way to be certain, but he sensed they were alone for the moment. The windows on the cabin were covered, making it impossible to see inside. Wind rustled the leaves as rain began to fall steadily. Thunder rumbled loudly, drawing the newest storm closer.

Jake stepped onto the rotting porch. Timing his action to the thunder, he discovered the door handle turned easily beneath his hand. He went through the door fast and low.

Ignoring the empty feel of the place, he used his training and checked every inch of the small cabin. Not until he was satisfied that the only thing sharing the place with him had more legs than he, did he allow himself to take in the empty bed, the dangling handcuffs, and the food remains sitting on a scarred old dresser.

A hollow feeling gathered in his chest even as the storm gathered momentum. Rain beat against the cabin. Jake turned back to the door. He was tempted not to show Amy what he'd found, but she needed to know. Still, he studied the scene outside before gesturing to where she waited. Immediately, Amy ran forward, wiping rain from her face as she entered the cabin.

He hated to dash the flicker of hope in her eyes. "It's empty," he said. "But your hunch was right. Someone was being held here." He led the way to the bedroom, his hand on the small of her back as she took in the scene.

Horrified, she twisted back to him.

"I don't know who was held here, Amy, or where they are now. But there's no sign of blood or a struggle."

"Not here," she whispered.

She was thinking of the scene back on the road just as he was. Please, God, don't let that have been his daughter's blood.

"We need to get Hepplewhite and that FBI agent over here," he said with more calm than he was feeling.

"We'll have to go back to the car."

"I'm pretty sure it was disabled, Amy. Someone had raised the hood. That's how I knew we weren't alone back there."

"Then what are we going to do?"

"What we were doing. Hike out to the road. The search teams should be assembled by now."

"Maybe Kelsey wasn't here, Jake."

He wished he could lie to her. "The second car belonged to Cindy Lou."

"But that doesn't mean—"

"Kelsey's birth certificate was on the floor inside the car, Amy."

"Why didn't you tell me?"

"I'm telling you now."

"But—"

"Amy." He took hold of her arms, forcing her to look at him. The wild panic slowly faded from her expression. "We have to get out of here and go for help."

Her inner struggle was painful to watch, but she took a deep shuddery breath and nodded. "I think…I'm finally beginning to understand, Jake."

"What?"

"Why you keep your emotions under such tight control. It's the only way you can survive in situations like this, isn't it?"

Jake squeezed his eyes shut and opened them to view her pain. "Yeah. It is. Come on. Same rules as before. Stay close and do exactly what I say, all right?"

"Yes. Sir."

He offered her a half smile in return. She had guts. And brains and beauty and spirit and—he was the biggest fool God had ever created. All these wasted years that she could have been part of his life. Years they could have spent raising their daughter together.

"Come on."

Jake opened the door. The rifle shot exploded along with the thunder. The bullet thudded into the wood above his head. "Get down!" He shoved Amy back inside and down, slamming the door shut before diving on top of her and rolling them as far from the door as he could. The next shot came through the door, over their heads, embedding itself in the far wall.

"Crawl toward the kitchen area!"

Amy obeyed instantly. Jake threw a glance around the spartan furnishings. A rusty ax sat next to the firebox and the dirty fireplace.

"There's no back door," Amy said fearfully.

"I know. We'll use the window over the sink. Move over into that corner." He half stood and ran for the ax.

"You won't fit."

He heard the rising note of hysteria. "Yes, I will."

Another shot whistled through the house. The direction of the sound had changed. Jake thought it had gone through the bedroom. Whoever it was obviously wasn't sure where they were and was probably testing to see if they were armed. It wouldn't be long before the shooter would come inside.

Jake yanked down the dark grimy curtains and swung the ax. Glass shattered to the accompaniment of thunder. The blade cut right through the sill. He swung it several more times, pretending his back wasn't screaming a protest, until not only was the window gone, but there was a hole large enough to accommodate his broad shoulders and the jacket he wore.

He was surprised that the sound hadn't brought the shooter running, but he wasted no time thinking about the reason. "As soon as you get outside, run for the trees." Dropping the ax, he lifted Amy as if she weighed nothing. He shoved her through the opening and followed on her heels, diving face down out the window.

Hot searing pain tore through his back and shoulder. Easy enough to ignore when the next pain might be a bullet tearing through skin and tissue, he decided.

They made it to the tree line without incident. Jake grabbed Amy's hand, half dragging her along. He didn't slow until the underbrush became too dense and the danger of falling outweighed the need for speed.

Jake tried to keep mental track of their direction so he could guide them back toward where he thought the main road should be. But he made no attempt to keep the road in sight. They would have to go the long way around that open section anyhow. With luck, there was only one person to deal with instead of two.

"Was it Ms. Perry?" Amy asked.

Jake doubted that a woman in her condition could fire a rifle with such accuracy. "I don't think so. The general didn't mention a rifle, only a gun."

If Gertrude Perry had kidnapped Kelsey, the old woman probably had a helper here in these woods. One that didn't want live witnesses.

"WHAT ARE YOU DOING?" Kelsey asked Matt as they stood outside yet another cabin. He'd managed to lead them a long ways from the one where he'd found Kelsey.

"It's okay, cuz. I'm breaking the window so we can get inside."

Kelsey trembled visibly. "But won't the owners be mad?"

"Yep. Here. I'll help you up, but be careful of the glass. Don't cut yourself."

"I don't want to go in there. It's dark."

And she'd just spent two days locked in another small, dark cabin. Matt understood.

"I'm going in with you, Kelsey. We've got to get out of this rain before we drown. Trust me, okay?"

Her head bobbed once. He knew she couldn't go any farther. She was soaking wet, cold, and scared out of her wits. Heck, if she wasn't, he was. They'd just witnessed a murder and nearly been killed themselves. Maybe he should be used to that after what he'd been involved in, but he wasn't. Matt didn't think a person could ever get used to being hunted.

What he did know was that they couldn't keep stumbling through the woods blindly. Sooner or later they'd hurt themselves or meet up with something more lethal than a startled deer.

Kelsey let him boost her over the sill. Matt had to work a little harder, but eventually, he wormed his broad shoulders in after her. He'd deliberately skirted all the cabins near the one where he'd found her in case the killer searched them. He'd actually spotted this one by accident. He only hoped it was far away enough from the others that the killer wouldn't find them right away. The problem was, with the rain and lower temperatures, he couldn't afford to drag her around any farther. Kelsey was only wearing a pair of shorts and a thin T-shirt. It would be pretty awful if he saved her life and then she died of pneumonia.

Matt was pretty sure they'd lost the killer a long time ago. He'd made Kelsey walk in the creek they'd stumbled over just so nobody could follow their tracks. But the water had been cold and rising fast enough that he worried about flooding. He decided they were safer in the woods.

His flashlight batteries had died last night, but maybe he could find some new ones inside this cabin. It was worth the chance. The cabin was dark enough that he had to rely on intermittent flashes of lightning to see around the inside. Kelsey stayed tight to his side. He could feel her shaking.

Fortunately, this cabin was in much better shape than the one where he'd found Kelsey. This one was clean and neat. There was even comfortable furniture and beds with blankets.

"Look around and see if there's anything to eat," he told the girl.

"We can't just take stuff."

"Sure we can."

"That's stealing."

He studied her indignant face in the next flash of lightning. "Not when it's an emergency. Don't worry, Jake'll pay 'em back once we're rescued."

"Are we going to g-get rescued, Matt?"

"Sure we are. Hey! Look what I found, matches and candles!"

"But we can't stay here. What if that person with the gun finds us?"

"How? *We* don't even know where we are."

He opened a few more cupboards, greatly reassured to discover tins of food on a shelf.

"Hey! We're really in luck. Soup. There's even crackers. And soda. Man, we're going to be fine. Hey, you're really shivering."

He could hear her teeth clicking together.

"Maybe we can find some dry clothes in the bedroom. Come on."

"Matt? How are we g-going to g-get home? My mom's going to be awful s-scared."

He'd led her into the bedroom, but the fear in her voice made him turn away from the mostly empty dresser drawers. "Hey, *cuz*," he said as kindly as he could. "I told you I'd get you outta this mess an' I will. But we're gonna be stuck here at least until the rain stops and we can see where we're going. Otherwise we might run into the shooter instead of a rescue team."

That possibility really worried him. "Maybe, while we're sitting here, the owners of this cabin will come and give us a ride back to town."

"D-do you think s-so?"

"You never know. You aren't going to wimp out on me, are you?"

"N-no."

"Okay, then. Step one, let's get some of this mud off our bodies. We're making a mess, tracking it all over like this. Then you can put on this shirt I just found and we'll hang up your clothes so they can dry."

"It won't fit."

He held up the flannel shirt he'd found in the closet. "Sure it will. Think of it as an old bathrobe."

Kelsey eyed it dubiously. "Can I wash my clothes out first?"

"Sure. We'll clean up, then we'll eat. We've got candles and…hey, that's an oil lamp. We have all the comforts of home. It's gonna be all right, Kelsey. I'll take care of you. I promise."

And he'd give anything—do anything—if Jake would just find them and get them out of this mess.

Chapter Ten

By the time Amy and Jake literally stumbled over Harvest Branch Road she realized he was in pain. Despite his protests, she stepped out into the two-lane road and flagged down the first car that approached.

Fortunately, the driver was Iggy Iverson. He and Clyde Newby were fixtures in Fools Point, having lived there since before she could remember. Clyde ran the movie theater while Iggy ran the gas station. Together the two men lived in a crazy-looking house at the far end of Main Street.

Iggy skidded to a halt in his newest refurbished car.

"Half the county's out lookin' fer you two. You wreck?" Iggy demanded.

"We got stuck in the mud off Rover's Lane. Jake hurt his back."

"Let's get you over to Doc Martin's."

Almost two hours later Amy stood beside Jake, listening to him argue with Dr. Leslie Martin. Fear and anxiety still churned Amy's system, but the police had taken control of the scene immediately. The woods were being searched. There was nothing more she could do except be certain Jake was okay.

"I'm fine," he told the doctor.

"That's the drugs talking."

"Well, I like what they're saying."

Leslie rolled her eyes. "You aren't going to listen to me, are you?"

"I just did."

"Mr. Collins, you can't live on painkillers. You have severely strained muscles that are far from healed from your earlier injury. You should be in the hospital."

"No."

Leslie turned to her. "Amy? Can you talk some sense into this mule?"

The intractable expression on Jake's face told Amy arguing was useless. "Forget it, Leslie. Just tell me the least harmful position to arrange the body when he falls over."

His lips twitched. "I won't fall over."

"Of course you won't. You can't even sit up," Leslie scolded.

"Watch me."

"Jake," Amy said, laying a hand on his shoulder before he could attempt to prove his words. "I can't take much more right now. How about if you lay here and rest while I call the hospital to check on my parents? Is it okay for him to stay here until then?"

Leslie scowled. "Yes, but I still think he should be admitted."

"Or committed," Amy agreed.

"Thanks," he said drolly.

"You don't have to prove anything, Jake. Why not give the muscle relaxants more time to do their job?" She squeezed the bridge of her nose as a headache pounded away. "Chief Hepplewhite and the detectives should have some information for us soon." She saw again that small dark bedroom and wanted to sob. "There's nothing more we can do at the moment."

Their gazes locked. Sorrow, frustration and anger

clearly showed in his expression. She suspected he saw the dread in hers just as easily. They were moving the searchers over to the woods. Why hadn't they heard something by now?

"Please, Jake."

He covered her hand and she had to close her eyes again, swallowing hard. In that brief moment, she felt they were united in a way they had never been before.

The police had promised to thoroughly comb the woods, but the latest line of thunderstorms was making the situation impossible now. Lightning strikes put the searchers at risk. The weather was due to break early this evening and law enforcement personnel were standing by, promising an all-out effort. Amy was terrified at what they might find.

"All right," Jake said as if sensing her thoughts. "When you come back, we're going home."

"Yes."

Leslie ushered Amy into her office and cut through the hospital red tape to reach the attending physician. Susan Thomas had improved enough to wake up, only to have such a case of hysterics when the police tried to question her that she had to be sedated. The cardiologist feared for her heart.

They expected Cornelius to come out of his coma anytime now. Amy's relief was tempered by the oppressing weight of fear for her daughter. She simply couldn't get the image of that room and the car fender out of her mind. She was caught between the need to wait here, close to where the search was progressing, and her desire to be with her parents. This nightmare had to end soon.

Amy and Leslie returned to the examining room to find Jake sitting in a chair, waiting for them.

"All right, hero," Leslie said. "I'll ask my receptionist, Jasmine, to give the two of you a ride home."

"The restaurant's right across the street. We can walk," Jake said.

"That's your idea of taking it easy?" Leslie demanded.

"I need to go home, too, in case you've forgotten," Amy cut in. "I want out of these wet, muddy clothes. We'll take the ride. Thanks, Leslie."

"He'll get my bill."

Jake stood slowly and stiffly. "It will be worth every penny."

Leslie's gorgeous young receptionist was more than happy to give them a lift. Amy had gone to school and even dated one of Jasmine's older brothers. The whole family was attractive, but Jasmine was incredibly beautiful—and genuinely nice.

Amy decided Jake was in more pain that she'd thought because there wasn't even a flicker of masculine appraisal in his eyes when he looked at Jasmine.

"I'm going to need a car," he told Amy.

"Iggy offered to rent us the one he was driving. He said he'd drop it by the restaurant if you want it."

"Remind me to buy him a case of Scotch."

"He'd rather have hubcaps," Amy said.

Jake smiled with his eyes. "I forgot about his obsession. I'll see what I can do."

"Don't encourage him," Jasmine protested. "I don't want to think where he'd put any more."

"Oh, I don't know. A fence made from hubcaps is pretty clever, even if it isn't original."

"It's an eyesore," Jasmine insisted. "Now he's trying to create siding for the house. They're going to have to pass an ordinance to stop him."

As they turned into the driveway of her parents' home, Amy's smiled faded and her heart began thudding. This was no longer the refuge of her youth. The house sat in utter darkness. There were no detectives keeping silent vigil inside tonight. The police no longer expected any phone calls and Amy suddenly didn't want to go inside. The very thought of staying there alone made her physically ill.

"Grab what you need," Jake said. "We're sleeping at the Perrywrinkle tonight." His hand rested comfortingly on hers.

Amy glanced at Jasmine, aware of the young woman listening. "But the hospital might call. Or the police—"

"Leave my number on your mother's answering machine. I already told Hepplewhite and that detective we planned to stay at my place. I'm not leaving you alone tonight and I need to check in at the restaurant."

Of course he did. Relief and gratitude mingled with the ever-present spark of physical attraction at the thought of spending another night with Jake.

"Do you want any help, Ms. Thomas?"

"It's Amy, Jasmine, and I don't think so, but you're welcome to come inside with me. You, on the other hand, should wait here so you don't strain your back," she told Jake.

Jake smiled at Jasmine. "She likes to fuss over me."

Amy felt the color mount her cheeks. "It keeps me from strangling him," she assured the amused woman. "I'll just be a minute."

Jake rolled his eyes. In the old days a minute had generally translated into half an hour. Motherhood had taught her a few things. As she mounted the steps, Amy was relieved to have Jasmine at her side.

The house was as empty as it looked. The police recording device had been removed. Amy tried not to look in that direction or think about the meaning behind its absence as she offered up a silent prayer again for the safe return of her daughter.

Amy pulled together an overnight case in record time and hurried back downstairs. She tended to the plants, her mother's two lazy old cats who had come out of hiding now that the house was quiet, and changed the answering message, surprised to find she wasn't embarrassed anymore. Not even when she and Jake walked into the Perrywrinkle and every eye in the place stared at them.

Jake led the way to the stairs, moving with painful stiffness. "Go on up. Matt's room is on the right. My room is next door. I'll see if Arly can pull together something edible for us."

"Better not let him hear you say that."

"Not a chance."

Jake had left the decision of where she was to sleep totally up to her. Amy didn't even hesitate. She took her bag into Jake's room and stared around at the military neatness of the place and the starkness of the furnishings. At least the bed was a double, she was relieved to see. She unpacked what she needed and headed for his bathroom. Like the bedroom, it was immaculate despite the old fixtures.

When she came out she felt clean and calm. Fear still rustled at the edges of her mind, but she had it under control. Jake was in the large room up front, watching Ben Dwyer set the small table with linens and china.

"Feel better?"

Amy nodded. She cinched her bathrobe a little tighter, uncomfortable at being so casual in front of a virtual stranger. But Ben smiled kindly, poured her a glass of wine and disappeared.

"I'm going to take a quick shower before the food comes up," Jake told her.

"Do you want any help?"

The instant the words left her lips, she wished she

could call them back. Jake raked her with a gaze that somersaulted her heart rate. That he could even think of sex now shocked her. More amazing was that she could think of sex now. He smiled. It was almost a caress.

"I'll be back."

Her mouth went dry. Memories flooded her of other times, other showers, and the slick soapy feel of wet flesh against wet flesh.

Amy sank down onto his badly worn couch and took a gulp of the light, fruity wine. The fire in her stomach intensified. Warmth spread to her limbs. She had loved him so deeply nine years ago. How could she even think about going there again?

Amy slowly sipped her wine. Things were different now. Older and wiser and armed with the knowledge of the way he'd been raised, she realized Jake ran because he'd never learned to trust. And he'd never learned how to express his emotions.

Certainly no one could doubt he loved his nephew. She'd watched him with the boy, seen the concern and the caring in his eyes.

And she didn't doubt for an instant that he wanted to know his daughter. His expression when he'd looked at Kelsey's baby pictures had revealed so many things about him.

Jake could love, but he showed it in his own quiet way. Ever since these events had started happening, he'd been there for her, Amy acknowledged. He was always touching her in silent support, offering her the reassurance of his presence whenever he could.

But could she live without hearing the words? Could she afford to love him all over again?

Did she have a choice?

A waitress arrived with a kind smile and proceeded to arrange rolls and fruit cups and two bowls of steaming soup on the table. Another waitress arrived with a water pitcher and more food. The small room became incredibly crowded, but they worked with quiet efficiency before they disappeared, her thanks ringing in their ears. The scents were heavenly, but she couldn't summon much interest in sitting down to actually eat.

"Allow me."

"Jake! You startled me. You always did move like a ghost."

Something dark crossed his features but was gone before she could analyze the expression. "A ghost?"

"You're right. Bad analogy. How about a stalking tiger?"

"Definitely has a more manly ring to it. But is that what you think? That I'm stalking you?"

Yes, now that he mentioned it. The room had been less crowded with the two women inside. Jake filled any area with the force of his presence. He held out a chair and waited for her to sit.

"Not exactly, but you have to admit there is something of the predator in you, Jake." His face took on that distant look that she'd come to hate so much.

"Does that bother you?"

This was no time to be flippant, Amy realized. Jake hid a real concern behind his mask. "No, Jake. In fact it's been rather reassuring lately."

She sat and he came around the table. His hair was wet but neatly combed and she realized he'd taken time to run a razor over his jaw. Her gaze lingered, noting the lines of strain still in evidence on his face. He'd changed into a white dress shirt, open at the collar, and another pair of dark slacks.

"Tell me something. Do you own any casual clothing?"

Jake glanced down in surprise. "Yes, but I'm going to

have to go back downstairs before we close for the night. I need to thank my staff for the job they've been doing. Ben and Arly in particular have gone above and beyond the call."

"Of course. I'm sorry, Jake."

"You have nothing to be sorry for. I'm the one who should be apologizing. I should never have led you into a situation like the one today."

"Funny, as I recall, I'm the one who led you."

"I was driving."

Gazing into his eyes she saw his concern and she strove to lighten the atmosphere. "Shall we fight over it?"

His tension eased and Jake lifted his fork. "I'd rather dig into this meal."

"Me, too." But she was lying. Her stomach wasn't at all interested in food when she couldn't stop thinking about her daughter.

"You have to eat something, Amy. You won't do the kids or your parents any good if you get sick."

"This from the man who should be in the hospital."

"I've seen enough of hospitals to last me a lifetime," he said quietly.

"I'm sorry, Jake." She picked up her fork and speared a stalk of broccoli. "I asked you once before, but we got interrupted. How did you come to own the Perrywrinkle?"

"I got the idea when I first came to Fools Point. I was looking for an investment opportunity and there aren't many places to eat this far out. Arly is a first-rate chef and I figured if I could hire him, I might just have a quiet little gold mine. Quiet appeals to me now."

Amy shifted uncomfortably, not sure how to respond to that statement or the intensity of his expression. She opted for asking a safe question. "How did you meet Arly?"

"I served under him a few years ago."

Amy swallowed a bite of veal and lifted her head, startled. "He was your commanding officer?"

"For a short time. We met again in Annapolis. He was working in a small café over by the harbor. We got to talking one night after the place closed and I laid out my plans. I asked him if he'd consider working for me."

"I assume a head chef's job pays better than working in a café?"

"Substantially," he agreed, the corners of his lips lifting.

"Do you enjoy running a restaurant?"

"More than I thought I would. What about you?" he asked. "Are you going to continue working as a translator?"

"No. I applied for a teaching job at Maryland and a couple of other places. My timing was poor since the schools had already hired their staff for the year, but there are plenty of jobs for people with multilingual skills."

"So you're going to stay in the area?"

"Yes. After Mom became ill, I realized I wanted to be closer to home. And Kelsey…" She took a deep breath and strove to keep her voice level and calm. "Kelsey needs a more stable environment…now that she's older."

Only, Kelsey might not need anything any longer. Amy fought back the burning need to cry.

"We're going to find her," Jake said firmly.

"I wish I could believe that." Amy set down her fork, no longer able to pretend she was hungry.

"Believe it."

"But all that blood…"

"Believe it, Amy. That blood could have come from

anyone or anything." He hesitated just a moment. "When we find her, will you let me be part of her life from now on?"

The memory of his marriage proposal echoed in her mind. She couldn't deal with that right now. "Of course."

His face relaxed and he resumed eating. Matt and Kelsey represented all the family Jake had. He needed them. But that wasn't reason enough to agree to marriage.

"If you're finished mauling that roll, would you like something else to eat?" Jake asked.

"I can't."

"Okay. How about coffee?"

"I'd rather have another glass of wine."

Jake reached for the bottle and winced. It was a small but subtle reminder that he needed to rest.

"There's a television in the bedroom," he told her before she could voice her concern. "I remember how you used to like watching TV lying down."

Obviously he'd noticed her things in his room, but this was the only reference he'd made to sharing a bed together again.

"I need to go downstairs and talk to Arly."

She started to remind him that he should be taking it easy, but caught herself. She wouldn't nag. Jake wasn't stupid. When his back hurt enough he'd do what he needed to do. His features softened and she saw his gratitude.

"Make yourself at home. I'll have the staff clean away everything but the dessert. We might want something later on."

Chocolate icing smeared on his chest.

She shook off the forbidden memory. "I can clean up."

"That's what I'm paying them to do. Besides, I'm a good tipper."

"Yeah?"

He touched her hair lightly. "Yeah."

Amy found herself smiling sadly in return.

"I won't be long."

She reached for her wineglass. Jake had kept it full, though he stayed with water—probably because of all the medicine he was taking. The wine and the food and just being warm and dry left her drowsy. Amy set down the glass and headed into Jake's utilitarian bedroom.

She pulled back the sheets, took off her robe, and lay down on a pillow that held his scent. She breathed deeply, feeling like a schoolgirl with her first crush. Jake was special. He'd always been special. Even empty, his room surrounded her with his presence, cosseting her.

Jake didn't know how to love, but she did. She could teach him what he needed to learn.

If only she knew where their daughter was.

JAKE WATCHED HER WAKE. He knew the moment she realized she was wrapped around his body, one leg thrown over his hip like the old days. Her arm looped around his shoulder as if to pull his face to hers. He watched her green eyes widen the moment she felt his erection pressing against her thigh through his briefs.

"Good morning."

She pulled back quickly. "I, uh…"

Because he couldn't help himself, he kissed her forehead. "You never were very coherent before you had coffee."

Jake rolled off the bed, ignoring the protest from muscles that had tightened overnight. "I'll take a quick shower and then you can have the bathroom." He knew her gaze followed him from the room.

As he soaped his hair, reveling in the feel of the warm water, he tried not to dwell on the night he'd just spent. Amy had been restless, tossing, turning, sometimes whimpering softly, but always relaxing beneath the touch of his hand. And it had been all he could do to keep that touch impersonal when what he'd wanted, what he'd longed to do, was to sink himself inside her and unite them once more.

He wanted more than sex, he admitted to himself. He wanted the right to have her in his bed every night, to be part of her life on a full-time basis. He wanted Kelsey to call him Daddy. He wanted the world to know this was *his* family.

He rinsed his hair and reached for the soap and washcloth. He'd do whatever it took to make that happen. Somehow he'd find a way to win Amy back. And this time he'd never let her go.

He was patting himself dry when he heard a sound that stopped him cold. Jake opened the bathroom door fully and listened. The sound of muffled sobs sent his heart plummeting. He raced into the bedroom.

"Amy?"

She was curled around the pillow, sobbing as if her heart had broken.

A sick dread filled his mind. He glanced at the telephone, but the receiver still rested in its cradle. He hadn't heard it ring, but he could have missed the sound over the noise of the shower.

"Is it Kelsey? Your parents? Sweetheart, what is it?"

She lifted her head, shaking it no. But no to what? Jake did the only thing he could do. He pulled her against his bare wet chest and cradled her, stroking her tenderly as all sorts of horrors filled his mind.

"Did someone call?" he asked softly when her sobs finally changed to dry hiccuping sounds.

"No, I—I'm sorry."

He kissed her head, wrapping his hand in her hair to stroke the back of her head. "Did something happen?"

"No." She gazed up at him, her watery eyes eloquent with her pain. "I just…I can't be strong anymore." Fresh tears leaked from the corners of her eyes. "They haven't called, Jake. I need…I want to know my daughter—"

"Shh. Hush." He pressed her head against his chest and rocked her gently until the new spate of tears was spent. Tears slipped down his own cheeks and he let them fall.

She was right. The police should have called by now. Every second that the search continued diminished the chances that news would be good. Amy wasn't a fool. She knew this as well as he did. The odds were high that Kelsey was dead.

Amy looked up at his face. Her fingers touched the wet path the tears had traveled. "You're crying," she marveled.

"Kelsey's my daughter, too."

She tugged his face down and their lips met. They were riding the ragged edge of emotion and it showed. This was no languid kiss of passion. Wickedly fierce, demanding, the hunger in her stunned him, but only for the briefest of seconds. Then it roused an instant, answering hunger that had been gnawing deep in his soul.

All the love, all the uncertainties, all the need inside of him, he poured into that kiss as he took her mouth with marauding intensity. Amy kissed him back with a frantic urgency that shattered his self-control.

Their mouths fused and mated the way their bodies longed to do. He didn't consciously remember running his hand beneath her T-shirt, until his rubbing hand cupped the fullness of her breast. He lowered his head to take the exposed nipple between his teeth.

She sucked in a breath of pleasure that pushed him closer to the point of no return as her hands desperately threaded through his hair. Her legs moved with restless abandon against his. She arched her back to offer him better access as he moved from one breast to the other.

They should stop. They had to stop. But he wasn't sure he could. He was intoxicated by the taste and scent of Amy.

Her hand skated across his damp chest and slid lower until her fingers closed over the hardness of his pulsing flesh. Before he could move, she replaced her hand with the heat of her mouth.

Desire coiled tightly inside him.

He needed her. Desperately. Completely.

"Amy!" It was close, but he pulled her up before he embarrassed himself. Large liquid-green eyes questioned him. "It's been too long, sweetheart. I won't last ten seconds if you continue doing that."

"I don't mind." She started to bend her head.

He captured it, framing her face with his hands.

"Don't stop. Please don't stop." She threw her arms around his neck and drew his face to hers. "Not this time. Please. I need you so much, Jake."

He groaned at her unconsciously wanton plea. All his good intentions dissolved in the air and he knew that he couldn't stop because he needed her every bit as much. This was Amy and she was part of him.

"No. I won't stop."

Her body was riper, fuller, more womanly now. She trembled as he pulled the T-shirt over her head. It was agony trying to go slow with a woman whose hungry passion matched his own. He wanted to drive himself inside her to quench the burning fire they'd started.

She shuddered when he paused to take first one nipple then the other into his mouth.

"Jake!"

She was so sensitive. She'd always had sensitive breasts. He loved touching her. But when his hand reached the junction of her thighs, it was her turn to stop him.

Her hand clenched his wrist. "It's been a long time for me, too," she said breathlessly.

A silly, giddy relief flooded him. "I'm glad." There had never been anyone in his life like Amy.

"Me, too," she whispered.

"You are so beautiful." Then he bent to place a string of kisses along her inner thigh.

It was the sort of foreplay that couldn't last. They were both too needy for that. Jake parted her legs with his knee and she pulled him down for a long, drugging kiss.

"Wait," she said as he started to position himself. She must have seen him wince. She surprised him by pushing him back gently.

"You need to rest your back."

"Later."

"Now." The heated promise in her expression stole his breath. The next kiss finished the job. Her mouth was hot and wet and so sexy he could have kissed her forever. Then she settled on top of him and he knew he didn't want this moment to ever end.

They went beyond a union of bodies as they moved together, finding the rhythm that had always been exclusively theirs. As she began to contract around him he was instantly lost, needing to pleasure her with an urgency that could not be denied.

They came together too quickly, with explosive passion that left them weak and damp and spent. Afterward she lay across his chest, eyes closed as he kissed her cheek and her hair lightly, gratefully. Finally she lifted her head.

Before he could articulate the emotions rolling inside him, the telephone rang. Amy jumped. Her stricken gaze flew to the telephone.

"I'll get it," he told her.

She slipped from the bed as Jake reached for the receiver. Amy quickly gathered her T-shirt. Color leached from her face as soon as she heard him greet Chief Hepplewhite.

"I'd like you and Amy to stop by the police station this morning," Hepplewhite said in his ear.

Alarm punched the air from his lungs. "The kids?"

"No. Sorry. We haven't found them yet. The heavy rain and the fog are slowing the search efforts. We've covered the immediate area where the cabins are clustered, but there are others spread out all over these woods and the mud makes walking difficult. We're doing our best."

The pressure eased. "I know but you have something?"

"I'd rather tell you in person."

"We can be there in ten minutes."

"What is it?" Amy demanded as he hung up.

"He wouldn't say."

"I'll be ready in three minutes."

They were dressed and outside in nine minutes.

"It's stopped raining," he said.

"Did Iggy drop off the car last night?"

Jake held up a set of car keys with a miniature hubcap attached. Outside, the morning was crisp and clear and cool. Arly's and Iggy's weren't the only two cars in the parking lot. The work crews had arrived and had already set up equipment around the root cellar.

"Should we talk about what just happened?" Jake had to ask.

She blushed, but didn't look away. "After we talk with Heppiewhite, okay?"

"Okay."

He started to guide her over to Iggy's lovingly restored vintage car when a sudden shout made them both turn toward the work crews. There was a flurry of excited commotion. All heads turned in his direction and one of the men started running toward them.

"Now what?"

"Mr. Collins!" Buddy was streaked with mud, but it was the expression on his face that warned Jake even before he uttered the next words. "Down in the pit. Mr. Collins, we got us another body."

Chapter Eleven

Jake and Amy didn't make it to the police station. Chief Hepplewhite came to them.

Despite the boards that had covered the opening after the gravel had been removed, several inches of water had collected in the bottom of the old root cellar. Almost enough to cover the sticklike figure of Gertrude Perry.

It was some time before the police chief was even able to acknowledge Jake and Amy. They both had to answer some questions, but no one had heard or seen anything. The police couldn't tell exactly when the body had been dumped into the recently cleared-out root cellar.

Amy was concerned that this new discovery would impact the search for the children, but she was assured that the search had commenced as planned. The Perry clan arrived and police requested a place inside the restaurant to speak with the family members. Jake called Ben Dwyer to come in early and give Arly a hand seeing to coffee for the officers and family members.

General Perry gave Jake and Amy a piercing look and an almost rude nod of acknowledgment as he strode past, posture stiff, lips in a fine tight line. His wife, Millicent, offered a weak smile in greeting, then quickly lowered her head to follow her husband. Eugene swaggered behind them, leaving Amy with a strong desire to wipe the smirk off his face. The only one who appeared to be grieving at all was the mayor, and Amy couldn't tell how much of that was put on for the inevitable arrival of the media.

Hepplewhite sank down onto a chair in the empty dining room opposite Amy and Jake. He took a grateful sip of the hot coffee. "You know, the irony is, I took this job because Fools Point was such a quiet, out-of-the-way little town."

He ran a hand over his face and eyed them wearily. "From what we could determine yesterday, it's pretty obvious your daughter was being held in the Perry cabin over near Rover's Campgrounds. There is no sign she was assaulted. In fact, from some of the evidence we collected, I'm going out on a limb by telling you I believe Miss Perry may have been the one holding her there."

"She said she had to protect the baby," Amy said, trying to still her hopeless panic. "Remember, Jake? She'd been staring down into the root cellar and I remember thinking at the time she meant Kelsey."

And now Gertrude was dead, so where did that leave her daughter?

"Looks like your instincts were correct."

"But if Gertrude Perry is dead—" Her voice broke. Jake touched her lightly. She took in a deep, shaky breath.

"Any idea where Kelsey is now?" Jake asked.

"Unfortunately, no."

"What about all that blood?" Amy asked.

"We're running tests."

"But it was human blood?" she persisted.

Hepplewhite looked at Jake, who nodded imperceptibly.

"Yes, but that doesn't make it Kelsey's or Matt's."

Jake slid his arm around her shoulders, but it didn't

help the coldness in her soul, even though she knew he shared her fear.

"Was that what you wanted to see us about earlier?" Jake asked.

"No, actually, I wanted to give you some information and ask a couple more questions."

Jake raised his eyebrows.

"I know, but it's what I do. Toxic mushrooms were in that casserole. Cindy Lou likes to garden and her aunt, Gertrude, liked to collect the vegetables with her. Gertrude may have added a few mushrooms she found growing in the yard."

"On purpose?" Jake asked.

Hepplewhite shrugged. "We can't know one way or another now, but chances are it was just a fluke. We're lucky no one has died so far."

Amy began to tremble despite the tight hold he had around her shoulder.

Hepplewhite sighed. "Amy, Dr. Martin says your mother was taking digitalis for her heart."

She nodded.

"Were either of your parents taking something for depression?"

"No. Of course not. They are two of the least depressed people you'll ever meet. You should know that." She frowned at him.

"That's what I thought. Both of them had ingested a substantial amount of a tranquilizer used to combat depression. The drug causes drowsiness, loss of balance and a skipped heartbeat among other things."

"My parents wouldn't be taking something like that! Especially not my mother. You can check their medicine cabinet if you like but I'm sure neither of them ever took antidepressants or tranquilizers."

"So someone slipped the medication into their food or drink, like you suggested earlier," Jake said.

Hepplewhite nodded. "That's how it looks. As it happens, Gertrude Perry was taking that particular antidepressant."

"Why am I not surprised," Jake muttered.

Hepplewhite inclined his head in agreement. "I really wish one of the helpful neighbors hadn't washed their dishes right away."

"Maybe it wasn't a helpful neighbor," Jake said. "Maybe the person who poisoned them cleaned up quickly to cover any traces."

"Good point. We're checking with others who were there, but in the meantime I'd like you both to think back. It would be helpful if we knew who picked up their plates and glasses."

Amy shook her head. "Mom was so sick, I didn't notice anything after she started vomiting. And Dad became ill almost immediately, as well."

"That's about how I had it figured. Mr. Collins?"

Jake shook his head. "We were dealing with the immediate situation."

"Amy, have you ever heard your parents or anyone mention Orin or Penny Budnell?"

"No, I don't think so."

"Orin Budnell was the caretaker at the Perry estate thirty years ago. His wife, Penny, was a local midwife who acted as cook and housekeeper for Gertrude Perry."

"A midwife?" Jake fastened on the word.

"Exactly. Orin Budnell died of a heart attack—right after building the gazebo over the root cellar."

Amy looked at Jake who squeezed her hand.

"General Perry arranged for Orin's cremation immediately after he died. He gave Mrs. Budnell a handsome settlement so she could move to a retirement center in Florida."

"A bribe?" Amy asked.

"Or, as the people in town saw it, a nice thank-you

for years of faithful service." Hepplewhite shrugged. "We'll never know because Mrs. Budnell's apartment was burglarized shortly after she moved in. Florida police believed she was surprised and killed during the commission of the robbery."

"Tidy," Jake said grimly. The two men exchanged knowing looks. "I take it the murderous robber was never caught?"

"That's right. And as a sidebar, there were no other reported burglaries in the community before or after that incident."

"Surprise, surprise," Jake said.

Hepplewhite bared his teeth. "Isn't it?"

"I'm certain the general's time could be accounted for."

"Absolutely. He was on base with his unit, waiting to be sent overseas."

Jake sat back. "Nice and convenient."

"But couldn't he have hired someone to kill those people?" Amy demanded.

Hepplewhite rubbed his jaw with a tired expression. "Anything is possible. Unfortunately, we need proof to build a case."

"And now Ms. Perry is dead," Jake said.

"My parents!" Amy suddenly gasped. "If someone is killing off all the witnesses..."

"Your parents have around-the-clock police protection inside their room," Hepplewhite assured her. "Even their medication is being carefully monitored to be sure nothing is tampered with. We're taking all precautions, Amy."

"This whole thing is so bizarre. If that woman in the root cellar died a natural death in childbirth, why would anyone kill people to cover up her death? And how does she connect to my parents?"

"Maybe it wasn't to cover up her death, but to conceal who she was," Jake said softly.

Hepplewhite's eyes gleamed approvingly. "That's the only thing that makes sense at this point."

"Are you any closer to an identification?" Jake asked.

"We've eliminated rather than identified at this point, but we're still working some leads. In fact, what I called you about this morning was that we'd like permission to take blood samples from you, Amy. And from your parents, Amy. We'd like to run some DNA comparisons."

"I don't understand. You want to compare us to the dead woman? Why?"

"Frankly, we're grasping at straws. There's a link here somewhere. Forensics takes time, but it's an accurate science. If the woman in the root cellar is related to anyone involved in this case, DNA may help us pin down her identity. We're asking the same permission from the general and his family. You can refuse if you're uncomfortable with this."

"No, I don't mind."

"Good. But I'd appreciate it if you'd keep this information strictly to yourselves for now."

"What's the latest on the search efforts?" Jake demanded.

"The dog teams are combing the woods," Hepplewhite said gently. "They tell me they hope to have the helicopter back in the air sometime this afternoon. We *will* find the children."

"But if someone is killing all the witnesses, what chance does my daughter or Matt have to survive?" Amy demanded.

"I know it looks bleak, but I believe both children *are* alive." Hepplewhite hesitated. After a second he seemed to come to a decision. "Normally, I wouldn't tell you this until we had something more definite. I don't want to raise any false hopes, but we're pretty certain Matt was inside the cabin where Kelsey was being held. We've got one clear muddy footprint on the porch near a window. It may belong to him. There's a possibility—but just a possibility, you understand—that Matt found Kelsey and rescued her. We discovered two sets of prints leading away from the house into the woods. Unfortunately, we lost them, but we have the dogs out tracking their path now. I think it's only a matter of time before we find them.''

Amy closed her eyes. A tear slipped past her defenses. Jake rubbed her back and she reached for his hand, squeezing tightly. It took several deep breaths for her control to return.

She opened her eyes, ignoring the sting of unshed tears.

''Thank you for telling us. If Kelsey is with Matt, he'll take care of her.''

Jake was surprised she had such faith in a boy she didn't even know, but he shared her belief. ''Amy's right. If they are together, Matt will do his best to keep Kelsey safe.''

Hepplewhite nodded. ''And we all know Matt is one very resourceful young man. Keep thinking good thoughts.''

As they stood, Jake slipped his arm around Amy, pleased when she leaned into his side. From the hall came raised voices. The three of them turned to witness General Perry glaring into the face of a Montgomery County detective.

''I told you, I do not consent. I consider that request an invasion of our rights. Any further dealings you have with my family will be done in the presence of our attorney.''

He paused, saw them, and shot a venomous glare straight at Amy. Then he strode for the main door.

''But, Dad,'' Cindy Lou protested. She had to hurry

after him so the rest of her protest went unheard. The other members of the family followed in their wake.

"Problem, George?" Hepplewhite asked the detective.

"The general doesn't wish to submit to DNA testing."

"And isn't that interesting."

"Yeah. So we'll have to do it the hard way." The detective shot a speculative look at Jake and Amy.

"Ms. Thomas has agreed to have testing done this afternoon. Did the general give us anything on the gun?"

The detective raised his eyebrows in surprise, but answered readily enough. "The gun found under his sister's body appears to be the one missing from his daughter's house. Ballistics will probably confirm it was the gun that killed her."

Hepplewhite nodded as if that was what he expected.

"I think...I'd like to go see my parents, if that's all right," Amy said weakly.

"Go ahead, Amy. I'd appreciate it if you'd stop by Dr. Martin's on your way. Leslie has already agreed to draw the blood samples for us."

"We'll head over there first, then," Jake told him. Amy nodded agreement. "I've closed the restaurant to the public, but you can let Ben or Arly know if you need anything. They're going to stick around here."

"Thank you, Mr. Collins."

Jake led Amy outside. The hole in the parking lot swarmed with police activity. A uniformed county officer had to let them out of the cordoned-off parking lot.

They stopped at the doctor's office so Leslie could draw a vial of blood, but it was a young nurse who actually performed the task. Jasmine looked nervous and explained that due to an emergency at the hospital, Leslie had left for the day. Jake said nothing, but worry pricked at him as he and Amy left. He wasn't totally unprepared when they reached the hospital and learned Amy's mother had gone into cardiac arrest.

She was in stable but critical condition. Amy left her bedside with swollen, red-rimmed eyes and Jake watched as she stood over her father's bed a few minutes later, holding his limp hand. The doctor's assurance that it was simply a matter of time before the older man woke brought little comfort.

"He looks so shriveled and old," Amy said, her voice suddenly breaking.

Jake folded her into his arms and let her cry. The policeman assigned to the room discretely watched in sympathy.

Amy was a strong person, but how much more could she take? Jake prayed Hepplewhite was right about the children.

They rode home in silence, each lost in their own thoughts.

Jake wasn't sure when he first noticed the sporty black SUV with the darkly tinted windows behind them, but he began to pay particular attention when the vehicle took the off-ramp for Fools Point. The SUV remained some distance behind him when he turned onto Maple Ridge Way, heading into town. Rapidly, the other vehicle began to close the gap.

Jake had learned a long time ago to listen to his instincts. Without warning Amy, he made the left onto Back Lake Road instead of following Maple Ridge all the way to Main Street.

"Jake? What are you doing?"

Amy followed his gaze to the rearview mirror. Then she twisted around in her seat for a better look behind them.

"Isn't that Eugene Perry's car? The one that ran me down in the parking lot the other night?"

Jake took a firm grip on the steering wheel when the SUV followed them onto Back Lake Road, racing up behind them.

"Hang on!"

"Who *is* that? Is it Eugene?"

"I don't know, but I'm afraid we're about to find out."

"Jake! He's going to hit us!"

"Make sure your seat belt is fastened."

Jake fed the Fury more gas. The restored car responded instantly, but the road was wet and covered with wind-blown leaves, making it dangerously slippery. Jake wasn't sure how good the tires were. Ahead was a sharp bend, after which they'd reach the narrow overpass where Rumble Creek fed into Trouble Lake.

"Oh, my God, Jake! He's got a gun!"

A glance in the mirror showed the barrel a rifle sticking out of the driver's window. Jake swerved into the oncoming lane, praying no one else was on the road.

"Get your head down!" he ordered, swerving again.

This time he saw the discharge as the rifle fired. Their car lost traction and skidded. He corrected, then had to slow for the turn before he wrapped them around a tree.

The moment he let up on the gas, the SUV bumped them from behind.

Amy gave a small shriek. She pressed the back of her hand against her mouth to keep from crying out a second time as the SUV rammed them again. Jake pressed her head down. A shot sailed through the back window and out the front windshield.

"Keep down!" he ordered, accelerating.

They went into the turn faster than he would have liked. The car started to slide. He managed to steer into the skid, but it carried him into the opposite lane again. There was no room to maneuver. Trees lay in ambush on both sides of the road. He straightened and the SUV hit them again with enough force to rock him forward against the seat belt. The tires hit a patch of wet leaves. Jake fought the wheel, struggling to maintain control. He nearly had it when the other vehicle smashed into their right rear fender.

The impact sent their car spinning off the road on the lake side. Miraculously, they missed the line of trees and careened down the embankment straight into Trouble Lake.

Jake threw himself as far across Amy as the lap belt would allow. Amy didn't even scream as they were jolted around and the car plunged into the cold water of the lake.

The sudden absence of sound left him momentarily stunned. Almost instantly, water rushed inside the car as the heavy vehicle began to sink to the bottom. Jake yanked off the seat belt and released the catch on Amy's.

"Are you hurt?"

She shook her head numbly. The car was filling quickly. Water was already up to the seats.

"Can you swim?"

"Yes."

"Then wind your window down, take a deep breath, and swim clear. Try to head for the overpass when you break the surface. You don't want to give him a clear shot at you. Got it?"

Amy nodded. He squeezed her hand and reached for his own handle, grateful that the car hadn't hit anything that would cause them to be pinned inside.

Their eyes met. They sucked in a last gulp of air before the water rushed over their heads. Jake felt Amy launch herself through the passenger window. The steering column made it a tight fit for him so he struggled with the door for a few precious seconds before it finally opened.

He shivered violently as he broke the surface with a gasp. Instantly he looked for Amy. Rumble Creek was dumping the recent rain into the lake in a fast-moving torrent. They'd submerged right in its path. The icy water made his back muscles cramp. Jake tried to relax, but he was too cold.

Once a strong swimmer, with his back in wicked spasm, Jake knew he was in serious trouble. He had little body fat to help with buoyancy. A choppy wavelet slapped him in the face. He began to choke, fighting incipient panic. Suddenly, Amy was there tapping him on the shoulder. He tried to tell her to get away, to save herself, but he couldn't manage the words.

"Listen to me. Jake. Listen. I'm going to put you in a carry. Don't fight me, okay? I know what I'm doing. Try to relax."

He managed to nod and choke all at the same time.

He'd never known Amy was trained in water rescue, but having learned the same drill himself, he was relieved to discover she knew what she was doing. He was able to stuff panic into the back of his mind and assist her efforts.

Even so, it was a struggle. At a hundred and ninety pounds of mostly bone and muscle, Jake was no lightweight. And he doubted Amy had done a lot of recent training for this sort of situation. The coldness of the water, the weight of their clothing, and the odds of getting shot all added up to a battle for every stroke.

He felt her tiring short of the shoreline. Spasms or no spasms, he was going to have to do more to help. Suddenly she faltered. For a minute he thought she'd been shot. Then he realized she staggered because she was touching bottom.

"Here! Ms. Thomas! Grab the stick. Come on! I'll pull you in."

Matt? The voice seemed to come from out of nowhere. Amy released him. The strong flow of the water threatened to sweep him off his feet again, but he planted them firmly in the rocky bottom and searched the road above for any sign of the black SUV. Matt had extended a long stick to Amy. Jake glimpsed Kelsey reaching for her arm.

His relief at seeing both kids unharmed was almost overwhelming. They were alive and safe. Now it was up to him to keep them that way.

Jake struggled out of the water. Moments later, Matt got Amy onto the rock-lined bank and turned his attention to Jake. With his help, Jake made it up the slope away from the rocks before he collapsed onto the spongy grass.

"I am damn glad to see you," Jake told the boy. "Where's the SUV?"

"It took off," Matt assured him. "We saw the whole thing."

Jake twisted to look at Amy. She clung to Kelsey, sobbing in relief. His throat constricted at the deep emotion on her face and he offered up a quick prayer of thanks that both kids were okay.

"You're all right?" Jake demanded gruffly of Matt. His own throat clogged with emotion.

"Yeah. We're both fine. Tired, but fine. What about you? Is your back okay?"

"I'll live. No medicine could be stronger than seeing the two of you alive and unharmed."

Matt looked shocked, then embarrassed, but also pleased. "Uh, thanks. Hey, you're turning blue. I've got a blanket in the car."

"What car?"

Matt looked momentarily disconcerted. "Uh. Don't be mad, okay? There was a whole line of them not far from where we came out of the woods. I, uh, sort of boosted one."

"There's an entire search team out looking for you. Didn't you see them?"

"No, and I didn't want to. I was trying to avoid people.

I didn't know who we could trust. Speaking of which, don't you think we'd better get out of here?''

"That's exactly what I think." Jake stood stiffly, trying to keep his teeth from chattering. Kelsey and Amy got to their feet, as well. Amy's arm stayed securely around her daughter.

"Are you two okay?" Jake asked them.

They nodded as one. Amy's entire face glowed with happiness.

"Thanks for the rescue," Jake told her.

She beamed despite teary eyes. "You're welcome."

"Matt has a car."

"Yeah," the youth put in enthusiastically, leading the way. "It's way cool. It's right up here on the road. We were coming around the other side of the lake when we saw you guys going in. Of course, we didn't know it was you, but the way the SUV took off, I knew it wasn't an accident. The driver knew we'd seen him so he headed toward town."

"Did you see who the driver was?" Jake demanded.

"No. The windows were tinted. I didn't even think to look at the tag number. I'm sorry, Jake." Anxiety filled his eyes.

"Don't worry about it. We know who the car belongs to."

"You do?"

"Eugene Perry."

"Are you all right, Matt?" Amy asked as they reached the road.

"Yes, ma'am. We're both okay, right, cuz?"

Kelsey nodded, firmly plastered against her mother's side. "Matt rescued me."

Amy's eyes filled with fresh tears. "I know. And I'll always be grateful to you, Matt."

The boy blushed again. Jake spotted the reconditioned

maroon Super Sport sitting by the side of the road. He stared from the car to Matt.

"You do know whose car this is, don't you?"

"Uh, yeah. I sort of figured Agent Coughlin might not press charges under the circumstances."

Amy gaped at him. "You stole an FBI agent's car?"

Jake found himself hiding a grin. "Let's discuss this at home."

"Uh, Jake. I'm not sure that's such a good idea. Me and Kelsey saw someone shoot old Miss Perry. Now they're trying to kill us."

"You actually saw her being killed?" Amy asked in horror.

"Who?" Jake demanded.

The boy shook his head. "We weren't close enough to identify the guy."

"Okay, get in the car. We need to get away from here." Jake went around the still-running vehicle and slid in behind the wheel.

"Maybe it was the same person that was driving that big black truck-thing," Kelsey said from the back seat where she snuggled next to her mother.

"You're probably right, Kel," Matt said approvingly. He turned to smile at her before twisting back to face Jake. "It was raining and foggy when I tried to lead Kelsey back to where I got your car stuck in the mud. The guy with the gun was wearing one of those big top-coats like Chief Hepplewhite wears. He had a hat that covered most of his face so we couldn't make out his features."

"But he saw us," Kelsey chimed in. "He shot at us! We had to run and run until we got lost. I was scared, but Matt found us another cabin—a nice one this time. It even had stuff to eat inside. Matt said you'd pay them back. Only, we had to break the window to get in. Are we going to get in trouble?"

Amy hugged her daughter tightly. "No, you will definitely not get in trouble. Matt deserves a medal for saving you and keeping you safe."

"Hey, she's a brave kid. And smart."

"Yes, she certainly is," Jake said.

"Mom, I'm sorry for everything. I was mad when you said we might have to leave Fools Point, and I acted like a jerk. Sarah said maybe...maybe Mr. Collins was my dad."

Jake saw her eyes slide toward his in the mirror and quickly look away.

"She said if he was, maybe it was on my birth certificate. I know I shouldn't have gone up to the attic without your permission, but I was mad. I thought if he was my real dad...I thought maybe he'd say we could stay. But I never got to ask him because old Ms. Perry grabbed me in the restaurant parking lot and I lost my birth certificate and I'm so sorry!" She got it all out in one long breath.

Amy hugged her tightly as the little girl began to cry. "It's not your fault, Kelsey. It's mine. I should have told you the truth a long time ago."

"Kel? Hey, kid, don't fall apart now, cuz," Matt said, turning around. "We gotta figure out what to do first, right, Jake? We can deal with this family stuff later."

Jake had never loved his nephew more than at that moment.

"Exactly right. We need to let Hepplewhite know you kids are safe, but," he added, seeing the immediate tension on Matt's face at the mention of the police officer, "we need to do it from someplace safe."

"Why can't we drive straight to the police station?" Amy asked. She looked from Matt to Jake. "You don't think Chief Hepplewhite—"

"We need to get the kids someplace warm and dry first," Jake said quickly. The coat Matt had described could have been a military coat rather than a policeman's.

But Matt had no love for the police no matter who they were. Jake would get more answers if he talked with the boy quietly first. Besides, he didn't know who was driving around in that SUV. The parking lot outside city hall was completely exposed. It would be safer to let the police come to them.

Amy couldn't know what he was thinking, but she didn't argue.

"There's no one at my mom's house anymore," Amy suggested.

"Your place and the restaurant are out. That's where the person in the SUV will expect us to go."

"Well, we can hardly check into a motel in this condition. And my purse was in that car. I don't have money, identification or anything."

"That's okay." Jake tried to tease. "We all know who you are."

"Very funny. In case you forgot, *your* identification is all wet! Explain that to a hotel clerk."

"Hey, I know where Agent Coughlin's apartment is," Matt announced. "No one would look for us there."

"He lives outside Frederick. I don't want to go that far from town, but you just gave me an idea. His sister, Kayla, still owns a duplex off Main Street. She's the real estate agent who sold me the Perry estate," he explained for Amy's benefit. "I'm pretty sure the upstairs of her duplex is still standing empty. No one will think it strange to see her brother's car in her driveway."

"But what if she isn't there?" Amy asked.

Jake and Matt exchanged knowing glances before he met Amy's stare in the mirror. "Let me worry about that."

Chapter Twelve

Kayla wasn't there. A hand-lettered sign on her office door said the office was closed until the following day and gave a number to call.

"Jake, you can't just break in," Amy protested when she realized his intention.

"Let me worry about that. You two keep your heads down and wait here in the car."

"But, Jake—"

"I'll be back."

Amy fumed, but her daughter laid a hand on her arm. "Don't worry, Mom. You said the people at the cabin won't be mad, so this Kayla person won't be mad, either."

"Uh, this isn't exactly the same thing, sweetie."

"Why is it different?"

Amy tried to come up with an answer for that and failed. She was miserably cold, wet and tired, and so relieved to have her daughter back safe and sound that she couldn't seem to think past her relief. She kept touching Kelsey to reassure herself her daughter was there and unhurt beyond a few scratches.

Jake and Matt disappeared around the corner. The unusual two-story building with its deep front and back porches, housed two identical apartments, one over top of the other. Kayla had lived in the upstairs until her marriage to policeman Lee Garvey. The lower level still housed her real-estate business.

The front door opened abruptly. Jake beckoned to them. Amy knew he and Matt must have broken a back window or something to get inside, but she decided she was too tired to argue. She and Kelsey ran onto the porch and followed Jake up a long steep staircase to a second front door.

"There's still some furniture, a few blankets, and other items in here," Jake told them. "And we're really in luck because there's a small washer/dryer combination thing in the kitchen. We can toss our clothes in and warm up while we're waiting."

"What about the police? Aren't we going to call them?"

"As soon as I find a phone," Jake said.

"Hey, Jake! I found a whole box of stuff she has marked to donate to charity back here under these old blankets. There isn't any guy stuff, but there might be something Ms. Thomas and Kelsey could wear while their clothes are getting clean."

Jake raised his eyebrows in question.

"Why not?" Amy said tiredly.

The men stripped down in the kitchen and wrapped themselves in two of the old blankets. Their clothing made a full load for the tiny machine, so Amy used the time to take a quick shower before donning a blouse and sweater and pair of slacks she found amid the used clothing pile. Kelsey also showered, while Amy fished out a bathrobe for her daughter to curl up in.

"Did you miss me?" Kelsey asked suddenly, sounding almost timid.

Amy hugged her daughter tightly. "With every beat of my heart, Kelsey. Jake and I were scared to death for you. We didn't know what had happened. I never want to live through anything like that again.''

''Me, either.''

Amy could almost hear her daughter thinking. She rested her chin on Kelsey's damp head and waited.

''Are you and Mr. Collins like…friends?''

Amy thought about all the ways to describe her relationship with Jake. She looked down at her daughter and smiled. ''Yes, Kelsey. We're friends.''

''Matt says Mr. Collins didn't know he was my father.''

''Matt's right. He didn't. I wrote him about you after he was sent overseas, but he never got my letters.''

''Is that why we lived over there all that time? So you could find him and tell him?''

Her daughter was entirely too perceptive. ''I did hope to meet him again, Kelsey. I wanted him to meet you and see what a wonderful daughter we had together.''

''Is he…you know…mad? I mean, when he found out about me.''

''No,'' Jake said softly from the doorway. ''He's thrilled to have such a beautiful daughter. I only wish I could have been there to watch you grow up all these years.''

''Really?''

Amy's heart wrenched at the eager note in her daughter's voice and the sad expression on Jake's face.

''Really.''

''Does that mean you're going to be my dad now for real?''

This was what they meant when people said their hearts swelled. Tears stung her eyes and Amy blinked them back rapidly. She had never known having a father meant so much to Kelsey. Or that having a daughter could mean so much to Jake.

She raised her gaze and found him watching her. He should have looked ridiculous wrapped in a big yellow blanket, but somehow he managed to look sexy and dangerously handsome instead.

"I'd like very much to be your father from now on."

Kelsey reached out for him as Jake came forward, sitting on the opposite side of his daughter. Watching the two of them hug caused a tear to leak past Amy's defenses. When she looked up, she caught Matt watching wistfully. Immediately, she patted the spot beside her.

"Come and join us."

"I—"

"I want to hear how you saved my daughter."

"I didn't really save her, Ms. Thomas." But he took a seat beside her almost gratefully.

"Would you be comfortable calling me Amy, Matt?"

"Well, uh, yeah, sure. Okay."

"You did, too, save me," Kelsey insisted. "Old Ms. Perry handcuffed me to that disgusting bed and left me there. I was scared until you came. Matt figured out how to get me loose."

"How did she grab you, Kelsey?" Jake asked, shooting Matt a look of gratitude.

"I was mad at Mom. I found your name on my birth certificate so I decided to ask you if you were my real dad. Only I saw old Ms. Perry standing alone by that pit where they found the dead bodies. She was crying and talking to herself. It started raining. I guess it was stupid, but I went over and asked her if she was okay. She just grabbed me."

Kelsey shuddered and Jake put an arm around her before Amy could move.

"She was awful strong. I couldn't get away. I screamed, but nobody came. I guess no one heard me. I struggled real hard, but she put handcuffs on me and then put something over my head. She shoved me in a car. I was real scared then because I didn't know what she was going to do to me.''

Amy's heart thundered as she pictured the scene.

''She kept talking, but it was like she wasn't really talking to me, you know? She kept saying 'sins of the father' and 'save the baby.' I didn't know what she meant, but she really scared me when she told me to be quiet or he would kill me.''

''Who would kill you?''

''I don't know.'' Kelsey shrugged. ''She just said she couldn't let him kill me.''

Amy looked at Jake. Eugene? she mouthed. Jake lifted a shoulder in a small shrug as Kelsey continued her recital.

''At first I thought she meant my father. You. But then she kept talking about all these other people. She wasn't making sense.''

''Did she mention names, Kelsey?'' Jake asked.

''Uh-huh. Lots of them.''

''Can you remember any?''

''Sure. All she did was talk about people. There was Marcus and Eugene. I remember that especially because I thought Eugene was a dumb name to give someone. She said those names a lot—like they were people she didn't like much.''

Jake again exchanged glances with Amy. Marcus or Eugene Perry could have driven the SUV. And ''sins of the father'' made it sound as if Eugene might be behind everything. But why?

''There were some other people named Orin and Penny,'' Kelsey continued. ''She said they were 'pathetically trusting fools, faithful to the end.' I'm not sure what she meant.''

Amy saw Jake raise his eyebrows at the mention of the former groundskeeper and his wife.

"Then there was Lola and Cindy Lou. I remember Grandma calling the mayor 'Cindy Lou' and I wondered if she meant her, but I couldn't tell. Old Ms. Perry didn't make much sense most of the time."

"She was crazy," Matt said flatly.

"But sometimes she acted like she knew what was going on," Kelsey protested. "She brought me stuff to eat and she'd touch my hair like she was trying to be kind. Like you do, Mom."

"Were those the only names she mentioned?" Jake asked.

"No. She said scrawny old Millicent didn't like her, but she didn't care. She said the woman was a stupid snob. She didn't like this Millicent person much, either. Once she even muttered something about Susan and Corny. She said it was too bad."

"What was too bad?" Amy asked.

"Beats me. She muttered that she'd tried to warn them one night. I don't know what she meant, but I kinda thought she was talking about Grandma and Grandpa. Only, when I asked her, she just went into that 'have to keep the baby safe' stuff. I finally realized she meant me. I was the baby she wanted to keep safe. It was spooky. She didn't want to hurt me, Mom. She was real confused. She even called me Amy a few times, like she thought I was you. She kept saying I was a poor little orphan."

An orphan?

Kelsey sighed in an adult manner. "I felt sorry for her, you know? She wasn't mean except when she locked me up. I think she was trying to keep me safe. Only I couldn't get her to let me go."

Amy stroked her hair and Jake patted her arm.

"You said she was real fixed on that 'sins of the father' part," Matt put in.

"Uh-huh. She'd say that, then she'd say he would kill us all. She acted scared when she said that part."

"The dude shot her," Matt said matter-of-factly. "I'd say she had reason to be scared."

Amy couldn't help herself. "Eugene?" she asked Jake out loud this time.

"Or the general," he agreed.

"You think one of them killed her?" Matt asked. "Wow, that's really messed up. I mean, they were family, right? I recognized some of their names."

"Marcus is Gertrude's brother. Millicent is his wife. Cindy Lou and Eugene are Gertrude's niece and nephew."

"And Orin and Penny are the Budnells," Jake reminded her. "The staff who died so conveniently right after the Perry's had the root cellar covered up."

"Hey, wow," Matt said, his expression alert. "Did somebody kill them, too?"

"Possibly," Jake said. "We know Penny Budnell was murdered shortly after her husband died of what they think might have been a heart attack."

"But we don't know why," Amy added.

"It has to have something to do with the bodies in the root cellar," Jake said.

"Kelsey said she mentioned a Lola. Think that could be the dead woman's name?" Amy wondered out loud.

"I'd take bets on it. She didn't use any last names, did she, Kelsey?"

"No. Not that I can remember."

"But why did Ms. Perry think she had to protect Kelsey?" Matt asked.

"Good question," Jake agreed. "Another good question is why you disappeared without telling me where you were going, Matt.''

''Yeah. I was afraid you'd be mad about that. The thing is, I saw old Ms. Perry taking a whole bunch of food off the table at the Thomas house that day. She was stuffing it into a bag and looking around like she didn't want anybody to see her. She acted so suspicious that it occurred to me that she was just weird enough to have taken Kelsey. You were busy so I decided to follow her. I didn't expect her to get into a car.''

He shook his head as if the memory still surprised him. ''Heck, I thought she was too old to drive. But there wasn't time to get you or I would have lost her. I figured I'd follow and come back and tell you where she went, you know?''

''Playing hero?'' Jake asked mildly.

Matt blushed, but nodded. ''Sort of. I knew how much finding Kelsey meant to you, so I figured I could bring her back for you. Only I got your car stuck in the mud. Then I sort of got lost in the woods.''

''Don't worry about it,'' Jake said kindly. ''So did I.''

''Really?'' Matt perked up in obvious relief. ''Well, eventually I found the cabin and Kelsey. It was late and raining pretty good so I figured we'd better wait until it stopped. I knew you'd come looking for me, so I thought if we made it back to the car we could wait there for you.''

''Matt said there might be bears in the woods,'' Kelsey piped up.

Matt turned beet-red, but gamely went on with his part of the story. ''I managed to find the car despite the fog in the morning, but Ms. Perry was standing there talking to some guy. All of a sudden he just pulled out a gun and shot her.''

"Yeah," Kelsey agreed. "And when she fell down, he saw us and came after us."

"We lost him in the fog," Matt continued. "But we got lost, too."

"You said the murderer was wearing a coat like Chief Hepplewhite's?"

"Yeah. You know the one I mean? The guy was tall. Kinda like you only thinner, I think. It was hard to tell 'cause of the coat."

Jake looked at Amy. "Hepplewhite wears a coat that looks a lot like a military coat."

"The general?"

"Eugene was also in the service."

"And the entire family is tall," Matt pointed out.

"So what are we going to do?" Amy asked.

A buzzer went off in the kitchen, making all of them jump.

"Let's start with dry clothes," Jake said. "I'll be right back. I need to pull the shoes out of the oven."

"You're baking our shoes?"

"Haven't you ever heard of filet of sole?"

Amy groaned and Kelsey giggled. Jake grinned at them.

"Hey, that's really bad, Jake," Matt said happily.

"Thank you." He ruffled Kelsey's hair and tugged up his blanket, heading for the kitchen. One end of the blanket trailed behind him.

This was the old Jake, Amy realized. The man who could tease her with bad jokes and puns and make love to her until she couldn't move. He hadn't disappeared, after all, he'd just been hiding behind that stern exterior he used to keep people at a distance.

It was time for him to let that part of his personality out on a permanent basis, she decided. She hesitated for a few minutes, then turned to the kids. "Why don't you two wait here. I'll go see if Jake needs any help."

TIME HAD RUN OUT right along with the luck. The police were pushing hard for DNA samples. Once they had those it would all be over. Everything would have been in vain. There would be no second star for his uniform. He'd be lucky if he didn't have to face a review board— maybe even a court martial. The Perry name would be ruined. Someone else would be mayor of Fools Point.

All because of a no-name slut. Why couldn't he have kept his pants zipped thirty years ago?

And why hadn't Budnell filled in that godforsaken pit after he dumped the bodies? He'd deserved to die of a heart attack. Because of his incompetence the bodies had come to light. It was a miracle they had stayed buried this long. No one had missed the woman. Not once in all these years.

It wasn't fair.

The sins of the father did have a way of coming back to haunt the present. Gertrude had been right about that.

There was only one thing left to do—one chance left. But it would have to be carefully staged. Even more carefully than killing Penny Budnell all those years ago. If Penny had known what she was doing in the first place, Lola and her kid wouldn't have died.

At least not in childbirth.

It was much too late for regrets now. Too late for a lot of things. But maybe, just maybe, the future could be saved—with a couple more deaths.

JAKE REPLACED the telephone receiver as Amy walked into the kitchen. He'd pulled on his briefs and his pants before he'd spotted the telephone over in a corner.

"Did you call Chief Hepplewhite?" Amy asked.

"I can't from here. The service has been disconnected." He reached for his shirt.

"That doesn't look dry."

"Everything's still damp, but they're wearable."

"Are we going to the police station?"

Jake frowned. "I thought you could stay here with Kelsey and Matt."

"Shouldn't we all go?"

"I don't like the idea of the four of us marching down the street with that SUV still out there."

"We could take Alex's car."

"That Super Sport sticks out like a sore thumb. I could break into Kayla's office and use her phone, but I thought I'd just run over to city hall for help."

"What about your back?"

Jake wished she hadn't reminded him. "Now that I'm warmer the spasms are better. What's wrong?" He lifted her chin and saw the concern in her eyes.

"It'll sound stupid."

"Tell me, anyhow."

"I'm afraid if you go alone, something bad will happen," she said almost defiantly.

Amy came willingly into his arms. Her wet hair was cold where it touched his bare chest, but Jake didn't mind. Holding her brought a sense of peace.

"Nothing's going to happen," he said against the top of her head. Instantly, she stepped back.

"You don't know that."

"No, I don't know that, but I'm going to do my best to insure that it doesn't."

He sought her mouth. Her lips parted in instant welcome even as her arms came up to circle his neck. A heady anticipation set up a staccato beat inside him. He'd intended nothing more than a light kiss, but Amy's mouth was fierce and demanding, eliciting an immediate response. He cradled the nape of her neck and deepened the kiss. She clung with an eagerness that couldn't be denied. Satisfaction swept him as she made a tiny, ardent sound against his mouth.

"Amy!" Her name was a whispered plea. He wanted her right here, right now, with a fierceness that shocked him. "We can't do this now."

Her fingertip traced his mouth with such innocent sensuality that he lowered his head to taste her again. Her response was intoxicating. He felt greedy with need. He caressed her breasts through the bulky sweater. Frustrated by the impediment, his hand slipped up and under the sweater and shirt below until he felt the softness of her skin. He slid his palm over her abdomen, feeling the muscles flutter beneath his touch. He took one perfect breast in his hand, rubbing lightly until the nipple budded, tight and firm against his palm.

Amy moaned softly. He smothered the sound in a slow, lingering kiss that pushed his control to the limits.

"I want you," he whispered.

"Yes."

Her eager acceptance required a will of iron. If they hadn't had two children in the other room…but they did.

He released her breast and pulled her body tightly against his chest. Her arms circled his waist. He knew she could feel his arousal pressing against her.

For what seemed like an eternity, they stood there without moving, banking the blaze they had lit.

He loved this woman. He suspected he always had. If he told her so now, she'd think it was emotion based on the moment. She couldn't know that the only time he felt free to be himself was with her. She would never believe how empty his life had been since he walked out on her all those years ago.

He needed her love the way a starving man needs food.

Only Amy staved off his abiding loneliness. With her he felt whole. And loved.

Not for the first time, he wished he was good with words. If only he knew how to share all the thoughts churning inside him. But then, the force of his need might scare her off and that was the last thing he wanted.

"We'll all go," he said softly.

Amy looked up at him with eyes softened by passion. "Yes," she whispered, stepping back unsteadily. "We'll all go. But Kelsey's clothes aren't done."

"We'll wait."

"Maybe—maybe you should just go."

"No. You're right, we'll all stay together."

Like a family, he added to himself.

"But we need to let everyone know the kids are safe. That car in the driveway could act like a beacon. You were right. It's distinctive."

Jake began buttoning his shirt. "Do you think Kelsey would mind going over there dressed in the robe and a blanket?"

"Probably."

They shared a smile.

"Little girls have a strong sense of dignity," Amy said.

"What about big girls?"

"Them, too, until some sexy man comes along and kisses them senseless."

"Sexy, huh?"

"Don't let it go to your head."

"You know, that first day, when I saw you wearing those earrings I gave you, I told myself things were going to work out."

Her smile widened. "They were supposed to discourage you."

"Nothing could do that, Amy. Not where you're concerned.'' He felt her tremble in his arms and exalted in the knowledge that things were going to work out for them.

Amy stepped into his arms slowly. ''I'll go talk with our daughter.''

EVENING WAS CLOSING IN as they left their safe haven, piled into the Super Sport and drove the short distance to city hall where the police station was housed. They were stopped at the traffic light when Amy suddenly gave a shout.

''Jake, look!''

At the gas station across the street, Eugene Perry climbed behind the wheel of a black SUV with tinted windows and sped off. He was not alone, though they couldn't make out who the passenger was.

''Should we follow them?''

He wanted nothing more, but he shook his head. ''No.''

''But that's the car that forced you into the lake!'' Matt said.

''And he's armed with a rifle. I'm not. Hepplewhite needed proof to act. I think we have what he needs.''

He turned into the surprisingly empty parking lot and rolled to a stop. Millicent Perry ran from the building toward them, waving her arms.

The fastidiously coifed, prim Millicent Perry they had come to know was gone. Her hair was awry, her jacket hung to one side, and her blouse was no longer neatly tucked into her tailored slacks.

''Help me! Please help me! There's no one inside and my husband is hurt. Please help! Please!''

''There's no one inside?'' Jake asked.

''I think he's dying! You've got to come! Please!''

''Come where? Calm down and tell me what's

wrong," Jake commanded. But Millicent Perry was beyond listening to anyone.

"Oh, God. There's so much blood. Someone has to help me." Millicent turned and ran for her car.

"Jake?" Amy asked.

"You and the kids go inside."

"No. She said there's no one in there."

"That doesn't make sense."

"I know."

Jake hesitated. They'd seen Eugene drive away, and there was no denying Millicent's sense of urgency.

"We've got to help her," Amy insisted.

"We don't know what's happened."

"Well, we can't just sit here."

"All right." Cindy Lou lived on the side street diagonally across from the Perrywrinkle. "When we get to the mayor's house I want all of you to wait in the car."

"I could come with you, Jake," Matt said quickly.

"No. I want you to stay with Amy and Kelsey." His unease grew as he turned onto Whylie Court. "Amy, get behind the wheel as soon as I get out. If you see the SUV or if anything looks or sounds wrong, take the kids and get out of here. Head for a public place and call 9-1-1. Don't take any chances."

"Jake, maybe this wasn't a good idea. I don't like this." Amy stared at the mayor's large house.

The street was almost eerily silent, the houses set far apart from one another. Millicent's car was the only vehicle in the driveway. The front door of her daughter's house gaped open in silent invitation.

Jake parked up on the street, ignoring the driveway. "I don't like this, either. Get behind the wheel and wait here. I'll be right back."

Years of training and experience had his every sense on alert. If he hadn't seen Eugene drive off toward the highway a second ago, nothing could have propelled him toward that front door.

Millicent appeared, gesturing frantically. "Please hurry!"

Jake mounted the porch steps.

"He's in the kitchen!" she cried.

The remembered odor of blood and death hit him as Jake rounded the corner. He was fully prepared for the sight of General Marcus Perry sprawled on the kitchen floor in a pool of blood. He didn't have to touch the body to know there was nothing he could do for the man. Still, thinking of Millicent, he started to bend to feel for a pulse.

The blow whistled out of nowhere.

Chapter Thirteen

Jake had a split instant of warning. Enough that the blow glanced off his head and caught him across the back. He went down on top of the general's body in a blaze of pain so intense he couldn't breathe.

When he could think past the fire in his back, his first dazed thought was that he should have let her hit him in the head. His second thought was to wonder what she'd hit him with. And then, as his head cleared, he was suddenly terrified, thinking of Amy and the kids.

"Hurry," he heard Millicent cry. "Mr. Collins said he needs your help right away. Please hurry."

Jake struggled to stand, slipping in the blood that pooled on the linoleum floor. Millicent was a far better actress than he would ever have given her credit for being. Jake had no doubt that Amy was even now heading into the house. It was that thought that gave him the strength to fight the pain and move.

He had to use a chair and the table to stand. Beads of sweat dotted his forehead. He closed his eyes for a second against the pain and the wave of nausea that made him sway unsteadily.

"Amy! Run!" he managed to shout. "Get away!" But he knew it was already too late.

"Jake? Oh, my God! Jake!"

Amy rounded the corner of the dining room. He saw Millicent start to swing a baseball bat toward the back of her head.

"Look out!"

Amy jumped aside before the words were out of his mouth. Either her reflexes were better than his, or she'd had some warning before he called out. The bat swished through the air, missing her and striking the wall a jarring blow.

Millicent dropped the weapon in favor of a .45-caliber handgun she pulled from her saggy jacket pocket.

"No!" Jake launched himself forward, knowing the distance was too great.

The gunshot filled the room with a clap of sound. Amy staggered back against the dining room table. Jake stopped abruptly as Millicent turned the gun toward him.

"Jake?" Amy whispered fearfully.

"Police!" Announced a sudden voice from the living room. "Drop your weapon!"

With a speed that astounded him, Millicent swung back toward the living room and fired. The officer's shot splintered a mirror on the wall at her back. In the remaining shards Jake saw the officer fall to the floor. Millicent fired a second time. Then she whirled back to face them.

Anger, fear and desperation lined her face. It was the desperation that scared Jake the most. That and the level way she pointed the gun at Amy.

"Millicent! Don't!"

He didn't have the mobility to reach her. Amy's hand was clasped to her thigh. Blood stained her skin and her dark slacks wetly.

"I have no choice," Millicent told them. "The police will think Marcus did it, then killed himself. Then it will all be over."

Jake put out a hand to steady himself against the table. "No. They won't. They'll know the general died first."

"He isn't dead. Is he?" Her pale lips parted in shock. Anger quickly flooded her face with color. "The bastard! That insufferable bastard! He wasn't supposed to die yet. That's why I shot him in the stomach. He told me gut-shot victims take a long time to die."

Jake tried to swallow and couldn't. She was insane. But it was a crafty form of insanity. She knew exactly what she was doing.

Where were the kids? Matt must have heard the shots. Would he be smart enough to get Kelsey and himself out of harm's way?

"He's dead, Millicent," Jake repeated.

"Are you certain?"

Jake managed a nod. He inched closer to Amy. His only chance was to get in front of her before Millicent pulled the trigger. Amy might have a fighting chance then.

"There must be some way to salvage this. I will not allow the family name to be destroyed," Millicent said.

"But you aren't even a real Perry," Amy said quickly.

Millicent's cold dark eyes turned to her. "The Perry name is mine by marriage. My children must carry that name. It means something in this town. And in Washington circles. I'm certain that is something a person of your caliber can't even imagine."

She was crazy. But she wasn't stupid. She held the gun rock-steady as she chewed on her lower lip.

"It's over," Jake said softly. "You just shot a policeman. There's nothing you can do to salvage this now."

"There has to be! I will not see *my* children suffer just because that rutting bastard couldn't keep his pants zipped. Why did that policeman arrive already? Did you go inside anyhow and tell them to come here?"

So the police *had* been manning the station. If he'd just checked first. "I'm sorry to say I wasn't smart enough to go inside, but the police were getting a court order for the general to give them a blood sample for DNA testing. My guess is, the man you shot was simply delivering the summons. He probably heard you shoot Amy." He glanced at her and saw the tight white line around her mouth. She was bleeding, but he'd seen worse.

"A court summons?" Millicent asked.

"I don't know any other way to account for his timely arrival, do you?"

"I cannot let that happen. If they test his DNA they will learn the truth." She sent Amy a glare of pure hatred.

"What truth is that?" Jake asked.

"I think I need to sit down," Amy said quietly.

"Yes. Sit down," Millicent said with icy anger. "Both of you sit while I try to think."

Amy's face was white, but as she pulled out a chair and sat down heavily, she winked at him. For a moment, Jake was stunned. Then he realized she was trying to tell him she wasn't hurt as bad as she was pretending.

At least he hoped that was what she was trying to say.

Jake pulled out his own chair and sank down beside her. He tried not to let Amy see him wince. Firmly, he pushed the pain to a pocket in his mind where he could close it away. He needed to try to analyze the situation. Millicent was angry and she was obviously nuts, but she was calm. The key was to keep her that way until help could arrive or he could convince her that their deaths would only make matters worse.

"There's only one solution. You'll have to go back to Trouble Lake and drown like you were supposed to. We're going to get in your car and—"

"This is the police! Come out with your hands up."

Matt *had* gotten help. Jake sent the boy a mental thanks while Millicent cursed. The stream of words sounded odd in such formal, Bostonian tones. She strode from his sight. Jake started to rise but Amy motioned him to stay put. Since she was in a better position to see, he obeyed. Seconds later he heard the sound of a round being chambered. A rifle blast shattered the stillness of the night.

"She had a rifle next to the television set," Amy whispered.

A second shot followed the first.

"How bad are you hurt?" Jake asked her.

"It hurts, but I'm fine. You're covered in blood."

Her deep concern warmed him. "It's the general's blood. She got me with the bat."

Millicent strode back to them, her face contorted in anger. "That should hold them."

"Go out the back," Amy urged. "Save yourself. You can be gone before they surround the house. We won't tell them it was you."

Millicent eyed her scornfully. "Do be quiet." She aimed the rifle at Amy. For a second, Jake thought she would squeeze the trigger.

"Do you have any idea how much I hate you?"

Amy gaped at her.

"You're a living reminder of what a philandering cretin I married."

"What are you talking about?"

But Jake suddenly knew as pieces started to slip into place. There was only one explanation that fit. He should have guessed the truth when he noticed the general had green eyes, too. That particular shade wasn't all that common. And Jake had even commented that Amy looked nothing like her parents in her baby pictures. He knew her father's secret. Even her mother's fear of the general was explained if he was right. Susan had been afraid Marcus Perry would take her child away from her.

Amy was the link they'd been looking for all along.

"She's talking about your real father, the general. Isn't that right, Millicent?"

Amy gasped. Millicent swung the rifle toward his chest. At this distance he wouldn't survive the first shot.

"Men are disgusting. That woman was a slut. A nobody. Yet he couldn't keep his damned pants zipped."

"My mother and the general were lovers?" Amy gasped.

"No. Not Susan. Lola and the general were lovers, right, Millicent?" Jake asked. "Cornelius and Susan adopted the baby that survived, didn't they? One died in childbirth, but Amy lived. A constant reminder that your husband was unfaithful."

Her eyes narrowed and her hands tightened on the rifle. "So Cornelius talked before he died."

"He didn't die, Millicent. You wasted the mushrooms and the medication you dumped in their drinks. I assume it was you who tried to poison them, right?"

"Be quiet."

"They're going to make it, Millicent. Killing us isn't going to do you any good at all. The police have a twenty-four-hour guard on them. The truth will come out now no matter what you do."

Millicent suddenly whirled and fired two rounds toward the front door. There was a scramble of sound and she disappeared into the living room again. The gun spat twice more. Glass shattered. Jake eyed the bat on the living-room floor. He was pretty sure he couldn't reach it before she could shoot him.

By now the police must either be getting ready to storm the house or setting up for a hostage situation. Jake prayed Amy was right about her leg wound being minor because she'd have to move fast, if the chance to escape ever came.

"The cop she shot got away," Amy whispered.

"Lucky cop."

Jake decided he'd gotten out of the military just in time. He'd definitely lost his edge and his timing. And if he wasn't careful and lucky here, he was going to lose his life, as well.

"The next time she goes toward the front door, run for the kitchen," he told Amy.

"I'm not leaving you!"

"I'll be right behind you."

"Stop whispering!" Millicent demanded. "If you try anything at all I will shoot you immediately. I need to think!"

"If you shoot us, you lose your bargaining power," Jake told her softly, calmly. "The police will storm the house and you'll be killed."

Her hand tightened on the rifle. Jake prayed it required a strong pull or she'd kill them without even meaning to.

"Lola should have stayed buried!" Tears clouded her eyes, but the gun never wavered. "That tramp ruined our lives. She refused to have an abortion. Marcus had to promise her a great deal of money to keep her silent. He talked Gertrude into hiding her until she delivered. He was up for promotion, you know. A scandal would have destroyed him. We would have been socially ruined."

"But Penny Budnell agreed to deliver the babies and Susan and Corny offered to adopt them, right? It wasn't such a bad plan," Jake said mildly. He hoped the shock on Amy's face wouldn't keep her from staying alert. They might only get one chance.

"It was stupid!" Millicent said angrily. "There is only one way to deal with people of that ilk."

She'd moved closer to the dining room, away from the

windows, but not close enough for Jake to risk trying to jump her.

"I would have handled the situation if he'd been man enough to tell me what a fool he'd been right from the start. But of course, he never did. Gertrude called me after it was all over and she was left to clean up the mess." Millicent wrinkled her nose in distaste.

"You mean, the bodies?"

"Of course not. I had no idea what Budnell had done with them. I foolishly believed he had dealt with the situation appropriately. After all, he and his wife could have been arrested for refusing to get Lola medical help when she began to hemorrhage. Fools! I cannot believe they gave the second infant to the *mailman* and then just watched Lola die while they stood there wringing their hands."

"My God," Amy whispered.

Jake reached for her hand. It was ice cold. The other hand pressed against her wound, but it didn't appear to be bleeding too badly. Still, she was going into shock. He had to get them out of here.

"So, you killed Budnell?" he asked.

"Of course not. Orin died of a heart attack. That was when Gertrude called me. Penny decided to make demands, you see."

"You set Penny Budnell up in a fancy condo and had her killed."

"Of course not. I killed her myself," Millicent said proudly. "And had I known there were twins, I would have removed the entire Thomas family, as well." She glared at Amy with undisguised fury.

Amy stared at her in horror.

"How did you find out?" Jake prodded.

"Gertrude, again. She began muttering to herself after the first body appeared. I began questioning her and quickly learned the rest of the story. Then I went to my worthless husband and demanded answers.''

The telephone rang, making them all jump.

''Want me to get that?'' Jake offered.

''Stay where you are,'' Millicent said sharply.

''It will be the police.''

''Be quiet!''

The answering machine clicked to life. Unfortunately, it was set too low for them to hear the voice that spoke into the machine.

''Why not talk to them? Maybe they can help you out of this mess,'' Jake suggested.

''I said to be quiet!''

''It's too late for that,'' Amy said, coming to life again despite her pale cheeks. ''The world is going to know the truth when the DNA samples come back.''

Millicent swung the gun back toward her. ''He was at least smart enough not to let them have any.''

''But now he's dead and so is Gertrude,'' Jake argued. ''They've probably already taken samples from her body. They can use those without permission.''

''No!''

He didn't know if they could or not and he didn't care. If he could just keep her off balance...

The telephone began to ring again.

''You were the wronged party here,'' Amy said coaxingly. ''The world will realize that. Look how many famous men have let sex supplant their common sense. The men are the ones people ridicule. Especially when they get caught. The women they wronged are looked up to and even admired for standing by their foolish husbands.''

''More deaths will only make the situation worse,'' Jake agreed.

He sensed Millicent waffling, weighing their words. He stood slowly. "Let me have the rifle."

"No!"

From out front, someone spoke through a bullhorn.

"This is Chief Hepplewhite. The house is surrounded. Pick up the telephone or we will make a forced entry."

Millicent's eyes glittered with an expression he couldn't read.

"You are wrong, Mr. Collins. One more death is still necessary." Her gaze went to Amy. "I am sorry my sister-in-law put your daughter through such an ordeal. I see now that I had lost control of the situation some time ago. Gertrude was quite correct. The sins of the fathers always do come to light."

She set the rifle on the chair at her back and pulled out the .45 before Jake could move. Pointing it at him, she walked forward. She was past him before he could move.

"Now!" he told Amy. "Run!" He shoved her toward the living room, standing to block her from Millicent. But Millicent never hesitated or turned around. She entered the kitchen with single-minded determination. It suddenly dawned on Jake what she planned to do. He turned back to the kitchen.

"Jake!" Amy cried.

"You were a miserable husband and a terrible father," Millicent said. "I'll see you in hell."

"Millicent! No!"

She put the gun to the roof of her mouth and pulled the trigger.

Amy screamed.

More shaken than he wanted to admit, he caught Amy before she could see the two bodies on the floor.

"Come on, let's get out of here before the police start shooting tear gas at us."

AMY SAT in the wheelchair between her parents' beds and tried to control her emotions. She'd had two days to come to grips with the situation, but everything was still overwhelming.

Her parents weren't really her parents. And she had had a twin who had died at birth. While she accepted both truths as fact, they didn't feel real. The entire past week was like some horrible nightmare that wouldn't go away.

She felt nothing but a remote sadness for the woman who'd given birth to her. Lola Carney had been a secretary working at the Pentagon when she'd met then-Lieutenant Marcus Perry. A product of foster homes, Amy chose to believe that Lola hadn't been a bad person, just a lonely woman struggling to survive the best way she could. Someday, perhaps, she'd take a closer look into her birth mother's past, but for now it was enough that Lola chose to give birth to her children and found two wonderful parents to raise them.

And those parents were wonderful people, hiding a terrible secret. Cornelius and Susan had wanted a baby so desperately that they'd agreed to the charade of pretending to be pregnant so they could secretly adopt Lola's baby. Amy knew there hadn't been enough money to go through a legal adoption agency. When Gertrude and Lola approached them, it must have seemed like a heaven-sent opportunity. And they'd been fabulous parents. Amy could never feel anything but love and gratitude for the way they had raised her. She could even understand why they'd never told her the truth.

Her mother had been so shocked when she heard about the bodies in the root cellar, Amy felt certain Susan hadn't known what had been done with Lola and the dead infant.

As for being a twin, the unreality of that made it a

tough issue to grasp. All Amy could feel was a detached sense of loss for the sibling she'd never known.

"We should have told you the truth a long time ago," Corny stated for the third time.

"I was so afraid," Susan Thomas said. "Orin Budnell told us the poor woman had died after giving birth to a second child. A boy, they said, but he strangled on the umbilical cord and they couldn't save him. We were sick about it, but there was nothing we could do. Orin brought you to us as soon as you were born. We never asked any more questions. We knew the whole situation was wrong and for a long time we lived in desperate fear. But we wanted you so badly."

"I'm glad you did," Amy told her fervently. "Lola Carney may have given birth to me, and Marcus Perry might have been my natural father, but you have always been and always will be my parents. A family is more than an act of nature," she reassured her mother.

Susan began to cry. There were tears in her father's eyes, as well, but he looked past Amy toward the door. She twisted around to see Jake, flanked by Kelsey and Matt, standing just inside the room.

"She's right, you know," he said in that soft quiet voice that acted like soothing balm. "It takes more than biology to be a loving parent. Amy was very lucky to have the two of you growing up."

"Jake. Should you be out of bed?" Amy scolded, backing up the wheelchair to give them more room.

"Nope," Matt said with a grin, "but Dr. Martin said she gave up. She said she was surprised she was able to keep him down this long."

"I hate hospitals," Jake informed the room at large, looking disgruntled.

"But your back."

"Is feeling just fine."

"Yeah. Until the pain medication wears off," Matt put in.

"Jake Collins—"

"Now don't you start nagging me, too. Between the kids and Leslie Martin, I'm feeling suffocated."

Amy ran her gaze over him with hungry intensity. He looked good. Better than good. He looked strong and sexy and capable. He looked like Jake, the man she loved more than words could express.

His gaze softened. The sternness of his features gentled as their eyes held, speaking without sound.

"I missed you," she told him.

I love you, she said silently with her heart.

"I missed you, too."

He loved her. He had to love her. A man couldn't look at a woman like that and not love her. She would make him love her. Because if he walked away from her again now, she wasn't sure how she'd survive.

"I didn't know you were up here. I came to talk to your parents," Jake said.

"Well, we're right here," Corny said with a trace of his old spunk. "Dr. Martin won't let us go yet, either."

"She likes being in control," Jake told them.

"I've noticed. I want to thank you for saving our girl and our granddaughter. Hiya, punkin."

"Hi, Grandpa!" Kelsey had perched on the edge of her grandmother's bed. "My dad has something to ask you," she said, bubbling with suppressed excitement. "And you have to say yes, Grandpa."

Amy felt her heart stutter. She'd never heard Kelsey call Jake "Dad" before. And the pride with which she'd uttered the word sent Amy's gaze skittering back to Jake. Only, he wasn't looking at her. He'd shaved and was formally dressed, she realized. Her heart began a wild pounding.

''Mr. Thomas, Mrs. Thomas, I should have asked you this question nine years ago, but I was young and really stupid back then. I'd like to think I've learned a few things since then and I'm hoping to rectify the dumbest thing I ever did in my life. I'd like permission to marry your daughter.''

A lump caught in Amy's throat. She would not cry, she vowed. She had already shed more tears than a summer storm, but his words brought her to her feet.

Jake finally turned to look at her. ''Aren't you supposed to be sitting down?'' he asked.

''Aren't you supposed to be asking *me* that question first?''

''I did ask you once, remember?''

''I remember. You said you'd ask me again when it was all over.''

''And I will, but I wasn't sure you'd say yes so I figured I'd get our daughter's permission and Matt's permission and your parents' permission first. Then I could skip the risk and go right for the marriage license.''

A wayward tear slid down her cheek. ''Oh, you did, did you? And I suppose they all said yes.''

Kelsey and Matt both nodded, grinning. Her father looked at her mother who was wiping her own tears and smiling at the same time.

''Hell, boy,'' Corny said, ''you've got my permission for what it's worth, but you'd better ask her, not us. This girl's always had a mind of her own. But I'd take bets on the outcome of this one.''

''Don't be so smug, Dad. He hasn't asked me properly yet.''

''If properly involves me getting down on one knee, Doc Martin might get her wish,'' Jake said wryly. ''They'd probably need a crane to get me up again and I'd end up in traction for sure.''

"You idiot." She brushed at the silly tears that wouldn't stop leaking from her eyes.

Jake closed the distance between them. "Will you marry me, bad back and all, and let Matt and me be part of your family?"

"That will blow your Mafia image in town."

He smiled with his eyes, stroking her hair back from her face with a hand that wasn't quite steady. "I'll take that chance. I'm not very good at the words, but I love you, Amy. I think I always have."

"I love you, too."

As his lips settled over her mouth in the tenderest of kisses, Amy heard Matt's voice.

"Looks like you two better hurry and get well. We've got a wedding to start planning."

"Yeah, and Jake says I can be the flower girl," Kelsey announced.

"Welcome to the family, Matt," Corny said.

"Yeah. Hey, thanks!"

"I think you should be a junior bridesmaid," Susan Thomas told her granddaughter. "That way Matt could be a groomsman. What do you think, Corny?"

Jake pulled back and gazed into Amy's eyes. "I think we ought to get out of here before they get around to naming our next child."

Her heart burst with love for this man. "They'll never miss us."

"What about your leg?"

"Bet it feels better than your back."

"No bets. We might have to get creative, but what do you say we go look for a room in this dump with a lock on the inside."

"I'd say I like the way you think, Mr. Collins."

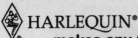

#1 *New York Times* bestselling author

NORA ROBERTS

brings you more of the loyal and loving,
tempestuous and tantalizing Stanislaski family.

Coming in February 2001

The Stanislaski Sisters

Natasha and Rachel

Though raised in the Old World traditions of their
family, fiery Natasha Stanislaski and cool, classy
Rachel Stanislaski are ready for a *new* world of love....

*And also available in February 2001 from
Silhouette Special Edition, the newest book in the
heartwarming Stanislaski saga*

CONSIDERING KATE

Natasha and Spencer Kimball's daughter Kate turns her
back on old dreams and returns to her hometown, where
she finds the *man* of her dreams.

Available at your favorite retail outlet.

Where love comes alive™